THE
CEMETERY
YEW

Also by Cynthia Riggs
in Large Print:

The Cranefly Orchid Murders
Deadly Nightshade

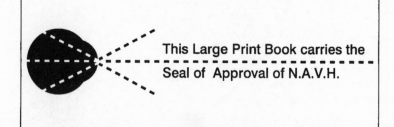

THE
CEMETERY
YEW

CYNTHIA RIGGS

Thorndike Press • Waterville, Maine

Published in 2003 by arrangement with
St. Martin's Press, LLC.

Thorndike Press® Large Print Americana.

The tree indicium is a trademark of Thorndike Press.

The text of this Large Print edition is unabridged.
Other aspects of the book may vary from the original edition.

Set in 16 pt. Plantin by Ramona Watson.

Printed in the United States on permanent paper.

Library of Congress Cataloging-in-Publication Data

Riggs, Cynthia.
    The cemetery yew / Cynthia Riggs.
      p. cm.
    ISBN 0-7862-5929-9 (lg. print : hc : alk. paper)
    1. Trumbull, Victoria (Fictitious character) — Fiction.
2. Women detectives — Massachusetts — Martha's
Vineyard — Fiction.   3. Martha's Vineyard (Mass.) —
Fiction.   4. Women poets — Fiction.   5. Aged women —
Fiction.   6. Large type books.   I. Title.
PS3618.I394C46 2003b
   813'.6—dc22   2003060104

FOR
DIONIS COFFIN RIGGS
POET

1898–1997

As the Founder/CEO of NAVH, the only national health agency solely devoted to those who, although not totally blind, have an eye disease which could lead to serious visual impairment, I am pleased to recognize Thorndike Press* as one of the leading publishers in the large print field.

Founded in 1954 in San Francisco to prepare large print textbooks for partially seeing children, NAVH became the pioneer and standard setting agency in the preparation of large type.

Today, those publishers who meet our standards carry the prestigious "Seal of Approval" indicating high quality large print. We are delighted that Thorndike Press is one of the publishers whose titles meet these standards. We are also pleased to recognize the significant contribution Thorndike Press is making in this important and growing field.

Lorraine H. Marchi, L.H.D.
Founder/CEO
NAVH

* Thorndike Press encompasses the following imprints: Thorndike, Wheeler, Walker and Large Print Press.

Acknowledgments

I feel sorry for any writer who doesn't have a plot doctor like Jonathan Revere. Not only does he know Robert Frost's poetry better than I do, but he can cajole me out of writer's block with a sympathetic, "Have you thought of . . . ?" followed by an improbable plot twist that often works. Thank you again and again, Arlene Silva. You know how much you have meant to me.

What would I do without my writers' group — Lois Remmer, our leader; Wendy Hathaway, our science fiction writer; and Brenda Horrigan, who's penning a historical novel that's sure to be a bestseller. You spot all sorts of stuff I've missed.

Thanks to friends and family and bed-and-breakfast guests, who've read and critiqued endless drafts of manuscripts. Special thanks to Carlin Smith, Alvida and Ralph Jones, and Ann and Bill Fielder.

Thank you, Nancy Love, my agent, who knows what publishers are looking for. Thank you, Ruth Cavin, my St. Martin's editor, the absolute tops in the field, for making my stories sharper and better.

While I've taken a few liberties with actual places, events, and people, my stories are fiction. I hope those of you who think you recognize someone realize that this is all make-believe. People in this book couldn't possibly exist, could they?

Thank you, West Tisbury Library — what would I do without you!

And, to all of you who've kept me going through some rocky times, thank you! You know who you are.

Chapter 1

Victoria Trumbull could feel the surf pounding on the south shore, a forerunner of heavy weather. She had hoped to get tulip bulbs planted on Jonathan's grave before the first frost. The sky had clouded over while she worked and the breeze now had a bite. She got to her feet slowly, using the handles of her kneeler for support. At ninety-two she was not as agile as she once had been. She straightened her legs slowly and stood tall.

While she worked, Victoria had been vaguely aware of a rhythmic sound on the far side of the cemetery. She reached for her fleece jacket and realized the sound was the clink of shovel blades hitting pebbles in the sandy Island soil and the swish of dirt landing on a growing mound beside a grave.

Then she heard the thunk of a shovel tossed onto the ground. One of the grave diggers, a slender young woman with long dark pigtails, climbed out of the grave and bent over the hole, hands on her knees.

"He's done it again, Ira," Victoria heard

her call down to someone still in the grave. With that, the woman — a girl, really — dusted her hands on her overalls and kicked her shovel aside.

Victoria picked up her walking stick and wended her way among the gravestones to find out what had happened. A man Victoria recognized as Ira Bodman clambered out of the hole.

"That's it for today, Denise," he muttered to the girl. "Let your father figure this one out. He's not paying me enough."

The girl, Denise Rhodes, flipped her braids over her shoulder. "What about her family?" She looked down at her grimy hands and wiped them on her dusty overalls.

Ira blew his nose on a red bandana he'd taken out of his back pocket. "Not our problem. Let the selectmen deal with it."

"I suppose we should fill the grave back in?" Denise sounded uncertain.

"Nope," said Ira.

Victoria had reached the big yew tree that overhung the grave and stopped to catch her breath. Denise looked up at her and smiled, a deep dimple showing in her cheek. "Hi, Mrs. Trumbull."

"What seems to be the trouble?" Victoria asked.

10

Ira pointed into the hole. Victoria took hold of a branch of the yew and looked down. The grave was about six feet deep. The straight sides showed neat layers of sand and clay. There was nothing at the bottom but sandy soil speckled with stones. A shower of sand and pebbles cascaded down the vertical sides.

Victoria stepped back from the edge and looked questioningly from Denise to Ira. "What's this all about?"

"Who knows." Ira blotted his forehead. "We were supposed to dig up a coffin that was buried here ten years ago. The family wants to move the remains to Milwaukee."

Denise indicated the large family plot enclosed by a boxwood hedge and a wrought-iron fence with the yew tree's branches spreading over one side. "The girl is a Norton cousin."

"Was." Ira put his bandana back in his pocket.

"Then where's the coffin?" Victoria asked.

"Good question." Ira shrugged. "Guess we need to ask Denny. He's the one who got the court order. He's cemetery superintendent, not me."

Denise leaned over and picked up her shovel.

Ira folded his arms over his chest. "One of us better go to Town Hall. You want to give your father the good news, Denise, or you want to wait here?"

"Are you kidding? I'm staying here to help Mrs. Trumbull." Denise took a last look into the open grave and followed Victoria, who was heading back to where she'd left her basket.

"I heard you say he'd 'done it again,' " Victoria said. "Who did what again?"

Denise sighed. "My father?" Her voice rose in a question.

"Yes, of course. Denny Rhodes, the selectman."

"He's cemetery superintendent, too, you know?"

Victoria nodded.

"Like, he's supposed to keep track of who wants to be buried where and next to who, you know?"

Victoria flicked a pebble out of her way with her stick.

"It would be gross to bury a person next to someone they hadn't spoken to in years," Denise added.

Victoria smiled. "And that's what your father did? Or didn't do?"

"Something like that." Denise turned and pointed to two identical marble grave-

12

stones, not next to each other, shoulder to shoulder, but lined up, head to foot. "My mom was always talking about how hen-pecked Mr. DeBettencourt was. It's like Mrs. D. was pretty domineering, you know?"

"She was certainly a strong woman," Victoria agreed.

"Well, my dad buried Mr. DeBettencourt at Mrs. D.'s feet. My mom says she's still bossing him around."

"It probably doesn't really matter now," Victoria said.

"It does, though. The DeBettencourt kids are bullshit. My mom went to high school with them."

"Can't your father have Mr. DeBetten-court moved to the grave next to his wife?"

"No. My brilliant father put Mr. Moreis next to Mrs. D."

Victoria paused to catch her breath. "Napoleon Moreis? He was their neighbor, wasn't he?"

Denise laughed. "My mom says Napo-leon and Mrs. D. had a thing going be-tween them, if you know what I mean." She looked at Victoria, who was leaning on her stick. "You okay, Mrs. Trumbull? Want to sit down?"

"No, no. I'm fine," Victoria said. "What about the girl you were supposed to exhume? You say she was a Norton cousin?"

"She committed suicide, like, ten years ago?"

"Oh?" Victoria looked puzzled. "I don't recall anything about a Norton suicide."

"I guess the family wanted to keep it quiet. They didn't put up a gravestone or anything." Denise lifted her braids and let them drop again. "Knowing my father, he's probably lost the records. I suppose he'll expect Ira and me to dig up the entire cemetery." She glanced at Victoria. "He has me digging graves as punishment."

"Oh?" said Victoria.

"You don't want to know, Mrs. Trumbull."

Back at Jonathan's grave, Victoria replaced her gardening tools in her basket while Denise waited.

"Is your granddaughter picking you up, Mrs. Trumbull, or do you need a ride home?"

"Elizabeth will be here in a few minutes, but thank you." Victoria glanced up at the heavy gray clouds that were moving in from the southwest. "I suppose the cousin's coffin has to be found quickly. It's going to do something tomorrow. Maybe snow."

"It's early for snow, isn't it?"

14

Victoria smiled. "Island weather," she said, as if that was all the explanation needed.

Ira stomped into Town Hall leaving a trail of sandy dirt behind him. He was a tall, sturdy man, and his footsteps shook the floorboards and rattled the ancient filing cabinets. Mrs. Danvers, the town secretary, looked up from her computer screen.

"Where's Denny?" Ira demanded.

Mrs. Danvers lifted her narrow shoulders in a shrug and checked the clock on the wall between the tall windows. "He should be here any minute. Want to wait?"

Ira plopped into Denny's chair, swiveling it. The chair squealed.

The clock clicked. Outside, a crow called. The phone rang. Mrs. Danvers answered quietly and wrote something on a notepad. After several minutes, she glanced out the window. "Here he comes now, Ira. He just parked his truck."

In a few moments, a stooped, black-bearded, potbellied man shuffled into the room. "Say, Ira!" he said. "Thought that was your pickup. The girl's coffin ready to go?"

"Nope," said Ira, swiveling the chair again.

15

"You better get on with it. Hearse is coming from off-Island tomorrow to pick the coffin up."

Ira pointed underneath the chair. "You need some WD-40 on this." He shifted whatever he was chewing to the other side of his mouth. "We found us a little surprise."

Denny sat in the visitors' chair next to his desk. "What kind of surprise, Ira?"

"Nobody was there."

"What are you talking about?"

Ira leaned back in the chair before he replied. "We got down six feet and there was nothing there."

Denny flushed. "Where in hell were you digging?"

"Right where you said. Next to old Simon." Ira swiveled the chair yet again.

"For God's sake, Ira," Denny shouted. "I told you two sites over." He got to his feet and leaned over his desk, his face inches from Ira's. "Can't you do anything right?"

"Back off, will you? I'm not deaf!" Ira's face was almost as red as Denny's. "Sit your fat ass back down." He took a scrubby piece of paper out of his shirt pocket, unfolded it, and handed it to Denny. "Here. Take a look at this." He stabbed his finger at the sketch map and the words underneath. "Next to old Simon, right? Under the yew tree, right? That's your handwriting, right?"

The phone rang. Mrs. Danvers said, before she picked up the receiver, "Will you boys please keep your voices down? Go outside if you *must* fight."

Denny examined the paper. Ira continued to chew. Mrs. Danvers told someone on the phone that a yard sale permit was ten dollars.

Denny tossed the paper at Ira, who refolded it and put it back in his pocket.

"So where's she buried, Denny?" Ira said. "Wasn't a gravestone there."

Denny started toward the door without replying.

"What d'ya want us to do?" Ira shouted at Denny's stooped back. "Dig up every coffin in the Norton plot? In the entire cemetery? Or what?"

Denny opened the door and said over his shoulder, "Fill it back in. Dig where I told you to dig. Two sites over."

"Something's fishy, Denny. Rotten. And I don't mean a corpse. You got a burial record for the girl? I ought to call up the DA or the governor's office. The Inspector General."

Denny stopped. "I wouldn't do that if I were you."

"Oh no?" Ira shouted. "You threatening me?"

"You start calling in state officials, Ira, and that'll be the last grave you ever dig." Denny shuffled out of the room and slammed the door so hard the crack in the glass extended all the way to the bottom.

Mrs. Danvers sighed. "This building has no privacy."

"My last grave, eh?" Ira got to his feet. "We'll see whose last grave it is."

As he opened the door, Mrs. Danvers called out to him, "The hearse is due on the first boat tomorrow. What do you want me to tell them?"

"Not my problem. Ask Denny," said Ira, and slammed the door. The glass fell out and smashed on the floor.

Bacchus, the toucan, was taking a bath in the kitchen sink when the phone rang. Before Dahlia Atherton could answer, the bird had knocked the phone out of its cradle with his beak, and was chortling into the mouthpiece. Dahlia picked the instrument out of a pool of water on the counter.

"Hello, hello!" she said. "Sorry about that."

The voice at the other end sounded

18

upset. "Red, Dahlia. On Martha's Vineyard."

"Is everything all right?" Dahlia asked.

"No," said Red. "You better get here quick. The coffin is missing."

"Missing?" Dahlia asked. "What are you talking about?"

"When they opened the grave, there was nothing there."

"Nothing?"

"They went down a full six feet. Nothing."

Dahlia thought for a few minutes. "Were they digging in the right place?"

"I went there afterward to check. The grave digger said he dug where he'd been told to dig, and there was nothing there." Red paused. Dahlia drew arrows on a piece of scrap paper and waited. "You wouldn't be playing tricks on us, by any chance, would you, Dahlia?"

"Good heavens, no. Is there a direct flight to the Island from Washington?"

"Not this time of year. You have to fly to Boston, take the bus to Woods Hole, the ferry to the Vineyard. Do you have a place to stay?"

"I'll call my cousin Howland," Dahlia said, and hung up.

Chapter 2

During the night, snow fell, a fluffy snow that clung to the cedars and filled the dried seed cups of Queen Anne's lace. Snow ticked against the kitchen windows, driven by the southwest wind.

Victoria was gazing out at the west meadow trying to think of a word she needed for her column when Howland Atherton drove up. He stamped his feet on the mat, shook the snow off his yellow slicker, and hung it on a nail in the brick-paved entry. When he came into the kitchen, a tall, elegant man, Victoria could see ice crystals glistening in his hair. Howland reached for a paper towel on the rack under the cupboard and rubbed his head with it.

"Help yourself to coffee and come join me," Victoria called out. She was sitting at the table in the cookroom, a small, bright room one step down from the kitchen. McCavity, her ginger cat, was asleep on her lap, his paws dangling over her knees.

"Here's your mail, Victoria." Howland

set a stack of envelopes and catalogs on the table next to her. McCavity looked up and yawned. "Quite a storm. Both the Pennsylvania and Mass Turnpikes are closed."

In Victoria's childhood, the cookroom had been her grandmother's summer kitchen. Now the small room was where she liked to write, a room filled with plants and baskets that hung from the heavy whitewashed beams.

Victoria had been working on her weekly column for the *Island Enquirer* when the elusive word stumped her. "I've got it," she said. "Purfle." Once she'd typed the word with two fingers she glanced at Howland, her smile framed by intersecting wrinkles.

Howland looked puzzled. " 'Purfle'?"

"Decorative edging. In this case, on a cello." When Howland still looked baffled, she continued. "I'm writing about the Island Consort's performance on Sunday."

"No one will know what it means."

"That's what dictionaries are for." Victoria pushed her typewriter to one side. "The storm doesn't seem bad to me. We've had only five or six inches."

"Buffalo's had twenty-two, and snow is still coming down. The storm is mostly to the west of us."

Once they'd dispensed with the weather,

Victoria told Howland about the grave diggers and the empty grave.

Howland rubbed his nose with his knuckle, a nose that was almost as large as Victoria's.

"Howland, do you know anything about a Norton girl who was supposed to have committed suicide ten years ago?"

"I hadn't moved back to the Island year-round yet. I was only here summers. If *you* don't recall her death, it probably never happened."

Victoria smiled faintly.

"They have no idea where she's buried?" he asked.

Victoria moved the pile of mail toward her and started to go through it. "They didn't as of yesterday afternoon."

Howland thought for a moment. "Is it possible that someone dug up the coffin earlier?"

Victoria shook her head. "The sides of the hole where Ira and Denise dug were still stratified. The ground had not been disturbed before."

Howland watched Victoria slit open her mail. "Was Denny a selectman at the time the girl was buried?"

"He's been in office at least twenty years."

The envelope Victoria opened was printed in fluorescent green. It read *Victoria Trumbull has won $8 million!!!* She shuffled through the flyers, peeled off a gold label that read *I accept $8 million!!!*, and stuck it on a spot that said, *YES!!!*

"Denise said this isn't the first time Denny buried someone in the wrong place," Victoria said as she smoothed the label.

"Who's Denise?"

"Denny Rhodes's daughter. She has a part-time job as a grave digger."

"A grave digger?"

"Denny is cemetery superintendent. I suppose he feels the job will keep her out of trouble." Victoria put the flyer in an envelope and set it aside.

Howland, who'd been watching with growing concern, said, "What are you doing?"

"I'm accepting the eight million dollars I've just won."

"That's a scam, Victoria. You don't believe all that stuff, do you?"

Victoria shrugged and looked at Howland through hooded eyes. "Someone has to win. Apparently I just have."

"Let me see that." Howland held out his hand for the flyers and started leafing through them. "You didn't even read the fine print."

"Of course not," Victoria said stiffly.

"A condition of acceptance is that you send them a check for twenty-five dollars."

"That's not much out of eight million. Pass me my checkbook, will you please, Howland."

Howland sighed. "You should know better." He moved the papers to the far side of the table out of Victoria's reach. "Denny's been in office too long."

"Why don't you run against him, Howland? We need some new blood in town government."

"Denny's not running for office this time. He's got another year to go. Noodles is up for reelection."

"If you run against her and win, you can oversee Denny."

Howland laughed. "No thanks."

Victoria drummed her gnarled fingers on the table. "You should call her by her proper name, 'Lucretia.' "

Howland laughed again. "The poisoner?"

"What have you done to upset her so?"

Howland made a wry face. "It's what I haven't done."

"Oh?"

"Ever since her husband left her for that

24

bartender, she's been trying to get even with him by acquiring a stable of male conquests."

Victoria examined Howland's hair with its silver streaks, his patrician nose, turned-down mouth, large off-center chin. "I see," she said.

"She claims she has a boyfriend, some guy from off-Island. A fisherman named Meyer. Nobody I know has ever seen him."

Outside, snow veiled the town center. The clock in the church steeple a half-mile away struck ten. McCavity slipped off Victoria's lap, sniffed Howland's trouser legs, and stalked out of the room.

"McCavity smells my dogs," Howland said. He leaned forward, elbows on the table. "I got a call last night from a cousin of mine in Washington who's suddenly decided to pay me a visit."

"A close cousin?"

Howland shook his head. "She used to spend summers with us before my parents died. Now I see her maybe once a year."

"I didn't know your family then. They were summer people. When is she coming?"

"On the late boat this evening. She's flying to Boston, then taking the bus."

"What about the storm?"

"The foul weather is mostly to the north

25

and west. She shouldn't have a problem."

"That's awfully short notice." Victoria drummed her fingers on the table. "How long does your cousin plan to stay?"

"She sounded as if she intended to be here indefinitely," Howland said.

Victoria refilled his coffee mug and set the pot aside. "That's putting quite a burden on you. Especially since she won't have a car, if she's flying in."

"That's not the worst part. She said she's been diagnosed with cancer and has been undergoing chemotherapy."

Victoria sipped her coffee, eyes half-closed. "This must be a difficult time for her."

Howland paused for such a long time Victoria thought he hadn't heard. Finally he said, "I've never liked Cousin Dahlia. You never knew her, but she was a domineering, self-centered kid, with a flair for self-dramatization, and she hasn't changed."

Victoria ignored his comment. "Has she finished her chemotherapy?"

"She's on a new course of treatment, said she's taking Taxol, a new drug that's supposed to be specific against her type of cancer."

" 'Taxol'?" Victoria looked up. "Why does that sound familiar?"

"I don't know. Taxol is a derivative of the Pacific yew."

"Yew," Victoria murmured. "The genus name for yew is *Taxus*. That's the explanation. Yew is terribly poisonous — bark, berries, roots, and needles." She started to reach for the pile of mail and stopped. "I suppose the drug is expensive?"

"Cousin Dahlia said she's moving in with me to cut costs. She'll have to go to the hospital once a week, and she wants to be treated here at the Vineyard. On the phone she was brave and noble beyond my endurance."

"I think that's wonderful of her," said Victoria. "And you, too, of course."

"Furthermore, Cousin Dahlia is bringing Bacchus with her."

"Bacchus?" Victoria glanced at him.

"Her toucan. She was in the Foreign Service, and when she was posted in Colombia several years ago, someone gave the bird to her." Howland grimaced. "An awful creature."

By evening, when Elizabeth, Victoria's granddaughter, came home from her job at the harbor, the storm had let up. Heavy clouds had moved to the east and moonlight sparkled on new-fallen snow.

Victoria looked up from her writing, knobby index fingers poised over the typewriter keys. "Supper is ready, Elizabeth. Lentil soup."

"What a day!" Elizabeth had moved in with her grandmother after a messy divorce — temporarily, she had said. But she'd found a job working in the Oak Bluffs harbor and was still here, apparently permanently. Victoria, who had reveled in her solitude, discovered to her astonishment that she enjoyed the company of her granddaughter.

Elizabeth looked down at her filthy jeans. "We're replacing mooring buoys with winter stakes. I'd better shower before I get this slimy green stuff over everything." She disappeared into the bathroom and Victoria heard the water running. She had almost finished editing her column when Elizabeth emerged.

"Did they find the girl's coffin, Gram?"

"I don't believe so." Victoria crossed something out and put down her pencil. "I understand the hearse was held up outside Buffalo. The girl was supposed to have been buried in the Norton plot under that big yew tree. But Denise seems to think the coffin could be almost anywhere."

"The grave diggers had better get busy if

28

the hearse is due soon."

"The grave diggers quit," said Victoria. "Ira and Denny had a falling out."

"No kidding! Denise, too?"

"She won't work without Ira. I gather Denise and her father had words." Victoria moved the pages of her column to one side. "I can't remember the last time it snowed this early in the year. It's only mid-November."

Elizabeth shook her head. "I suppose Noodles . . ."

"Lucretia," Victoria corrected.

"Well, I suppose they have to find the coffin. I mean, if you want to rebury a loved one, you're not going to give up until you find her. What do the Nortons think about all this?"

"That branch of the family moved off-Island some time ago. I suppose that's why they want to rebury the girl."

"What about the open grave?"

"Ira refused to fill it in." Victoria fastened the cover onto her typewriter and stowed it next to the bookcase.

The phone rang. Elizabeth passed the handset to her grandmother. "It's Howland."

"Has Cousin Dahlia arrived yet?" Victoria asked him. "What did you say,

29

Howland? I can't understand you because of the dogs."

"The noise is not the dogs," Howland growled. "It's Bacchus."

"Bacchus?" Victoria asked loudly.

"The toucan," Howland shouted. The barking increased. ". . . the dogs . . . Bacchus . . . them up."

"I'm sorry, I can't hear you."

The noise stopped. "Is that better?"

Victoria sat down again with the phone at her ear. "What did you just do?"

"I've shut myself in the broom closet. I picked up Cousin Dahlia and that god-damned toucan and a half-ton of luggage at the boat. But when we got to my house, Cousin Dahlia said she's allergic to my dust."

"Your house isn't dusty. Not very."

"According to her, she can't sleep here because of my housekeeping, and she won't move in until I vacuum."

"Well," said Victoria. "I suppose it's good to have an excuse to clean up once in a while."

"I have a favor to ask you, Victoria."

"Of course."

"You rent rooms occasionally, don't you?"

Victoria smiled. "Would you like me to

put Cousin Dahlia up until you finish cleaning? I'd be glad to."

"Are you sure, Victoria? This might take several days."

"I can use the extra money," Victoria said. "Besides, that will give me a chance to get acquainted with her. I know very little about summer people."

"As if anybody would want to," Howland muttered. "She'll have that toucan with her."

"The toucan is in a cage, isn't it?"

"Most of the time."

"I don't see why that would be a problem," Victoria said. "Do you want to bring her over now? If you haven't eaten, we have plenty of soup."

"I don't think she's had supper. We'll be there shortly. And thanks, Victoria."

By the time Victoria hung up, Elizabeth had already set an extra place at the table. "The downstairs bedroom is made up, Gram. I'll check to make sure there are fresh towels."

A short time later, Victoria heard a car drive up and then a series of yips and barks that marked the toucan's progress from car to house.

Victoria opened the door to greet them.

A tall, hefty woman stood in the entry,

31

stomping snow off her boots. She was wrapped in a bulky down coat and was wearing a multicolored knit cap that covered her ears and stopped just above her eyes. "You must be Mrs. Trumbull. I'm Dahlia Atherton." She held up a large cage draped with a paisley shawl. "And this is Bacchus." Inside the cage, the toucan was making a fearful racket.

Victoria held the door open and said over the noise, "Come in and welcome."

"Thanks so much, Mrs. Trumbull. It's good of you to take us in like this."

Howland, carrying two suitcases, followed Cousin Dahlia into the house. "The downstairs bedroom, Victoria?"

Victoria nodded.

"I'll help with those," Elizabeth said.

Dahlia set the cage on the kitchen floor and unwrapped the shawl. The toucan stopped barking briefly, blinked in the light, glared at Victoria out of one eye, and slashed his beak across the bars of the cage.

"What a fine bird," said Victoria, admiring the toucan's enormous beak. "Will my cat disturb him, Dahlia?"

"Will Bacchus disturb McCavity?" Howland muttered as he passed them on his way out to the car.

Dahlia laughed. "Really, Howland!" She turned to Victoria. "Bacchus needs to be where it's warm. Perhaps in the kitchen?"

Howland stopped at the door. "No!" he said.

Dahlia frowned and looked from Victoria to Howland and back. "I'm afraid the bedroom may be too drafty for him. He's a tropical bird, you know, of course."

"The bedroom will be fine," Victoria said. "I can turn up the heat a bit. The first floor has central heating."

Dahlia shrugged off her coat and turned to Victoria. Her cap had slipped over her eyes and she pushed it back. "I hope you don't mind if I keep this on. I'm undergoing a course of chemotherapy."

"So I heard. It's certainly a cheerful hat."

"One of the boys in my Sunday school class knitted it." Dahlia patted her head. "I'd like to wash up, if I may. My bathroom is, where?"

Victoria opened one of the doors that led off the cookroom. "Right here. You'll be sharing it with Elizabeth and me."

"You don't have private baths?" Dahlia asked.

Howland returned with another suitcase. He snorted. "They had an outdoor privy until recently. And chamber pots in each room."

"How quaint!" Cousin Dahlia stepped into the bathroom. "If you'll excuse me."

Elizabeth carried another large suitcase into Dahlia's room. The toucan, which had been silent for several minutes, started barking again, a harsh noise that went on and on and on.

Howland scowled. "I don't know how long this cleaning project will take, Victoria. A good long time, I hope."

"It's fine, Howland. I'm glad to help out."

That evening, Lucretia Woods and Denny Rhodes, two of the town's three selectmen, were working on correspondence at the big table in Town Hall.

The wall clock clicked off the seconds. Melting snow dripped steadily from the eaves. An occasional car swished by on the wet road in front of the building. Next door the town clock in the church steeple struck eight.

Lucretia had returned to the office after celebrating her fortieth birthday. Her face was slightly flushed and she was holding back a silly smile.

"Your boyfriend get back in time for the

party?" Denny asked as she was hanging up her coat.

"He called."

"Where's he at now?"

Lucretia pulled her long, straight hair into a ponytail and fastened it with an elastic. "He called from Seattle."

"So he says." Denny hobbled over to the table and sat.

"What do you mean by that, Denny?"

Denny waved a hand dismissively. "Forget it."

Lucretia glared at him, but he was looking at the papers in front of him. "I suppose Atherton showed up with a birthday present? A ruby necklace, perhaps?"

Lucretia's flush deepened. "I didn't invite Howland Atherton."

Denny looked up and smirked, his lips a pink smear in his beard. "Trying to play hard to get, eh?"

"Shut up, Denny!"

"Ooooh!" Denny grinned. "Guess I touched a nerve."

After they had worked for several minutes, Lucretia pushed her papers aside. "Ira is making a big deal about the missing coffin."

"Ira dug in the wrong place."

"Where *did* you bury the girl, Denny?"

"Two sites over. I told him that." Denny moved a paper from the top of the pile in front of him and studied the one underneath, lifting his head to peer through the lower half of his bifocals.

"Fortunately, the snowstorm held up the hearse," Lucretia said. "What do you propose to do now that Ira and your daughter have quit?"

Denny continued to thumb through his papers. "Wait until the snow melts and then hire somebody to dig two sites over, that's what. Last job I ever give Denise," he mumbled. "Teenagers! The hearse will have to wait."

"I want to see the burial records for the girl, Denny."

"Ask Mrs. Danvers. She keeps them."

"You're cemetery superintendent."

"For crying out loud, Noodles. She's the record keeper."

Lucretia persisted. "Ira said he's submitting a complaint to the District Attorney."

"Ira's full of horse manure." Denny wet his thumb and turned the page he was reading.

"Are you sure the girl is buried two sites over?"

Denny looked over the top of his glasses

at the other selectman. "Lay off me, will you, Noodles."

Lucretia flushed again, two bright spots high on her cheekbones. She flicked her ponytail off her shoulder. "The whole town's talking about the missing coffin."

"Let them talk." Denny picked up the letter in front of him with both hands and studied it.

"You may think you run this town, Denny, but you don't. Ira's got a right to complain to anybody he wants."

"We'll see about that," Denny said, not looking at her.

"You'd better find that girl's coffin, Denny, before the hearse gets here. The snow can't hold them up more than another day or two at the most."

Denny went back to his papers, his face rigid. "That's my business as cemetery superintendent."

"It sounds to me, Denny, as if this is selectman's business, not yours."

Denny examined another page. "Then bring it up at tomorrow's meeting."

"For heaven's sake, Denny. Stop being such an ass. This can't wait."

Denny looked at her again. "You know the open meeting law. No chance meetings. This," he pointed down at the tabletop,

37

"constitutes a chance meeting."

Lucretia pushed her chair back and stood up. "I'm going home. I just hope you don't drag Ephraim and me down with you."

Denny didn't respond. Lucretia shrugged into her coat and stalked toward the door. "Turn out the lights and lock the door when you leave."

Denny lifted up a hand. "No point in locking it. Tell Mrs. Danvers to get the glass replaced, will you? Ira broke it on his way out yesterday."

"That's not what I heard," said Lucretia. "Tell Danvers yourself." She shut the door firmly behind her and went out into the moonlit night.

"Many happy returns!" Denny called out to her back.

Chapter 3

That night Victoria woke to the sound of the siren in the firehouse a quarter mile down the road, and a short time later she heard the rumble of the new pumper as it approached her house. When she turned on her light the clock read two-thirty.

McCavity had taken over almost a third of her bed. She nudged him out of the way and swung her feet onto the cold floor. She pulled on the sweater she had draped on the back of the rocking chair, leaned on the windowsill, and looked out the open window.

In a few minutes the truck passed by the house and turned onto Old County Road, red lights flashing. The engine noise faded as the truck went down Scotchman's Bridge Lane.

Victoria went back to bed, but couldn't sleep. The truck hadn't returned. The fire at the dump must have flared up again. At least she hoped it was the dump fire, not somebody's house. Who did she know who lived out that way? Ever since she had been a child, she had worried about fire. Village houses were wooden and most had ancient chimneys, the old bricks held together with oyster shell mortar.

She got up again and found the down comforter in her closet. She tucked the blanket around McCavity, who had spread out still farther on her bed; she finally slept, uneasy about a fire somewhere in the direction of Scotchman's. The fire must be at the dump. The mountain of brush and stumps had been smoldering for weeks. Spontaneous combustion, the fire chief had told the selectmen after a neighbor had complained.

At breakfast the next morning she asked Dahlia if the fire siren had awakened her.

"I didn't hear anything," Dahlia replied. "Apparently the siren didn't bother Bacchus, either." She broke off a piece of her blueberry muffin. "By the way, do you suppose we could turn the heat up just a bit? Bacchus is not used to New England weather."

Elizabeth checked the thermostat. "It's set at seventy-four. You want it warmer than *that?*"

"If you don't mind." Dahlia adjusted her knit cap and pursed her lips. "It's kind of you to take me in on such short notice. I simply couldn't stay in the house the way Howland keeps it."

Elizabeth scowled.

"And I have another favor to ask of you. Be sure to say 'no' if you'd rather I didn't."

Elizabeth looked down into her coffee mug. Victoria murmured something that sounded like, "Of course."

"I give Bacchus a bath in my kitchen sink every morning. He enjoys bathing." Dahlia nibbled her muffin.

Elizabeth raised her eyes from an examination of her coffee mug. "You want to give that bird a bath in *our* kitchen sink?"

"Bacchus and I will wait, naturally, until you've had a chance to clear the dishes."

Elizabeth started to say something, but Victoria interrupted quickly. "Yes, certainly, Bacchus may have a bath."

Elizabeth stared at her grandmother, who smiled.

After they'd put away the dishes and had provided Cousin Dahlia with a clean sink and a bath towel for Bacchus, Victoria and Elizabeth bundled up the rubbish to take to the dump. They could hear Bacchus stropping his beak on the bars of his cage.

Elizabeth's usually sunny face was dark as they backed out of the parking spot under the now bare maple tree. "I see what

41

Howland means about that woman and her toucan."

They turned onto Scotchman's Bridge Lane.

"Dahlia and Bacchus will be here for only a day or two." Victoria pointed at a patch of snow under an overhanging cedar tree. "The snow is almost entirely gone now, only a bit left on the north-facing banks."

Elizabeth grunted. "I think they'll be with us more than a day or two."

Victoria tugged down the visor and peered at herself in the small mirror. "I've forgotten my earrings."

"We're only going to the dump, Gram. You look fine." Elizabeth waited for a car to pass on State Road, then turned right. "Howland told me the cleaning woman refused to come until he'd cleaned first."

"Howland likes to exaggerate."

"I wouldn't blame him for stretching out the cleaning for a few more days. We'll roast to death with the heat turned up the way Cousin Dahlia wants it for that bird."

Victoria stared straight ahead. "I think the warmth is for her, actually, Elizabeth, and she prefers not to admit it. Chemotherapy sometimes makes people feel cold. The chemicals affect nerve endings. She really is a brave woman."

Elizabeth glanced sharply at her grandmother, then beyond her out of the windshield. "Look at that smoke. I thought they'd got the dump fire under control."

Victoria swiveled around to see. "I heard the fire engines early this morning. The fire must have flared up again."

A thick plume of smoke rose above the bare trees. When they approached the dump, fire engines and hoses blocked the road. Anthony Rebello, the fire chief, waved them to one side. "You'll have to go around by the back road, Mrs. Trumbull."

"What happened?" Victoria asked.

"I don't know." Anthony, a tall craggy man with a heavy beard, jerked his head toward the mountain of stumps, branches, and dead trees that towered over the shingled building next to the road. "The fire must have reached something more flammable than the brush. Maybe pine pitch. Who knows."

Victoria leaned her head out of the window and saw, high above, smoke and flames snaking out of a dozen places among tree roots and branches. Patches of snow contrasted with the dark jumble of decaying brush and the bright flicker of the fire.

Anthony held up a hand to stop the vehicle that was following Elizabeth's car, then bent down and said to Elizabeth, "You'll have to move. Let the fire equipment through. You know the back way?"

Victoria nodded. "The old Dr. Fisher Road."

"The road's pretty rough," said Anthony. "People who live there keep it that way. They don't want the road used as a shortcut." He straightened up and beckoned to the waiting fire truck. "Take care now, ladies."

" 'Ladies,' " muttered Elizabeth as they backed out of the access road, passing the Chilmark fire engine. The driver held up a hand in greeting to Victoria.

Elizabeth made the circle of almost four miles over a badly rutted road before they reached the dump by the back way. Mr. Lardner, the dump-master, was waving his arms vigorously at an elderly couple in a red Volvo station wagon. Mr. Lardner was enormously fat and was encased in voluminous trousers and a tent-like maroon poncho that hung down to his knees. The woman at the wheel of the Volvo was listening with an occasional polite "Ahh!" or "Ooh!" The man next to her was watching silently.

"They'll never put that out," Victoria

heard the dump-master say. He nodded at the fire behind them. "It'll have to burn itself out, like those coal mines that burn for a hundred years."

"Ooh!" said the woman.

"Yessir," Mr. Lardner went on, "believe you me, I seen a lot of fires, and the way this one started up again is no spontaneous combustion."

"Really!" said the woman.

Mr. Lardner extruded a red-sweater-clad arm from under the poncho and waved toward the smoldering mountain in the near distance. "Looks to me like a fire bug."

"Ahh!" said the woman.

The man in the passenger seat looked over his shoulder at Elizabeth's car. "We'd better move," Victoria heard him say to the woman. And to Mr. Lardner, "Have you punched our dump ticket yet?"

"Right you are," said Mr. Lardner, handing back the book of tickets. "Nice to see you."

Elizabeth edged the car up to the dump-master's shack. "Do you have any idea how long we'll have to use the back road?"

Mr. Lardner lifted massive shoulders. "No idea. The way the fire started up again, they're not putting it out in a day or two, let me tell you." He reached for the ticket book Elizabeth held out to him, and as they drove away he said, "Have a nice day, ladies."

"What's with these creepy guys?" Elizabeth mumbled. " 'Ladies.' Bunch of pigs."

"What's wrong with being called 'ladies'?" Victoria asked. "Would you prefer 'girls'? Or 'women'? Or 'honey'?"

Elizabeth sighed. "It's their whole attitude."

Victoria settled back in her seat. "There are more important things to fuss about. Think of Howland's Cousin Dahlia."

Elizabeth steered around a deep rut. "She told me she was half-owner of Howland's house. I had no idea the house wasn't his alone. That's awkward for Howland."

"I was thinking of Dahlia, not of Howland. He'll have to come to terms with the situation. That house is large enough for both of them. He's had it to himself for about ten years."

When they got home, Bacchus was still bathing, dipping his large beak into the sink, flailing his wings, and splashing water to the right, where the paper towels hung limply, and to the left, where Victoria kept her wooden spoons in a pitcher. Dahlia was sitting at the kitchen table, reading the

Island Enquirer. She looked up with a pleased smile as Victoria and Elizabeth came into the kitchen.

Elizabeth stopped abruptly and Victoria almost bumped into her. "Everything is soaking wet!" Elizabeth stared around in dismay.

"He's having such a nice time, I didn't want to cut his bath short," Dahlia said. "He hasn't bathed like this in days."

"I should hope not." Elizabeth set the empty trash container on the floor with a thump.

Dahlia folded the newspaper, which was wet in spots. "I'll clean up, of course. And I'll buy a new paper."

Victoria sat down in the captain's chair by the door, opened her coat, and fanned herself. "That's not necessary. The paper will dry out."

"Quickly, in this heat," Elizabeth mumbled as she stowed the trash basket in the closet under the back stairs.

"I did turn the thermostat up a bit," Dahlia said. "I didn't want Bacchus to catch cold. I'll turn the heat back down to seventy-six."

"Seventy-six!" Elizabeth exclaimed and went over to the thermostat. "The temperature's up to eighty now. Can't you put a

47

doggy sweater on Bacchus?"

"That's a marvelous idea," Dahlia said.

Victoria had taken off her coat and the sweatshirt emblazoned with "Alice Rock" she wore underneath. "Why don't we set the thermostat back down to seventy-four, which is warmer than we like, and let you use one of those oil-filled radiators in your room. That way, you can keep your room as warm as you like." Victoria corrected herself. "As warm as Bacchus likes."

"Splendid," said Dahlia. "I'll clean up later. First, I believe I'll let Bacchus rest." She glanced at Elizabeth. "He's still recovering from the trip."

Elizabeth made a sputtering sound, and Victoria interrupted her. "What a good idea. I'm sure that will settle him after that nice bath."

"I need to make a few calls. I hope you don't mind if I take the phone into my room."

"Not at all," said Victoria.

Bacchus, back in his cage, started barking.

Elizabeth put her hands over her ears. "How can you stand that racket?"

"He'll settle down after a day or two." Dahlia patted the side of the cage as she headed toward her bedroom. "He's not

48

used to his new surroundings."

Elizabeth rolled her eyes. "I'll get the radiator. Where do you keep it, Gram, the upstairs closet?"

Victoria nodded. "She really is suffering, Elizabeth."

"As Howland would say, 'Yeah, yeah.' She'll recover and live to be a hundred."

After Elizabeth settled Dahlia in her room with the cordless phone and the radiator, Victoria surveyed the kitchen sink. "I suppose we'd better clean up the feathers and water."

"And bird droppings," said Elizabeth.

"He did make a mess, didn't he?"

Dahlia tossed her knit cap onto the twin bed next to the one she slept in, passed her hand over her scalp, kicked off her shoes, and sat at the small table under the east window with the cordless phone. Bacchus was making soft chuckling noises.

She reached the answering machine for Rose Haven Funeral Home. "This is Dahlia Atherton calling for Mr. Crossley. I'm on the Island now . . ."

Someone picked up the phone. "Dahlia, Red here. When did you get in?"

"Last night on the late boat. What's the problem?"

"I can't talk now," Red said. "Let me call you back."

"I don't have my own phone. Can we meet somewhere? I left my car in Washington, and don't have a rental car yet." Dahlia moved the curtains to one side and looked out at Victoria's fishpond and the bare trees beyond. Two ducks landed on the pond with a splash.

"Where are you staying, Dahlia, at your cousin's?"

"I'm at Victoria Trumbull's."

"I know where she lives. I'll stop by and pick you up in an hour or so."

"I don't think that's wise," Dahlia said. "I'll meet you at Alley's store. By the way, you haven't heard from Emery, have you?"

"Should I have?"

"I've been trying to reach him all morning. I keep getting his answering machine."

"He probably got called out on a job."

"Maybe so," said Dahlia, and hung up.

Chapter 4

That afternoon, Elizabeth was emptying kitchen scraps onto the compost heap on the other side of the maple tree when Howland drove up. He eased himself out of his car. His face was covered with soot. Sweat had run down his forehead and cheeks, leaving pale streaks. His dark turtleneck and musty-looking pants were dusted with a pinkish powder.

Elizabeth put the compost bucket on the ground and stared at him. "What happened to you?"

"Chimney fire," he muttered. "I was trying to get the house hot enough for Cousin Dahlia and that damned bird and the creosote in the flue caught fire."

"What's the pink stuff?"

"Goddam fire extinguisher."

"Come on in, Howland, and I'll fix you a drink."

"There must have been a blockage near the roof, because all of a sudden, soot and smoke poured back into the house."

Elizabeth laughed.

Howland turned on her. "Every god-damned thing downstairs is sooty. The ceiling. The walls. The floors. The furniture. It'll take me weeks to clean up. All on account of . . ."

Victoria opened the kitchen door. "Coffee?" she asked.

"Scotch." Elizabeth retrieved a bottle from the cabinet under the coffeemaker and poured Howland a strong drink.

He took a large swallow and wiped some of the soot from his face with the paper towel Victoria handed him. "How did you two make out with Cousin Dahlia?" he asked.

"Dandy," Elizabeth replied.

"Fine, Howland, just fine," Victoria added. "I think we've come to some agreement about the temperature."

"Did you know the dump fire flared up again last night?" Elizabeth asked.

Howland shook his head.

"Anthony thought the fire might have reached something highly flammable, like a pocket of resin," Victoria said. She examined Howland. "You're welcome to take a shower before we go to the selectmen's meeting."

"Thanks, I will." He finished his drink with a few long swallows and stood. "The water in my house is off."

Elizabeth raised her eyebrows. "How come?"

"The smoke detectors tripped and blew the fuses, including the one to the water pump."

"I'll get some of Granddad's clothes, okay, Gram? I think they'll fit Howland."

"Thanks. You're coming to the meeting, Victoria?"

Victoria held up her notebook in response.

On their way to Town Hall, Victoria commiserated. "It must be difficult to learn you have a co-owner."

Howland slowed at the Brandy Brow triangle to let a car pass. "That was a big surprise. I've always believed my grandmother left the house to me. Dahlia's always been welcome to come for vacations, and she has. But I never figured she'd claim half the house and move in with me."

He parked in the semicircular drive in front of Town Hall and helped Victoria out of the car.

Inside, she sat down on the long bench in front of the selectmen's table as she did every week. And every week she had an odd sense of time standing still. Town Hall had been Victoria's school when she was a child. Now, more than three quarters of a century later, she could still feel the pull of her hair in its tight braids as she turned her head to watch Mr. Mitchell pace that same green-painted floor, hands clasped behind his back. Mr. Mitchell had introduced her to poetry. She could still hear him reciting Longfellow. When she looked out of the window, the view of the church was the same. She could hear children's voices. Not so very long ago she was one of those children.

Denny hobbled around to the back of the table and nodded to Victoria. The clock on the opposite wall clicked. Lucretia, this year's chair, looked up at the clock and seated herself at the head of the table. She shuffled papers in front of her without looking at either Victoria or Howland, who was sitting next to Victoria on the bench.

"I suppose Eph's running late as usual?" Lucretia glanced at Denny. He nodded. She looked at her watch. "I'll give him another couple of minutes, and then we'll begin without him."

Denny shrugged. "Okay with me."

The door banged open and three oyster fishermen trooped in. One, Fred Mayhew, pushed his baseball cap up with his forefinger as a polite gesture to Victoria. She moved closer to Howland, and the oysterman sat next to her. Victoria breathed in the iodine smell of seaweed and muck and salt-soaked clothing. The others seated themselves on wooden chairs behind the long bench.

Victoria looked up from her notebook to see Casey O'Neill, the police chief, enter. The chief, a stocky young woman with shoulder-length red-blond hair, stopped and examined the broken glass. "What happened?" she asked Lucretia.

Lucretia pursed her lips and looked down at her papers. "You'll have to ask Mrs. Danvers."

"Not a break-in, I hope," the chief said to Mrs. Danvers.

"Overenthusiasm," Mrs. Danvers replied.

Fred Mayhew shifted to give Casey room, and she sat next to Victoria. Casey had appointed Victoria her deputy after realizing how little she, the new chief and an off-Islander, knew about the convoluted relationships of the townspeople. Victoria knew almost everyone — where they lived, who was related to whom, and who wasn't speaking to whom. Furthermore, Victoria was related to half the people in town.

A weathered man wearing steel-rimmed

glasses followed Casey. "How do, Mrs. Trumbull," he said.

"Mr. Cooper," Victoria replied, and moved closer to Casey. "There's plenty of room."

Lucretia glanced over her shoulder at the wall clock. "The meeting is in session."

Midway through the complaint against the crowing of Mr. Cooper's roosters, Ephraim, the third selectman, sauntered in.

Denny was telling the complainant, "That's what roosters do. They crow. Something hormonal." He moved his chair slightly so Ephraim could get by. "What say, Eph?"

"Not bad," Ephraim replied.

Ephraim was at least ten years older than Lucretia, and several years younger than Denny. He sported a bushy mustache and one gold earring, and was chewing gum. He sat next to Denny, set his reading glasses on his nose, and shuffled the papers that Mrs. Danvers had set at his place. He looked over the top of his glasses at Lucretia. "I move we take the rooster complaint under advisement."

Mr. Cooper shook his head, stood up, glared at Ephraim, and stalked out, slamming the door behind him.

After the selectmen voted to approve a proposed extension of the oystering season, Fred Mayhew and the others clumped out, closing the door gently.

"Next on the agenda," Lucretia glanced at her papers, "is the missing Norton girl."

"Who in hell put that on the agenda?" Denny demanded.

"I did," Lucretia replied.

Denny flung his pen onto the papers in front of him.

Ephraim shifted his gum to one side of his mouth. "What's the status of that?"

"The hearse driver, who'll be driving the remains back to Milwaukee, contacted Mr. Crossley, the new assistant at Rose Haven. Mr. Crossley is coordinating the move."

"The hearse still held up by the storm?" Ephraim asked.

"Let me finish." Lucretia held both hands up, palms toward her. "The roads have been cleared and the hearse should be here tomorrow or the day after, at the latest." She turned to Denny. "What do you propose to do about finding the remains, *Mr.* Rhodes?"

Denny was drawing boxes in the margins of the paper in front of him, punching holes in the centers with his pen.

Ephraim put his hands behind his head

and leaned back. "I guess we're assuming the coffin is definitely buried in the Norton family plot?"

"We're not assuming anything," Lucretia replied.

Denny continued to doodle. "The girl was buried two sites over. I told Ira that."

Ephraim set his chair down. "Right," he said. "Get Ira to dig two sites over, then."

"Ira quit," Mrs. Danvers said from her desk behind the bench. "He and Denny had words."

Ephraim yawned, showing his wad of chewing gum. "Why don't you just apologize to him then? No big deal. Grave diggers are artists. Temperamental. Tell him you're sorry."

"The hell I will," said Denny.

Mrs. Danvers spoke up again. "I called Ira's home. No answer."

Ephraim set his chair back down. "Call Luke Mayfield. He's got a Bobcat. He can dig up the entire Norton plot in a couple hours."

"You can't do that," said Mrs. Danvers.

Denny drew circles around the holes in the center of his squares. "Two sites over."

"Oh shut up," said Lucretia.

Victoria raised her knobby hand.

Lucretia nodded at her.

Victoria stood carefully. "I don't recall a Norton girl committing suicide ten years ago. Which girl was she?"

Denny peered at her over his glasses. "That's not germane."

Lucretia glared at him. "Who was the girl, Denny?"

Denny continued to draw on the papers in front of him. "Mary Jane Smith," he mumbled. "All that's on the record."

"No it's not," said Mrs. Danvers. "The name is not on the record."

"Who were her parents?" Victoria persisted. "Or grandparents? I don't recall any daughter or granddaughter by that name in the family."

"I'm sorry, Mrs. Trumbull. We're getting away from the issue, which is where is the coffin?" Lucretia waited for Denny's response.

He looked up from his doodling. "Authorize Luke to dig until he finds the girl."

"Is that a motion?" asked Mrs. Danvers.

"Yes," said Lucretia.

"Seconded," said Ephraim.

"You need to get permits," said Mrs. Danvers.

Lucretia asked sweetly, "Would you see to that, Mrs. D.?"

Victoria could hear Mrs. Danvers writing behind her.

After they had voted unanimously to have Luke dig until he found the coffin, Lucretia moved her papers to one side. "I have a problem I'd like to address." She cleared her throat. "It's not on the agenda."

"That's okay. Go ahead," said Denny.

Ephraim chewed his gum.

"I'd like a vote to remove a member from one of our committees."

"Who? Which committee?" Denny asked.

Ephraim yawned.

Lucretia fixed her gaze on the papers in front of her, two bright pink circles high on her cheeks. "The Substance Abuse Committee."

Howland crossed his arms over his chest and crossed his right leg over his left. Victoria noticed that his big toe showed through broken stitching on his shoe.

"Go on," said Denny. "We're all ears."

Lucretia scratched her head with the end of her ballpoint pen. "This member contacted our state representative without permission from me. Us," she corrected.

Denny leaned forward on his elbows. "The state rep?"

"Frank Perelman," said Ephraim. "Lives

in Oak Bluffs. Actually the state rep's rep."

"Mr. Perelman called Mrs. Danvers."

"Yeah?" said Denny.

Howland put both feet flat on the floor, uncrossed his arms, and sat forward. "May I speak to that?"

"I'm not through, Mr. Atherton."

Howland sat back, crossed his legs again, and began to shake his foot. Victoria turned her head to look up at him.

"Order, please!" Lucretia tapped her gavel on the table.

Howland stood up. "Madam Chair."

"Sit down!" said Lucretia. "I'll recognize you when I'm through."

Howland sat.

Lucretia dropped her voice to a lower level. "Mr. Perelman informed Mrs. Danvers that this *person*, who represented himself as a town official, was rude and offensive."

At this, Howland stood again. "Madam Chair, I am obviously the member of the Substance Abuse Committee in question. I called Mr. Perelman to ask a technical question. I most certainly was neither rude nor offensive."

Lucretia banged her gavel. "As of this moment, Mr. Atherton, you are no longer a member of that committee." Lucretia's cheeks were bright pink. She held her lips tightly together. Victoria noticed for the first time that Lucretia had a double chin.

Howland stood. Casey shifted her legs to let him by. Before he reached the door, he seemed to reconsider, turned, went back to the bench, and sat next to Victoria again. She sketched a smiling face in her notebook and showed it to him. He looked down briefly, crossed his arms, crossed his legs, and stared straight ahead.

At the selectmen's table, Lucretia examined papers in front of her. The skin around her mouth was white.

Ephraim looked over his glasses at Lucretia, examined his own set of papers, and chewed thoughtfully.

The clock in the church steeple next door made a slight rumble and then struck five. Victoria looked at her watch.

"Next on the agenda is approval of minutes." Lucretia's voice was tightly controlled.

"Let's get out of here." Howland held out his arm to Victoria. "I need fresh air."

Before they shut the door behind them, Victoria whispered, "The town clock is five minutes slow."

Chapter 5

The sun set, lighting the sky for a few minutes with a brilliant orange glow that abruptly faded. November darkness closed in. Howland hadn't said a word on the way back from the selectmen's meeting, and Victoria knew better than to interrupt his thoughts.

"I'll return the clothes tomorrow," he said, when he dropped her off.

"There's no hurry."

Victoria hung her coat on the back of a kitchen chair and went into the bright parlor, where Elizabeth had lit a fire. The parlor had an oddly assorted collection of furniture. A drop-leaf desk to the right had belonged to the ancestor who'd built the house. He had worked on his bills at that desk before the Revolutionary War, two and a half centuries before. Under the two front windows was an ornately carved Victorian sofa, with horsehair stuffing seeping out through worn upholstery fabric. In front of the sofa was a 1950s glass-topped coffee table, to the left, a mouse-colored wing chair, and to the right, a caned rocking chair. Under the west window was a bench on rockers where generations of mothers had worked on their mending while rocking their babies to sleep.

Elizabeth put their drinks on the coffee table and sat on the low wooden chair next to the fireplace. Victoria settled in the wing chair with McCavity in her lap, paws tucked under him.

The fire hummed. The selectmen's meeting seemed a long time ago. Victoria watched with amusement as Elizabeth stared at the portrait above the sofa, moving her head back and forth. The portrait had hung in the cabin of Victoria's grandfather's ship, and was of a black-haired woman clutching a blanket around her. The woman looked as though she'd been pulled out of the sea, half drowned. Or maybe she *had* drowned. As a child, Victoria had moved her head from one side to the other, just as Elizabeth was doing now, to see if she could escape the drowned woman's eyes.

Elizabeth met her grandmother's amused look and laughed. "How was the meeting, Gram?"

Victoria told her, and by the time she finished, Elizabeth was angry.

"Can Noodles do that? Can she simply kick Howland off a committee like that? Unilaterally? Did Denny and Ephraim sit there like toads while Noodles was chewing out Howland?" Elizabeth's voice was getting higher and louder. She jabbed the poker at a log, releasing a shower of sparks.

Victoria shifted McCavity to a more comfortable position. "I suggested to Howland a few days ago that he run against her next April."

"I hope he does. That would be the first time Noodles has been opposed in, what, ten years?"

"He said he won't run."

Elizabeth continued to poke the fire. "Whenever someone does run against the good ole boys — or good ole girl — it's as if they're threatening the whole fabric of this town. You'd never guess we're part of a democracy."

"I believe we're part of a republic," Victoria said. "Where's Dahlia?"

"She went for a walk. While you were at the meeting that toucan barked for half an hour. I can't wait for Howland to wring its neck."

Almost on cue they heard a few tentative yips from Bacchus, and then Dahlia appeared in the doorway, tugging at her cap.

"Would you care to join us for a drink?" Victoria called out to her.

"That would be nice, thank you," and when Elizabeth got up from her low chair to get the drink, "Plain juice, please." Dahlia held her hands out to the warmth of the fire.

"How was the walk?" Victoria asked.

"I went up to Alley's store, stopped on the way to watch the swans. The sunset was gorgeous."

"I'm sorry I didn't know you'd be out after dark, or I'd have let you take one of the flashlights."

"I didn't need one." Dahlia seated herself on the sofa under the portrait. "The moon on the snow made everything quite bright." She smiled up at Elizabeth, who had returned with a glass of juice. "How was the meeting?"

Elizabeth grunted. "That arrogant chairperson."

"Chairperson?" Dahlia looked from Elizabeth to Victoria.

"Lucretia Woods," Victoria said. "One of the selectmen. She was really quite rude to Howland."

Dahlia looked puzzled. "I don't understand."

Elizabeth sat down again, folding her legs like a stork alighting. "Neither do we."

Victoria said, "Howland was more upset this afternoon than I've ever seen him."

"I think Noodles has the hots for him," Elizabeth said.

Victoria frowned. "Howland mentioned this morning that Lucretia has been courting him."

Elizabeth sneered. " 'Stalking' is more like it."

Dahlia slipped off her shoes, put her feet up on the couch, and covered them with her voluminous skirt. "Howland is really quite an attractive man."

Elizabeth stirred the fire. "One summer when I was a kid, seven or eight, I guess, I had a crush on Howland. He must have been in grad school then." Firelight flickered on Elizabeth's face. She toyed with a half-burnt log that had fallen to one side, then set the poker down. "Someone told me Noodles — sorry, Gram, Lucretia — already has a gentleman friend. A fisherman named Meyer something."

Victoria thought for a moment. "I wonder why she's so upset with Howland then?"

"Maybe because he's rejecting her," said Elizabeth.

Dahlia smoothed her skirt. "Perhaps Lucretia is protesting too much?"

Victoria set her drink on the table. "Lucretia is quite a pretty woman when she smiles. She and Howland would make an attractive pair."

"Fat chance," said Elizabeth.

By the next morning, much of the snow had melted and a heavy ground fog had settled over the meadow, like grayish-white soup. From the cookroom window, Victoria watched the fog lap against the entry's stone steps. The pasture cedars floated out of the mist. Trees and telephone poles looked insubstantial, held up only by the thick, low cloud.

Victoria heard a vehicle bounce on her rutted driveway, and when the police Bronco pulled up in front of the door, she could see only its top.

She got to her feet to greet the chief.

"I can't stay, Victoria. I know I promised to take you to the hospital to read to the elderly, but I have to be around while they're looking for the girl's coffin. The hearse is due on the late boat." She watched Victoria rummage around in her cloth bag. "I don't suppose you want to come, do you?"

68

Victoria had already found her blue baseball cap and was setting it on her head. She studied her reflection in one of the small windowpanes in the dining room. The mirrored gold lettering on the cap read, "West Tisbury Police, Deputy."

Casey laughed. "Guess I have my answer. I don't know how long this will take, so you might want to call the hospital."

The fog lay evenly over the fields and meadows, patchy on the road. Casey drove in silence to the cemetery, past the small shingled police station and the mill pond. Victoria could see the pale forms of swans sailing in and out of the mist, two snow-white adults and one adolescent cygnet, half-gray, half-white.

Casey slowed as she drove between the granite gateposts at the entrance to the cemetery. Several vehicles clustered next to the big yew — Denny's red pickup, Ephraim's blue pickup, and Lucretia's red Volvo. Luke was unloading his Bobcat from the back of his truck. Another pickup pulled in behind them as Casey parked the Bronco.

Victoria turned to look. "It's Ira. I wonder what he's doing here?"

Casey helped Victoria out of the passenger seat. "Rubbernecking, I guess."

The open grave was directly in front of the ancient yew tree. To the left of the tree was a marble stone with "Simon Norton, 1854–1931" carved in lichen-covered letters.

Victoria stared at the gravestone.

"What do you see, Victoria?" Casey asked.

Victoria didn't answer. She was studying the stone.

"Victoria?" Casey leaned toward her and put her hand on her deputy's sloping shoulder.

"Something's not right," Victoria said finally. "I'm not sure what, but I suppose it will come to me."

Later that night, Beanie, whose job was to direct vehicles onto the ferry, hitched up his trousers, settled his baseball cap on his head, and strode over to the ferry slip. He could barely make out the lights of the *Islander* through the fog. The ferry rounded the jetty and entered the harbor, playing a searchlight over the fog-shrouded hulls of vessels anchored on either side of the fairway.

A teenage girl wearing a yellow slicker had followed Beanie out of the brightly lit terminal onto the dark wharf.

"Right on time, ma'am," he said pleasantly, checking his watch by flashlight. "You expecting company for the weekend?"

"My boyfriend," the girl answered. "He lives here. He went to America for the day."

"Yeah?" said Beanie. "Drive up to Boston?"

She shook her head. In the dim light Beanie could see she had large blue eyes with thick lashes. "He took the bus," she said. "He thought he might drive a friend's car back." When the girl smiled, she looked familiar to Beanie.

"Aren't you Denise Rhodes?"

She nodded.

"Your father's Denny Rhodes, right? The West Tisbury selectman?"

"Yuck." She shrugged, stuck out her tongue, and moved away from Beanie toward the vehicle gangplank.

"Better stand back," Beanie told her. "Cars come off the boat in a wicked hurry. Can't see much. Fog and all."

Beanie stationed himself next to the winch that ratcheted the gangplank up or down, depending on the tide.

The *Islander*'s bow door was open. Beanie could see vehicles lined up inside. He glanced quickly at the upper deck where passengers waited, faces barely visible in the diffuse light. The ferry's hull squealed against wood pilings. Beanie lowered the car ramp. Before he directed cars and trucks onto the Island, he checked that Denise was clear of traffic, then signaled with his light. Behind him, passengers were disembarking. Beanie heard Denise call to someone.

"Bye," she said. "Guess he didn't bring the car after all." She ran toward the passenger ramp.

Trucks rumbled over the uneven steel gangplank, carrying lumber and shingles and canned goods and appliances and produce, the necessities of Island life. After the trucks, cars drove off, first from one side of the ferry, then the other.

Something was holding up the line. Movement stopped, although Beanie could see vehicles still on board. The problem seemed to be a stalled vehicle, a hearse. A couple of deckhands directed cars around it and after a bit of backing and filling, things moved again.

By now, all of the passengers had left the boat. Beanie, who usually liked to listen to their greetings, hadn't noticed the sounds around him. The hearse was not moving. He called out to one of the deckhands, "*Dead* battery, I suppose?"

No one answered. A deckhand cupped his hands against the windshield to see inside. Someone tried the door. The door was locked.

"Where's the driver at?" Beanie called out.

A deckhand turned and lifted his shoulders.

"Still in the snack bar?" Beanie asked. "Someone better get him down pronto. We gotta load the next trip."

A stocky redheaded man Beanie hadn't noticed before walked across the traffic lane and stood next to him. "What seems to be the trouble?"

"Stalled hearse is holding things up."

"A hearse?" the man said. "A *hearse?*"

"Yes, sir. Driver's not with the vehicle."

The man turned up the collar of his dark windbreaker. "Where *is* the driver?"

"Good question. They're checking the snack bar now. He mighta lost track of time. Had a couple of beers."

"He doesn't drink," the man said.

"Better step aside, sir. We have to get the hearse off the boat so we can load the next trip."

The man paced a short distance from Beanie, then back again. His voice had an edge to it when he asked, "Hadn't you

73

better check on the driver?"

Beanie shrugged and dialed his cell phone.

A tall heavyset woman joined them, and the redhead looked at her with surprise. "Dahlia — what are you doing here?"

"I wanted to meet the hearse," Dahlia said. "Is there some trouble, Red?"

"Mort's missing."

"What about the hearse?"

Red nodded at Beanie. "They're going to tow it off the boat."

"Let's wait in the terminal," Dahlia said, and she and Red left Beanie, who shook his head and muttered something about off-Islanders.

Within a few minutes the tow truck had arrived and moved the hearse to the parking lot, out of the way of cars that were being loaded in a hurry. The schedule had been delayed for twenty minutes.

Red returned to Beanie, who was directing trucks onto the boat, tearing tickets and handing the stubs back, apologizing for the delay, joking with drivers. He tapped Beanie on the shoulder. "Mister!"

"Yes, sir?" Beanie said with a touch of impatience. "We're behind schedule, and I can't talk to you now."

"Something's happened to the hearse driver."

"I can't help you, sir." Beanie handed a ticket stub back to the driver of a large semi. "Schenectady?" he asked.

"Rochester," the driver answered. "The snow belt."

"Take care," Beanie said as the driver lifted a hand in salute and drove onto the boat.

Red continued to stand next to Beanie.

"Sir," said Beanie, losing patience, "talk to the guy in the ticket office. Not me."

Once the last car had been loaded, the ferry's large door clanged shut. Beanie hooked the chain across the slip. The ferry backed out, the distance between boat and land grew, and Beanie watched until the lights disappeared in the fog. He strolled over to the terminal building and went inside. Dahlia and Red were sitting on one of the wooden benches next to the window.

"Driver of that hearse has gone missing," Beanie told the ticket seller.

The ticket seller said, "Wouldn't be the first time a driver had himself a couple of beers, forgot he'd left a vehicle below, and remembered it once he'd taken a taxi to where he was going."

"But a hearse?" Beanie said. "Forget a *hearse?*"

Chapter 6

One more ferry was due from Woods Hole, and after that the ticket office would be closed. A dozen people milled around the waiting room, buying tickets, shifting luggage, talking to each other, speaking on cell phones.

Red stood by the window and looked at the hearse, which was parked beside a tall hedge. He was about Dahlia's height, and had the same stocky figure. His hair, once a carroty orange, was now a subdued red, streaked with gray. Boyish freckles had become age blotches across his lined face.

He turned from the window and sat again. "Do you have an extra key?" he asked Dahlia in a low voice.

"I have no need for a key. Didn't you bring yours with you?"

Red grunted. "I left it in the pocket of my black suit coat, which is in the Rose Haven hearse, which the undertaker, Toby, drove off-Island this afternoon."

Dahlia laughed.

"It's not funny. We need to get into that hearse."

Dahlia adjusted her hat. "I think it would be wise to wait until the terminal closes for the night."

"You're probably right." Red stood again. "Let's get a cup of coffee. The diner stays open late."

They walked the short distance to the ArtCliff and sat at a table where they could make out a few diffuse harbor lights.

Dottie, the waitress, hurried over. "Can I get you folks something?"

"Two coffees," Red said. "Black."

"Regular or decaf?"

"Regular." Red waited until she left. "I doubt if they even checked to see if Mort was in the hearse before they towed it off the boat."

"You don't suppose he *is* in the hearse, do you?"

"I can't see through those damned tinted side windows," Red said.

"I don't believe the windshield is tinted."

Dottie returned with coffee. "Would you care for anything else?"

"No, thanks," said Dahlia.

Red peered out into the fog. "The last ferry's just leaving." He stirred sugar and

77

cream into his coffee. "Have you reached Emery yet?"

"I've called several times, but keep getting his answering machine."

They finished their coffee in silence. Red wadded up his paper napkin and pushed his chair back. "We'd better get moving. We probably can see through that windshield. You'd think the deckhands would have checked to see if anyone was still inside."

"I'm sure they did," said Dahlia, "and didn't see anybody."

Dottie bustled over with the check. "Be careful out there. Real pea-souper tonight."

The terminal's yellow night-lights cast weird multiple shadows that lengthened and shortened as Red and Dahlia moved across the wet brick pavement by the empty taxi stand. The November-bare trees cast skeletal shadows on the hearse.

"Where's your car?" Dahlia asked.

"At Rose Haven. I expected to drive back with Mort." Red turned up the collar of his windbreaker. "Mort might have had a heart attack. Maybe he left the engine running. Carbon monoxide, you know."

"Perhaps he fell overboard," Dahlia said.

"Don't say that."

The parking lot lights barely illuminated the inside of the hearse. Red cupped his hands around the windshield. The driver's seat was empty. "The light's too dim to see if he's in back." Red moved away from the vehicle. "We've got to get hold of Tremont."

"Has Tremont arrived on the Island yet?"

"I saw him at the grocery store three or four days ago," Red replied. "He's staying at that motel on Beach Road."

"You have your cell phone?"

Red shook his head. "We can walk there. The motel's across from the diner."

They entered the brightly lighted motel lobby and asked for Tremont Ashecroft.

"I haven't seen him for several days," the clerk at the registration desk told them. "But I've been off," she added. "So I wouldn't have."

Red leaned his elbows on the desk. "He hasn't checked out, has he?"

The woman flipped through a ledger she retrieved from under the desk. "Nope. He's paid up through the end of this week."

"Would you check his room for us?" Dahlia asked. "We're concerned about him."

The woman looked at them carefully. "I

79

suppose so." She lifted a key from a board behind her desk. "I'll be right back."

She returned in a few minutes. "His clothing and papers are still there." She hung the key back on its hook. "Want to leave a message?"

Red started to say yes, but Dahlia shook her head. "We'll try him again later," she said. "Thank you."

While Dahlia and Red were trying to locate Tremont Ashecroft, Elizabeth was buying milk and eggs at Cumberland Farms, which was open until midnight. Victoria waited in the car. The store's display windows were festooned with purple and white crepe paper and large, hand-lettered signs: GO VINEYARDERS! BEAT THE WHALERS!

"Where's the game this year?" Elizabeth asked the boy at the checkout.

He eyed her strangely, as if she'd come from an alien world. "Nantucket."

He rang up the groceries and Elizabeth bagged them. "Are you going to the game?" she asked.

"Sure. Everybody is. The Steamship Authority is putting on a special boat. Didn't you go to the game last year?"

"I wasn't here then."

The boy relented. "Nantucket played here. Beat us good. This year, we got a chance." He handed Elizabeth the receipt. "Have a good evening, what's left of it."

Victoria was working on her crossword puzzle with the dome light on when Elizabeth returned with the groceries.

"I wonder where Dahlia's been all day," Victoria said.

Elizabeth grunted. She waited for a car to pass and pulled into Five Corners.

"Don't be so hard on her, Elizabeth. I feel sorry for Dahlia. She's used to having her own way and she's used to having money. Now that she is ill, she must worry about every penny."

Elizabeth grunted.

Victoria gazed silently out of the car window. Fog distorted the passing trees. Their headlights picked out golden beech leaves among bare oaks and maples. "Denny said the hearse was scheduled to arrive tonight."

"They still haven't found the girl's coffin, have they?"

Victoria shook her head. "Something didn't seem quite right at the cemetery this morning." She was quiet for a few moments. "I have a feeling I saw something significant."

They passed through the wooded stretch outside Vineyard Haven. On their right, lights reflected off the fog hovering over the cropped grass of Nip 'N' Tuck Farm. On their left, yellow sodium lights at the new fire station illuminated open doors and empty stalls.

Elizabeth slowed the car. "The firefighters must still be at the dump. One of the customers at the store was complaining about the smoke."

"I don't see how they can hope to extinguish the blaze," Victoria said. "That stump pile has been rotting for thirty years or more. No wonder it caught fire."

"The dump-master says the fire was arson."

Victoria shook her head. "Mr. Lardner doesn't understand compost heaps."

At the dump, firelight flickered through the fog. Dim figures moved about, silhouettes that became three-dimensional when working lights flashed on them. Voices called and responded. Flames hissed and crackled, engines throbbed, a bulldozer rumbled and clanked. The fire smelled acrid.

Elizabeth shifted gears. "I've got to move on. There's a car behind me."

A few minutes later they turned into Victoria's drive, parked, and went into the house. Elizabeth lit a fire in the parlor, and they relaxed with drinks.

Victoria suddenly set her glass on the coffee table and stood up, dislodging McCavity, who'd been dozing in her lap.

"I've got to call Casey. I just realized what was wrong."

Elizabeth looked up. "You mean at the cemetery?"

But Victoria had already disappeared into the cookroom. She turned on the table lamp and dialed Casey's home number.

"I know what was bothering me," Victoria said when Casey answered.

Casey sounded groggy. "What?"

"You know how I said at the cemetery that something wasn't right?"

"I just woke up," Casey mumbled. "I fell asleep in front of the TV. What did you say?"

Victoria sat down. "The gravestone was in the wrong place. Someone moved old Simon Norton's stone."

"What?"

"The stone used to be way over to the left of that big yew. Now it's almost in front of the tree."

Casey was silent.

83

"Someone moved the gravestone," Victoria repeated.

"A Halloween prank?"

"I don't know," Victoria went on. "Someone planted sod around the base, so the stone looks well established."

"I'm not awake yet, Victoria."

"It didn't strike me at first," Victoria continued, "because of the grass."

Casey sounded as though she was beginning to wake up. "You think this has something to do with the girl's coffin?"

"I can't imagine what else it would be. Someone didn't want the coffin found. How many places did they dig this morning?"

"Three more."

"And found nothing."

"Okay, Victoria. I can't think straight at the moment. I'll talk to Denny tomorrow. Pick you up around ten?"

Casey and Victoria met with Denny at Town Hall the next morning. Condensed fog dripped from the eaves. Denny stood up when Victoria entered and listened to her.

"Victoria, I know you mean well, but this is something you don't need to concern yourself with." He leaned his hands on his desk and studied some papers. Victoria unbuttoned her coat and sat down.

"Old Simon's gravestone has been moved." She emphasized each word.

Denny sat again. "Look, Victoria, I'm busy. I'm right in the midst of something." He turned to Casey. "Anything I can do for you, Chief?"

Casey said, "I'm here with Victoria."

"You've got to find that coffin," Victoria said.

Denny leaned back in his swivel chair. "I'm working on it."

"The coffin is under Old Simon's stone."

"Old Simon is under his stone. That stone has been there for three quarters of a century."

"No it hasn't," Victoria insisted. "That stone used to be to the far left of the big yew. I've put lilacs on his grave every Memorial Day since he died. His stone has been moved."

Denny sighed. "I don't have time for this."

Victoria watched him through hooded eyes. "You've looked in all the supposedly empty plots to the right of the stone and found nothing."

"That's right," said Denny.

"It won't kill you to look under his stone."

Denny sighed. "Okay, Victoria. Okay. You win. I'll ask Luke to dig there. Now can I get back to work?"

Victoria glanced at the papers on his desk, which had slid aside, uncovering a half-done crossword puzzle. She tilted her head to look at it, and said, "A three-letter word for a food scrap is 'ort.' " She lifted herself out of the chair. "Did the hearse arrive last night?"

Denny shifted the papers back on top of his crossword puzzle. "The driver's supposed to call me around noon."

Victoria buttoned her coat as she headed for the door, Casey behind her. "Maybe you'll have found the coffin by then."

Denny grunted.

At the door Casey turned. "Where's Mrs. Danvers?"

Denny didn't look up. "Seeing about glass for the door."

The three selectmen were already at the cemetery when Victoria and Casey arrived after lunch. Toby, the undertaker, waited by the open grave. His sparse dark hair was combed carefully across the top of his scalp. His windbreaker stretched tightly over his dark suit coat. His red vest showed in the V of the jacket. Luke Mayfield's

Bobcat had unearthed a metal coffin.

Denny shuffled over to Victoria. "I got to give you credit, Victoria. The coffin was where you said, under old Simon's stone." He muttered something that Victoria barely heard that sounded like, "Damned kids." Denny turned to Toby. "I guess you heard about the hearse driver not showing up?"

Toby sighed. "That's why I'm here."

"Where's Red now?" Denny asked.

"He called in sick." Toby cleared his throat. "Lucretia asked me to take care of the exhumation on behalf of the Milwaukee family."

"She's not in charge. I am." Denny thumped his chest. "Red picked a hell of a time to get sick." He shuffled away from Toby, then back again. "I told the Vineyard Haven police to have the hearse towed to Tiasquam Repairs here in West Tisbury."

"Curious as hell, driver gone missing like that." Toby peered down into the hole as he directed the two workers, who had positioned a hydraulic lift over the grave. "Okay, boys. You got the belts underneath?"

The coffin, an inexpensive model with the panels stamped in a waffle pattern, came up level to the surface. Clods of sandy earth dropped back into the grave. The curved top was mottled with a scrofulous-looking fungus — green, gray, and dirty pink. Streaks of blood-colored rust had run down the sides. A panel at the foot of the coffin, made of two thin pieces of sheet metal riveted together to make it look heavier than it was, had been fastened to the rest of the coffin with rusting sheet metal screws, and the panel shifted slightly as the coffin was moved.

Lucretia watched Denny, who was staring down at his feet, his hands folded sanctimoniously in front of him. Victoria heard a car go by on Deadman's Curve. A sudden raw breeze blew the fog into ragged streamers that fluttered around the tombstones. Toby's two helpers put on heavy leather work gloves, slid the coffin onto a gurney, and wheeled it to the hearse.

Toby turned from one member of the silent group to another. "You know, don't you, the state ordered us to open the coffin?"

No one responded.

Toby went on. "See you at the funeral home, then. Back entrance. Next to the loading dock. Plenty of parking."

Victoria looked questioningly at Casey,

88

who shrugged. "This is all new to me, Victoria." She paused. "You don't have to come inside the funeral parlor, you know. You can wait outside in the Bronco."

Victoria flicked a stone with her lilac-wood stick. "I wouldn't miss this for the world." Droplets of fog had condensed in her hair, like small diamonds. She glanced behind her. A branch of the yew moved slightly, releasing a shower of water into the open grave. Victoria shivered.

"Want my jacket?" Casey asked.

"I'm fine. I need to keep moving, that's all."

The cars, the pickups, and the police Bronco followed the hearse out of the cemetery and back the way they'd come, past the mill pond and Victoria's house. They continued on beyond the airport, where the runway lights glowed through the fog, and the convoy turned onto Airport Road. They passed gaunt silvery dead pine trees, killed by a fungus years ago. Mist twisted around the base of the trunks and writhed in the bare branches above. Casey stopped at the flashing red blinker. Victoria shivered again.

Casey looked at her. "I've got an extra windbreaker, Victoria. I'll pull over so you can put it on."

"Thank you, but I'm not cold. Really."

"I guess I know how you must feel." Casey turned onto the Vineyard Haven Road. "I can't imagine what the body is going to look like after ten years. Nothing but bones, I suppose. Or maybe it'll be dried up, like a mummy."

They slowed as they went past the high school. The sign out front, decorated with masses of purple and white balloons, said in enormous letters, BEAT THE WHALERS!!

"The football game, the football game," Casey mumbled. "When do they find time to study?"

She followed the others into the driveway of the white clapboard funeral home a mile or so beyond the high school. A vine with a few blasted roses twined on a rail fence at the front of the place. They parked at an industrial loading dock, where Toby's men had already set the coffin. Casey and Victoria went up the steps and through a small door into a chilly gray space that seemed part factory, part operating room.

The cement floor, painted a shiny battle-ship gray, sloped toward a drain in the middle of the room. The cement block walls were smoothed with thick paint, a lighter gray than the floor. A stainless steel sink and counter ran along one wall. An operating room light hung from the ceiling in the center of the room, casting dark shadows on the faces of the group standing uneasily against the wall, some distance from the hanging light and the stainless steel table underneath.

Victoria studied the room. It was cold and bleak and sterile and dispiriting. She blotted her dripping nose, sniffed, and recognized the acrid smell of formalin. Embalming fluid. She could see through an open door into what looked like a closet, where there was a stack of folding metal chairs, boxes and bottles on steel shelves, and a starched lab coat on a hanger on a rack.

Toby's helpers wheeled the gurney with the coffin on it next to the table. "That's fine. Stop right there," said Toby.

Casey was the only one of the group to move. She took a folding chair from the closet and opened it for Victoria, who sat with a nod of thanks. The room was deathly quiet. Victoria could hear the hum of an air conditioner, keeping the room even colder than the chilly November day.

Toby took off his windbreaker and suit coat, hung them in the closet, and put on the lab coat. "That's good," he told the workmen. He buttoned the white coat, fixed a surgical mask over his nose and mouth, and pulled on latex gloves.

He glanced around at the people who were still standing. There were two Victoria didn't recognize, who must be state officials. "You better all take seats," Toby said. "This may not be pleasant." He walked around the coffin, inspecting it.

Metal chairs scraped on the concrete floor.

"Let me have the pliers, Nick." He explained to the others, now seated, "I have to break the seal."

The group was silent while Toby worked. Casey sat next to Victoria. Lucretia and Ephraim were on the other side of the room, far away from Denny. Victoria heard someone move a chair behind her.

There were several metallic snaps, and then Toby handed the pliers back to the helper. "That does it." His voice was muffled. "Put on masks and surgical gloves, both you guys, then give me a hand."

Victoria folded her arms tightly over her stomach to quiet its rumbling.

Toby and Nick forced the lid back slowly. Hinges squealed.

Victoria sat forward. Everybody else was still.

Toby pushed the lid all the way back. He stared into the open coffin. "I'll be damned," he muttered. "I'll be goddamned."

"What is it?" asked Lucretia, standing up.

Denny, too, stood, and shuffled toward the coffin.

"Get back," said Toby. He turned to Casey. "Chief, you better look at what we got here."

Casey was already on her feet. Victoria levered herself up stiffly and followed. Ephraim stood by his chair, chewing.

Casey peered cautiously into the coffin. "Lord!" she said. Victoria, too, looked in.

The interior of the coffin was brightly illuminated by the overhead light. When Victoria's eyes moved reluctantly from the mildewy sateen lining to what she expected to see reposing in the center, she turned to Casey in astonishment. "Sandbags?" she said. "Just bags of sand?"

Casey unfastened her cell phone from her belt. "The stuff may be more than sand, Victoria." She started to dial. "I've got to call Howland Atherton right away."

Lucretia, who had been staring into the coffin with a blank expression, looked up abruptly at Casey, her face suddenly alive. She snapped at the chief. "No, you don't,

Chief O'Neill. I won't have you contacting Atherton." Her cheeks flushed. "He's no longer on the Substance Abuse Committee." She thrust both hands into her trenchcoat pocket.

Casey continued to press buttons on her phone. "Sorry, boss." She stepped away from the open coffin, the phone next to her ear. She held her hand over the mouthpiece. "Atherton's a fed."

Lucretia's face suddenly lost its color.

"He's with DEA," said Casey. "Drug enforcement."

Chapter 7

Toby shucked off his mask, gloves, and lab coat, took his suit coat off its hanger, buttoning it over his stomach, and ushered everyone into the public rooms, which were considerably warmer than the room where the coffin rested. The public rooms were tastefully decorated in subdued shades of blue and ivory with touches of rose, and smelled of gardenias.

While everyone else waited inside for Howland to arrive, Lucretia beckoned Denny outside and confronted him in the parking lot. Tendrils of fog rose from the asphalt.

"What were you thinking of?" she demanded. "You knew full well what was in that coffin, didn't you? A million, two million, three million dollars' worth of drugs? Cocaine, Denny? Or heroin?" She paced away from him and back again. "Are you crazy? You'll be sent away forever. And you'll drag Ephraim and me down with you. Didn't it occur to you they'd find out? You ass! Where did you get the stuff, anyway?"

Denny shuffled over to his pickup, its sides slick with condensation, and leaned against it for support. "I had no idea the Norton girl wasn't in the coffin. No idea at all." He took a blue bandana out of his pocket and wiped his forehead.

"Who's going to believe you after the fuss you made about the exhumation? What do you have, an IQ of seventy-five? Of *forty*-five? A three-year-old wouldn't have been so stupid."

"I can explain." Denny held up his hands as if to ward her off.

"What's to explain?" Lucretia's face was bright red. She jabbed her finger at him. "It's pretty clear, I'd say. And now you've got Howland Atherton involved. Why didn't Casey tell us he was a federal drug agent? We're police commissioners, after all. Her bosses. I'll have her ass kicked out of town. I'll make sure she never gets another chief's job in the commonwealth."

Denny held up his hands, palms out. "Calm down, will you?"

"Calm down! Calm down? You have to be kidding!" She pointed at the loading platform. "Millions of dollars' worth of drugs sitting in a casket on an autopsy table in there," she thrust her face next to

96

his, "and you obviously knew all about it. Buried for ten years, Denny? I suppose you *forgot* where you'd buried your stash?" She took a breath.

"Believe me, I had no idea it wasn't the girl." Denny slapped his chest. "The family called me from Milwaukee . . ."

"Baloney!" Lucretia spun on her heels. Her coat swirled about her.

"Hear me out, will you, Noodles?"

"Don't you dare call me Noodles."

Denny lifted his hands from his chest and held them out, shoulder-high, palms toward her. "They said the girl had committed suicide. The family wanted her buried here in West Tisbury. No fuss."

"Who was 'they'? I suppose you made sure the person who talked to you was who he said he was?"

"It was a she. Upset. I couldn't see upsetting her any further."

"Sure, Denny. Sure. Never occurred to you there was any hanky-panky, did it? I suppose you drove to Milwaukee to pick up the remains?"

He shook his head. "They drove the hearse here. I met them at the Steamship Authority dock in Vineyard Haven. Two guys from the Milwaukee funeral parlor."

"Did they give you a death certificate? In

case you forgot, Denny, you need a death certificate."

"Yeah, certainly they gave the certificate to me, and I entered the information into the record book."

"And the name was?"

"Mary Jane Smith."

"My God, Denny. 'Jane Doe.' Only there was no body." Lucretia looked heavenward to where the low scud raced below the overcast. "Just millions of dollars' worth of dope. I suppose somebody paid you off for being so sensitive to the bereaved?"

"They didn't pay me off," Denny said defensively. "They did, however, give me a gratuity."

Lucretia laughed. " 'Gratuity'! That's what is known as hush money, Denny. How large was the 'gratuity'?"

Denny stepped forward from the support of his truck, tripped on a pebble, twisted his foot, and winced. "Damn!" He leaned back against the truck again.

Lucretia was unsympathetic. "How large a gratuity, Denny?"

"That's all it was, a 'thank you' to me for my trouble."

"How much?" Lucretia stood with both hands on her hips.

"Five thousand."

"Five thousand *dollars?* My God! Five thousand dollars for a couple of hours of sneaking around?"

Denny leaned forward and ran both hands down the sides of his knees. "I worked a hell of a lot more than a couple of hours. I had to open the grave . . ."

"You did that yourself? Didn't that seem odd to you?"

Denny straightened up. "Certainly not. The family didn't want a big to-do." He bent again and continued to rub his knees. "It took me half a day just to open the grave."

Lucretia passed a hand over her hair, spreading droplets of moisture. "I can't believe what I'm hearing. So this hearse driven by a couple of goons disembarks from the ferry, you follow the hearse to the West Tisbury cemetery . . ."

"I led the way, actually."

"You led the way to the cemetery, the three of you — there were two guys in the hearse?"

Denny nodded.

"The three of you unload the coffin, lower it into the ground, and shovel dirt on top of it?"

"And then I resodded the site."

Lucretia stepped away from him. Then

turned. "All with your bad knees, I suppose."

"They were okay then."

"Just out of curiosity, what happened to your knees?"

"An accident," Denny muttered.

"What kind of accident?"

"I fell. Actually, I fell into an open grave."

Lucretia erupted in a peal of laughter.

"It's not funny," Denny said.

"How long ago did that happen?"

"While we were burying the Norton girl."

"*Not* the Norton girl. *Drugs*, remember?" She thrust her hands into her trenchcoat pockets. "Sounds to me like a drug deal — break his knees by shoving him into an open grave."

"It was an accident," Denny said. "Besides, I didn't break my knees. I tore the cartilage."

"Yeah? Who shoved you?"

"Get real, Noodles."

Lucretia looked up as a white Renault came up the drive and parked at the loading dock. Howland got out, slammed his car door shut, and took the steps, two at a time, into the room where the coffin lay. Lucretia jerked her head in the direction of the dock. "Now you've got *him* involved." She started back toward the funeral home and said over her shoulder, "I suppose I have to be pleasant to him."

Denny snickered. "What's with you and Howland? He throw you over for a younger chick?"

"Don't be any stupider than you already are."

"Now, now, Noodles. You're overreacting." Denny grinned as he limped toward the loading dock. "You've got to expect raging hormones at your time of life. That's all it is. Hormones."

Lucretia swung around with an expression that should have warned Denny, and slapped him so hard his glasses flew off and landed, unbroken, on the asphalt. Then she spun around and stalked up the stairs and into the building.

Howland paused inside the door. The coffin's lid was propped open. The overhead light illuminated the contents — three large sandbags where the body should have reposed. The coffin had been cordoned off with fat blue velvet ropes on stainless steel stanchions.

Casey stood at the head of the coffin, talking on her cell phone. She nodded at Howland and covered the mouthpiece of the phone. "More problems at the dump." She took her hand away and spoke into the phone. "Junior, I may be tied up here at the funeral home for a while. See what the fire chief needs from us, will you?" She listened, made some notes. "Call me after you've talked to Anthony." She put the phone back in its case on her belt. "They're going to bulldoze the stumps right down to bare ground to put the fire out."

"How long are they talking about, weeks?" Howland asked before he turned to the casket.

"Probably." Casey nodded. Then, referring to the coffin, she said, "Nobody's touched it. Toby and his helpers were wearing gloves. Nobody else even came close."

Howland straightened up. "Where is everybody?"

"In the viewing room or parlor or whatever. Where it's warmer. Lucretia and Denny are outside."

Howland's mouth turned down. "I saw them." He looked up from a quick examination of the three sandbags. "This doesn't seem typical of a drug stash, but I'll call in the techs." He located Toby's phone next to a glass-fronted cabinet filled with boxes of absorbent cotton and tubes and jars of makeup.

After he hung up he checked his watch. "The techs will be on the five o'clock boat. You'd better have one of your officers guard this until we know what's what. I assume Toby can lock up securely."

Casey nodded.

Howland opened the door that led into the public rooms. "I'll speak to them. I don't want anyone talking about this until we know what's in the sandbags."

Lucretia and Denny had joined the others who were seated on chairs drawn up in a circle. Lucretia looked up as Howland entered, bringing with him a gust of cold air and the smell of embalming fluid. He noticed her quick glance, saw her half close her eyes, then turn her head with a flick of ponytail.

As the police chief came into the room behind Howland, Lucretia stood up. She was several inches taller than Casey. In a low voice she said, "Chief O'Neill, would you mind telling me why I wasn't informed about this?" She gestured at Howland.

Casey looked surprised. "I believe you knew as much as the rest of us."

"I mean about Mr. Atherton."

103

"Sorry. I wasn't at liberty to divulge anything."

Two bright pink spots appeared on Lucretia's cheeks.

After Howland talked with the group in the public room and then dismissed them with a warning not to discuss anything, Casey and Victoria got back into the Bronco and headed away from the funeral home.

Victoria stared straight ahead of her. "What's the matter with Lucretia? She was certainly unpleasant."

Casey shook her head. "I don't know, Victoria. In the short time I've known her, she's changed. As though power has gone to her head."

"Power? The position of selectman in a small village hardly seems like the seat of power."

"It's all relative," Casey said. "I have to stop by the dump. Junior says there's a problem of some kind."

Junior Norton, Casey's sergeant and the son of the former police chief, had assumed he would take over his father's job when his father retired. Instead, the selectmen searched for a new chief off-Island, and appointed Casey — not only an off-Islander, but a female. The situation had been tense for several weeks. But Junior had adjusted. Casey was a professional, after all. And so was he.

Casey was quiet for several miles as she drove, and Victoria watched the thinning fog on either side of the road without saying anything either.

Finally Casey spoke. "What's with those two, anyway? Something personal? I mean, were they having an affair or something?"

"I think the problem is just the opposite. They *weren't* having an affair. Lucretia apparently made some overtures that Howland rebuffed."

"She's already got a boyfriend. Why does she want Howland?"

"You heard that Lucretia fired Howland from the Substance Abuse Committee at the selectmen's meeting?" Victoria turned to Casey.

"Yeah, I know, Victoria. I was right there with you. Everybody in town's heard," said Casey. "And that's what I mean. Why?"

"It must be embarrassing for her now she's found out he's not simply a well-intentioned citizen with time on his hands," Victoria said.

Casey slowed as they neared the dump. Smoke wafted into the air, mingling with the thinning mist. Junior met them at the chain-link fence that surrounded the dump. His normally sunny expression was grim. There were dark circles under his eyes. His face was smudged.

Casey wound down her window and leaned her elbow on the frame. "What's happening, Junior?"

Junior motioned a fire truck around the Bronco and bent down to talk to Casey. "They've been lifting stumps off the top of the pile with a cherry picker and moving stuff from around the base with a bulldozer. You better look at what they found."

Casey raised her eyebrows. "Oh?" She parked the Bronco out of the way of the fire trucks. "Wait here, Victoria."

"I'm coming too," Victoria said.

The ground around the stump mountain was muddy, black, and stony. The air reeked of partially burnt wood. Victoria picked her way carefully over the uneven ground behind Junior and Casey, testing the stones with her stick before she stepped on them. Smoke issued from two dozen spots above them.

Victoria looked up at the grotesque burial ground of trees that had been ripped out of the Island soil to make room for more houses. The dead trees were younger than she was. Most of the Island land had been sheep pasture when she was a girl. She remembered when she could view the sea from almost any high ground in West Tisbury or Chilmark. There had been only a few isolated wood lots then. These foot-thick dead trees had been saplings when she and Jonathan met.

The top of the brush pile was not as high as it had been two days before when she had come to the dump with Elizabeth. Fog and smoke mingled on the slopes of the mound and wrapped around the jagged branches and tree roots high above her. Victoria could feel the heat.

"Over here, Chief. Watch your step, Victoria," Junior warned, offering his hand to her.

Victoria tightened her hold on her stick. "I'm fine, thank you. Don't let me hold you up."

The stump mountain was one of several large mounds — sand, gravel, topsoil, and broken-up concrete. The angle of repose of each pile differed according to its material. The stump pile was the steepest and highest.

Casey, Junior, and Victoria stepped over hoses and around puddles. Over the noise of generators, engines, radios, and people shouting, there was a steady, disconcerting hissing and crackling far above them.

As they rounded the gravel mound, Victoria saw a group of people standing quietly. The group parted as they approached, and she could tell that someone was lying on the ground.

"Hurt bad?" Casey asked Junior as she hurried forward.

"The dozer uncovered him. Near the base. Dead. For at least a couple of days."

"Lord!" said Casey. "Any idea who he is?"

"Nope. The temperature's been low enough so the body hasn't started to decompose. The fire smoked him some, but he's not been burnt."

Victoria edged closer. The body was evenly blackened by smoke and soot, but she could tell the man was wearing once-tan cotton trousers, new work boots, and a heavy wool jacket.

Casey turned to Junior. "Who's medical examiner this week?"

"Doc Jeffers. I called him after I called you."

"Someone find a box or something for my deputy to sit on," Casey said to the people who were still standing around. "This may take some time."

A firefighter hurried off and came back with a plastic milk crate he turned upside down for Victoria. Once she was seated she looked around at the ground, the vehicles, the hoses, the footprints, the trampled mud.

"Not much of a crime scene now," said Junior.

Casey shook her head in dismay. "Where's the guy who uncovered the body? I need to talk to him."

Chapter 8

Dahlia emerged from her room later that afternoon and returned the telephone to its cradle on the cookroom wall.

Victoria, washing McCavity's bowl at the kitchen sink, watched her with concern. "Is there anything I can do to make you more comfortable, Dahlia? We really don't mind turning the heat up a bit more — if you think Bacchus needs the warmth."

Dahlia smiled. "Thank you, Victoria. The heat's fine. I'm worried about something else."

"You haven't contacted your friend yet?"

Dahlia shook her head. "Emery's a business acquaintance, not really a friend. But that's not what's bothering me. I'm sure I'll hear from him."

"What sort of business is he in?" asked Victoria.

Dahlia went over to the east door and looked out before answering. "He's with a government agency in Washington."

Victoria laughed. "Must be the CIA."

Dahlia didn't respond, and Victoria

dropped the subject. "Would you like a cup of tea? Elizabeth made oatmeal cookies this morning before she left for work." Victoria wiped out the kitchen sink and hung up the dish towel.

"Thank you. You've been awfully kind, Victoria. I'll be sorry to leave here." Dahlia turned away from the door. "I'm not sure how well Howland and I are going to get along."

Victoria poured tea into two mugs and took them to the cookroom, where Dahlia was sitting. "I'm sure things will work out, Dahlia. Howland is used to living alone, and so are you. That house certainly is big enough for two people."

Dahlia sipped her tea. "Nice. Tea is just what I needed. I plan to move tomorrow, if he's finished cleaning."

"What will you do about transportation?" Victoria asked. "Howland's and your place is really quite isolated."

"I've arranged to lease a car." Dahlia looked at her watch. "I'm to pick it up in Edgartown in about an hour."

"I wish I were still driving." Victoria scowled at the thought of the license she no longer had. "I'd have given you a ride." She snapped her cookie in half and bit into it.

"Howland is taking me to the car rental

111

place. He should be here any minute."

"If Emery calls, do you want me to give him a message?"

"No thanks, Victoria. I need to speak with him."

Just then, Howland drove up. When he came through the kitchen door from the entry, Bacchus started barking. Victoria took another mug from the cupboard.

Over the noise in the other room, Victoria told Howland about the body at the dump.

"Really!" Dahlia's face paled. "In the dump?"

"On the brush pile that's been burning for almost a month."

"Any idea who it was?" Howland asked, stirring milk and sweetener into his tea.

"They hadn't identified the body last I knew," Victoria said. "Doc Jeffers thought he'd been dead two or three days. The weather has been cool. Cold, really. Then the fire smoked him, so he's quite well preserved."

Dahlia murmured, "I wonder how the body got there?"

"I imagine the police are wondering that, too," said Howland.

"Not where I'd dispose of a body, certainly." Dahlia brushed cookie crumbs into a small pile in front of her. "You wouldn't happen to know if they've found that girl's coffin yet, would you?"

Victoria was about to tell her where they had found the coffin, when Howland interrupted. "Have they taken the body they found at the dump to Falmouth for an autopsy, Victoria?"

"Doc Jeffers examined the body on site, and then Toby arrived with the Rose Haven hearse."

"Why Falmouth?" Dahlia asked.

"We don't have facilities on the Island for an autopsy," Howland said.

Victoria again started to tell Dahlia about the coffin and what they had seen at the funeral parlor. "This morning Casey and I . . ." Howland's expression stopped her. She finished, "I've been awfully busy today."

"Did you get a look at the body, Victoria?" Howland asked.

"Yes. It was a man. I couldn't tell what he looked like, whether he was black or white, or what color hair he had." Victoria paused, thought again about the coffin and its contents, then changed the subject. "How's the house, Howland?"

"Spotless. It's never been this clean."

Dahlia plucked at a speck of lint on her skirt. Howland's mouth turned down, and Dahlia tried to smile. In the guest room Bacchus continued to bark.

Howland stood suddenly. "We'd better pick up your rental car, Dahlia."

"I'm sure Bacchus will get used to you when we've settled in." Dahlia pushed her chair away from the table.

"How long do toucans live?" Victoria asked, as she walked them to the door.

"Fifteen years or so. Not as long as parrots."

"Does Bacchus make a different sound if he likes someone?" Victoria asked.

"He chortles like this" — Dahlia made a throaty chuckle — "and he sidles along his perch like this." She demonstrated, her full skirt swishing. "He puts his head to one side and peers at you through the eye on that side. Like this."

Victoria laughed.

"And the other eye?" Howland said.

"I suppose he's aware if something creeps up on him from that side," Dahlia said. "They're very bright birds."

The fog had cleared by the next morning, but the sky was overcast with dirty gray clouds. Casey phoned. "Sorry I haven't called sooner, Victoria, but between those bags of stuff in the coffin and the body at the dump, I've been busy. I need to talk to you. If you're not tied up, I'll stop by in a half hour."

When Casey arrived, Victoria was standing on the stone step, her cap at a jaunty angle, her lilac-wood hiking stick in one hand, her cloth bag in the other.

Once they were on the road, Victoria waited for Casey to say something. "I don't know which end is up, Victoria. First that exhumation, then the sandbags in the coffin that may be a fortune in drugs. Now the body at the dump." She slowed to turn onto Old County Road. "The body was on the edge of the stump pile, covered with brush. Someone had poured kerosene on the pile, which is why it blazed up again."

"Yet the body didn't seem burned," Victoria said. "I wonder who the dead man was?"

"I suppose the killer figured the fire would get to the body soon enough. Until it flared up again and the neighbors called in an alarm, the fire department wasn't doing anything more than monitoring the blaze."

Casey checked the rearview mirror, and continued. "Then we have the weird stuff

115

about the coffin. You know the Norton family. What about the dead girl who's gone missing?"

"I've told anyone who would listen that I've never heard about a Norton suicide."

"You would have, wouldn't you?"

Victoria nodded. "Everybody would have. You can't keep a thing like that quiet on this Island."

"Assuming the body *was* a Norton girl who killed herself, how come there are bags of something in her coffin? Was the body removed in Milwaukee or here?" Casey lifted her hair from the back of her neck. "I honestly don't know where to begin. The state police have responsibility, but somehow I feel I ought to help unravel the puzzle."

"Howland came by last evening to pick up Dahlia," said Victoria. "He hadn't heard about the body at the dump."

"He didn't mention the stuff in the coffin in front of Dahlia, did he?"

"No, and he shushed me when I started to tell her."

"That's good." Casey turned left onto Scotchman's Bridge Lane. "We're heading for the dump, by the way."

"What's happening at Rose Haven?" Victoria asked.

"The DEA technicians from the mainland arrived with a huge van and they're at the funeral home now, checking fingerprints. Then they'll analyze whatever is in the sandbags."

"What else could the contents be but drugs?" Victoria asked. "Someone went to a lot of trouble. Too much to simply bury bags of sand."

"The body may have been stolen, for some reason." Casey lifted her fingers in greeting to a passing car. "If Denny is right, the coffin was buried about ten years ago. You'd think a lot of people would be hot on its trail if the stuff is heroin or cocaine."

"Do drugs spoil?"

"I honestly don't know," Casey said. "Was the Norton girl involved in some kind of drug deal? Her death might have been murder, not suicide. Or perhaps she died of a drug overdose, which would explain why someone didn't want the body found."

"Then why put the drugs in the coffin?" Victoria thought for a moment. "Denny didn't seem to be faking his astonishment when there was no body."

"If the stuff in the sandbags *is* drugs, someone would have gone to a lot of effort to recover them," said Casey. "Too late now the DEA is involved." Casey rolled down her window and adjusted the outside mirror. "I'm surprised no one unearthed the coffin before this."

Victoria tapped her fingers on the window frame. "I wonder who moved Old Simon's stone and why? The stone was moved after last Memorial Day, when I put flowers on the grave."

"You think someone moved the stone to throw someone else off the trail? Doesn't make any sense, Victoria. Why wouldn't a second party — or a dissident — simply dig up the coffin?"

"Hardly. During the day, someone's often there, tending a grave the way I do. And at night, any activity would be suspicious. Would they have dug up every grave in the cemetery?" She glanced at Casey, who was watching the road. "Break the seal on each coffin? Open it up? Peer in? Then close the coffin again, fill in the grave, and resod it? After the first two or three unexplained opened graves, people would be concerned."

Casey slowed as they approached Humphrey's bakery in North Tisbury. "Look at the way these people park. No consideration at all." They inched past a half dozen four-wheel-drive vehicles that stuck out into the road. "I ought to ticket them all, but to hell with it."

"What are we going to do at the dump?" asked Victoria.

"I want to ask Anthony what the firefighters need in the way of traffic cops and morale-boosting," Casey replied. "Now the body's gone off-Island, there's not much we can do but wait. In the meantime, we have this other problem about the bags of stuff in the coffin."

"We don't need to worry about trampling the scene at the dump, do we?"

"No, Victoria. The state guys have finished. You can poke around all you want. I'll see if I can find the fire chief. Someone needs to relieve him."

The ground was even muddier and more churned up than it had been the previous day. Victoria worked her way carefully between the burning pile and the gravel mound. On the back side of the stump pile, a cherry picker lifted off smoldering tree trunks, and a bulldozer shoved them to one side, where the firefighters hosed them down.

Victoria could smell the smoke and hear, deep inside the mound, a steady disconcerting rumble. The sound and smell reminded her of the volcano she had visited once in Hawaii. She felt the heat as she moved cautiously to where the body had lain. She scuffed at the ground with her stick, not knowing exactly what she was looking for, turning over small stones, swinging the tip of her stick through the mud, bending down occasionally to examine some small thing that looked different. She found a button, an ordinary metal button like the ones that fasten the waistband on jeans, and put it in her cloth bag.

The slight depression where the body had lain was still visible, with a thin sprinkling of charcoal and ash forming the remembered shape of a human being. She knelt in the soft ground, using her stick to lever herself down, and started to sift the sandy mud with her gnarled fingers, all around the barely discernible outline. She started at the indentation where the man's head had been, and almost immediately found a short grayish-blond hair. She put it in a sandwich wrapper in her cloth bag, and continued searching from his head down along where his shoulders had rested. He'd been on his side, Victoria recalled. She shifted slightly, her knees beginning to ache, and picked up another handful of soil. She found a penny. She moved slightly and picked up another handful.

"Ouch!" She had pricked her thumb on something sharp, a stick or a piece of metal or broken glass.

Gently, she brushed the mud off her hand and there, in her palm, was an enameled pin. She got slowly to her feet, and propped herself on her stick while she wrapped the pin in a tissue without looking at it, put it in her bag, and hustled as fast as she could to where Casey was talking with an exhausted-looking fire chief.

"The neighbors are bitching," Victoria heard Anthony mutter. "Complaining because we haven't put the fire out yet, and they're getting sick on the smoke, they say, and they're frightened to death the fire will spread. Christ! We're doing all we can, for God's sake. And we're all volunteers."

"Go home and get some rest, Anthony," Casey said. "Someone else can take over."

"It's my fire in my town. I can't drop the responsibility in the lap of Chilmark or Tisbury."

"Yes you can. Go home. Come back later tonight, if you have to." Casey noticed Victoria. "What's up, Deputy?"

"I'm going to the Bronco." Victoria held up her cloth bag.

121

"Okay. I'll be there in just a second."

When Casey joined Victoria a few minutes later, Victoria showed her the button, the hair, and unwound the tissue from the pin. The pin was about the size of a pumpkin seed, and about the same shape. She rubbed off the mud until they could see its outline in gold and the iridescent black and blue enamel.

Casey examined the pin. "It's a bird with a large beak."

"A toucan. Like Bacchus. What a strange coincidence."

"Coincidence, my foot," Casey muttered. "I don't believe in coincidences. Let me have the pin, and I'll give it to the state police. Don't mention what you found to anybody."

"What about Howland?"

"You can tell him."

When they got back to the police station, Howland was waiting for them, sitting behind Casey's desk.

"Drugs?" asked Casey. Howland got up and relinquished the chief's seat. He held the visitor's chair for Victoria.

"Ordinary sand," he said. "Quartz sand. Nothing else."

Victoria unbuttoned her coat and took off her baseball cap. "Why would someone put bags of sand in a coffin?"

Howland sighed. " 'Why' is anybody's guess. Perhaps there had been a body there, and someone removed it. Maybe someone substituted sand to give the coffin weight." He walked over to the window and looked out at the mill pond. "I've sent a sample back to the lab, where there's a soils scientist. The grains are sharp and angular, so the sand doesn't look like Vineyard beach sand. Beach sand would have rounded grains." He shook his head. "But I'm no geologist."

Victoria looked at Casey, her eyes bright. "Where do we go from here?"

Casey sighed. "Not 'we,' Victoria. The state cops." She reached for the phone. "I'll try to reach the Norton family in Milwaukee. See what they can tell me."

"And the coffin?" Victoria asked. "What happens to that?"

"Toby wants the coffin out of the funeral parlor, so we'll store it someplace until we know what's going on. Probably in that shed behind Town Hall. The shed has a padlock." She punched in the information number for Milwaukee. "I hate making calls like this." While she waited for an answer, Casey put her hand over the mouthpiece. "Show Howland what you found, Victoria."

Victoria searched through her cloth bag and brought out the tissue-wrapped pin. "I wiped off the mud and soot without thinking about fingerprints."

Howland examined the pin with a small hand lens he took out of his pocket. "It's a toucan, all right. The damned things are dogging me."

"Bird-dogging," Victoria murmured. "I suppose the pin is evidence of some kind?"

"Possibly," Howland said.

Casey was talking softly on the phone, her back to Victoria and Howland.

"What about the selectmen?" Victoria asked.

"What about them?" Howland closed up his hand lens and slipped it back into his pocket.

"Should we tell them about the sandbags and the toucan pin?"

"I've told them I'd let them know before the results of the analyses are released to the public."

"Once Denny knows, you won't be able to keep him quiet," said Victoria.

Howland's mouth turned down. "I think we will," he said.

Chapter 9

When Lucretia came into Town Hall after lunch, Ephraim was at the copier. He was wearing a large purple and white button that read, VINEYARDERS! She stopped inside the door. "I see you got the glass fixed, Mrs. D. Thank you." She shut the door carefully. "More paperwork, Eph?"

Ephraim grunted. "Computers were supposed to put an end to this stuff. You going to the game tomorrow?"

"I was until Sonny got kicked off the team."

"Yeah? What did he do this time?"

Lucretia turned away. "Pot."

"So? Three quarters of the kids at the school smoke pot."

"They're not on the football team."

"You ought to go to Nantucket anyway. You're a public figure. Show the flag."

"I might. I'm hoping Meyer will be on-Island."

"Your fisherman friend?"

Lucretia nodded.

"Where's he been, West Coast?"

"Yes, he was in Seattle last time he called."

Ephraim moved his chewing gum to the side of his mouth. "Invite him along. The Vineyarders have a chance this year. Should be an exciting game." A light on the copier blinked. Ephraim opened a door on the bottom of the machine and added paper to the empty tray. "I don't think I've ever met the guy." He pushed a button and the machine started up again.

Lucretia hung her coat in the closet and lifted her ponytail from the back of her sweater. "He's shy. Not shy, exactly, reserved I guess. We don't go out often."

"Shame he can't get a berth on a vessel out of Menemsha or Vineyard Haven. Get to see more of him. Bring him around sometime so we can meet him."

Lucretia smiled.

"I don't even know what he looks like. You got a picture?"

She shook her head. "I haven't actually known him that long. Almost three months." Lucretia went to her desk, which was on the other side of the room from Denny's, and absently riffled through her own papers. "He's tall, about six foot one, slender, broad shoulders like a swimmer."

"Must be in good shape. Does he fish pots or lines?"

"I don't know." Lucretia went on. "He's got blond hair and blue eyes that look as if he's focusing beyond the horizon. From being at sea so much, I imagine."

Ephraim collected the copied pages, lifted the lid of the machine, and took out his original. "How old a guy is he?"

"Older than me. Maybe forty-five or six?"

"Well, bring him around. I'd like to meet him. Maybe go for a couple beers in Oak Bluffs."

That afternoon, dozens of teenagers were festooning purple and white crepe paper streamers over cars and pickup trucks in the high school parking lot. Dozens of boom boxes blasted a cacophony of sound off the school's brick walls. Kids shouted and laughed and flung purple and white pom-poms at one another.

Sonny stood on the sidewalk, hands thrust deep into his pockets, watching the activity sullenly.

Denise danced up to him shaking long purple and white ribbons that twisted around his neck.

Sonny brushed the ribbons away. "Get out of my face."

Denise laughed. "You can't *not* go to Nantucket, Sonny."

"Sez who?" Sonny spit off to one side.

"Says everybody. You're, like, part of the team."

"That's not what the coach says."

A tall kid with his hair cut so short it was impossible to tell its color pounded Sonny on the back.

Sonny turned to him. "What d'ya say, Tris."

"Guess you showed Coach T who's who. If we lose on account of you not being on the team, we can thank him."

"Guess so," said Sonny.

Tris held his hand up, and Sonny reluctantly slapped a high five, then put his hand back in his pocket. Tris moved on.

"Come on, Sonny," Denise said. "We need your support."

"Sitting on the bench? Watching, you know, freshmen splash around in the mud? No thanks." Sonny started to walk away.

Denise tugged on the back of his sweatshirt. He pulled away from her. "What do you want?"

She stepped in front of him, hands on her hips, ribbons trailing on the ground.

"You, like, got what you deserved, smart-ass. You pushed Coach T too far. Everybody knows you smoked where he'd catch you. In the locker room? Bright!"

"So he, like, throws me off the team before the game?"

"He didn't have a choice."

"He made his point, okay?" Sonny kicked a stone. His bootlaces trailed on the ground. "I'm not going. That's that."

"Come on, Sonny."

"Lay off me, will you?" He started to walk away again, then turned. "Look who's calling who a smart-ass." He jabbed a finger at her. "Like, how many graves you got to dig before your old man lets you off?"

"You should know. You oughta be there too."

"I'm not as stupid as some people. He never caught me."

"I like grave digging. Ira's cool. He, like, does all the work." Denise fluttered her eyelashes. "He feels sorry for me."

"Yeah?"

"He says kids knocked over gravestones at Halloween before he was born. Outhouses, too. I told him you put the stone back."

"So you had to tell Ira."

"Ira knew already. I told him you sodded the grave, too."

"Thanks a lot."

"Ira said it looked good. As if, you know, the stone had never been knocked over."

"Big deal," said Sonny.

"Ira says you should be doing community service too."

"Ira, Ira, Ira," said Sonny, and walked away.

Howland's house was at the end of two miles of dirt road, perched on a bluff that overlooked Vineyard Sound. A raggedy lawn sloped gently from the back of the house down to a rock-strewn beach and a ramshackle dock, where Howland had tied up his sailboat when he was a boy. On either side of the lawn, wild grapevine and viburnum formed a tangled thicket. Each spring the thicket encroached on the cleared area, and Howland would hack at the brush with a razor-sharp machete he kept in the garage.

The house itself, intended originally as a summer retreat, was U-shaped with two wings pointing toward Vineyard Sound. In summer, Howland ate his meals on the terrace between the two wings, sheltered from the prevailing southwest winds. While he ate he could see boat traffic — ferries heading to and from Woods Hole, white sails of sailboats, an occasional large yacht, fishing boats on their way to Georges Bank. From the terrace he liked to watch the weather move in over the Elizabeth Islands, which hung like a chain from the elbow of Cape Cod.

In winter, his house was austere, almost impossible to heat. When a nor'easter blew in, the winds whipped up whitecaps on the sound and howled and shrieked around his house, rattling windows, wailing down the tall chimney, and sucking away any warmth. How would Cousin Dahlia stand it?

His unheated bedroom was at the end of one of the wings, the one to the right as he faced the house. To get there, he went through what used to be servants' quarters and was now storage space and his study. His bedroom windows looked out on the boats, Vineyard Sound, islands, and weather. Winter nights, he would settle into bed, tucked in between his two large comfortable dogs, who grunted, snored, and hunted dream game.

The wing on the left was empty and had been for years. That was where he would put Dahlia. Howland wasn't even sure how many bedrooms were in that wing. He seldom went there. During childhood summers, the house had been filled with his parents' friends, his friends, and Cousin Dahlia and her friends. As he recalled, Dahlia could fill the house, all by herself, with her only-child demands.

He had always believed the house was his. However, Dahlia had sent him a copy of his grandmother's will recently, and Dahlia, apparently, was co-owner. Somehow he had never imagined living in this house with her. She liked society swirling about her and concentrating on her. She liked acting out whatever role suited her surroundings. Howland preferred his dogs and his solitude.

Every day he drove out into the world of the Island, down his two miles of rutted road to do his errands, get the mail, meet his business contacts, and call on Victoria Trumbull. When he drove back home, he welcomed the sight of every familiar rock, every squirrel's nest, every patch of green moss, every tree, every clearing among the trees, as though he'd been gone too long. Once home, he'd walk the beach with his dogs, Bowser, who was mostly black Lab, and Rover, who was mostly German shepherd. He'd toss sticks into the water for them to fetch. Or he'd hack at the wilderness with the dogs supervising, or read in front of the fireplace in the small cone of warmth, the dogs curled up on the window seat.

Howland was still on call as a consultant to the DEA, covering Cape Cod and the Islands. Drug activity on the Vineyard tended to be small time and he didn't usually get involved. The exception had been some time ago when Victoria uncovered a major drug ring.

He didn't know much about what Dahlia had been doing between the years of their long childhood summers and the present. He never discussed her career as a Foreign Service officer with her. In between assignments, she'd spent her vacations on the Vineyard, as he had, up until ten years ago, when he moved to the Island full-time. Whenever Dahlia had visited, Howland occupied himself with his own affairs.

He thought about the changes to come in his life while he loaded wood from the woodpile into the cart. Housecleaning was only the beginning. She would take over, claim that she wouldn't impose on him except for what her doctors had advised.

What about meals? Would she expect to join him at his solitary, peaceful dinners?

Would she expect him to cook for her? Worse still, would she cook for both of them? Expect him to be home according to her schedule? Howland thought about his lost privacy and flung a log into the cart so hard it bounced out and onto the ground. Bowser, the Lab, looked up at him, eyes sad triangles under furrowed brows.

Well, today was the day she would move in. He'd gone with her yesterday to pick up a rental car, so at least she wouldn't depend on him for transportation. She'd stopped by this morning with the toucan and left its cage on the side of the kitchen sink, where the bird was barking its wretched head off. He'd fired up the woodstove in the dining room, set clean bed linens out for her — damned if he'd make her bed for her — and was thinking how he could defend some portion of his territory.

Victoria was right. The house was large. But it had common areas, and he didn't intend to hide out in his wing just because Dahlia had come to stay.

While Howland was wondering if he should expect Dahlia to show up for lunch, Dahlia and Red were eating quahog chowder at the ArtCliff Diner, seated at the table by the window. They were only vaguely aware of the men at the large round table on the other side, joshing Dottie, the waitress, who was joshing back.

"If I'd thought for a minute they'd find the coffin when they did, I'd never have taken sick leave," Red told Dahlia.

"How could we know?"

"We've got to find Tremont. Where in hell could he have gone? Is he double-crossing us? And where's Mort? Are they in this together?"

Dottie left the round table and came over to Red and Dahlia's. "Everything all right? How's the chowder?"

Red nodded, his mouth full.

"Lovely," said Dahlia.

"Need more crackers?"

Red wiped his mouth on a paper napkin. "No thanks."

"You folks visiting?"

"I work at the funeral home," said Red.

Dahlia smiled. "An extended visit for me."

Dottie held her pad ready. "Nice, this time of year. Quiet. Want dessert? Home-made blueberry pie and cranberry crisp."

Dahlia looked up. "No, thank you."

Red shoved his mug across the table. "I'll have more coffee."

"Sure thing." Dottie moved away.

Red spooned up the last of his chowder. "They're taking the coffin to the shed behind Town Hall as we speak. When I called in today, Toby told me that Denny — the selectman, you know?"

"I know who he is."

"Denny was going to move the coffin in his pickup."

Dahlia thought for a moment. "That's probably better than the funeral home. But I'm afraid the shed is locked."

"That's no big deal."

Dahlia finished her chowder and set her spoon on the side of her bowl. "Did Toby say what they were planning to do with the coffin? Can we offer to buy it?"

"That would look pretty strange," Red said.

"We have to take a chance, Red. Maybe I can buy the coffin for my own use. Or for a planter. It would make an unusual planter on Howland's terrace. Geraniums, white petunias, and blue ageratum."

"Where the hell can those two be?" Red muttered. "And what do they think they're doing?"

Dottie came back with the coffee and filled Red's mug. "Change your mind about the pie? Last summer's blueberries, and fresh-baked this morning."

"I believe I will have a small piece," said Dahlia. "Thank you."

When she brought the pie, Dottie peered out of the window. "They're calling for a storm. Nor'easter. Hope it doesn't affect the game."

Neither Dahlia nor Red answered.

"You sure you won't have some pie, sir?"

Red shook his head. "You can bring me the check."

"Sure thing," said Dottie, toting up the bill and setting the check facedown next to him. "Take your time. Not much business this time of year."

After Dottie left, Dahlia asked, "You haven't heard any more about the body at the dump, have you?"

"Toby went to Falmouth for the autopsy while I was on leave, looking for Tremont." Red slapped his wadded-up napkin on the table. "People don't just vanish the way those two have. They must be in this together. Where in hell could they have gone?"

"They wouldn't double-cross us." Dahlia pursed her lips. "By the way, you haven't heard from Emery, have you?"

"He was supposed to get in touch with you, not me."

Dahlia looked at her watch. "I have to get back. I forgot to tell Howland I wouldn't be home for lunch."

The toucan's barking was making both dogs skittish. They followed Howland wherever he went, from Dahlia's room where he had taken extra blankets, to her bathroom where he had taken clean towels. He climbed the steep stairs to the second floor to get a book, and they followed him, nails clicking on the painted stair treads. He carried wood from the cart, stoked the fire in the dining room stove, and tripped over them. He made himself a sandwich, and they sat as close to him as they could get while he ate. When he finally went into his study to work on his computer, taking long slow strides so he wouldn't acciden- tally step on a paw, they went with him, their hot flanks pressed close against his legs.

"That damned bird's spooking you, isn't he?" Howland said, rubbing the ears of first Rover, then Bowser. "He's enough to spook anyone."

Dahlia had left Bacchus's cage in the kitchen, and the toucan's yips and barks echoed down the long hall past the empty servants' quarters and into Howland's study. There was nowhere he could go to escape the constant racket.

He shut down his computer before he had even opened one of his files and patted the dogs, which were sitting with their heads on his knees. "Come on, fellows, let's go for a walk."

The dogs were at the front door before he reached it, tails wagging, noses pressed against the glass.

He talked to them as he headed to the beach down the wide shaggy lawn. "I don't know what's worse, Bacchus or his mistress. It's going to be a long few weeks. If I have anything to say, she's going to cut her time short. By one helluva lot."

The dogs bounded ahead of him, raced back again, knocked each other down, growled, chased things Howland couldn't see, fetched sticks for him to throw.

Howland's beach was protected from the wind by the headland to his right. Breaking waves hissed and roared far out on the sound. When he looked toward the Elizabeth Islands, all he could see was wind-driven spray that formed a layer of mist. The air had a peculiar milky tinge. Overhead, mackerel-patterned clouds, the fore-runner of a storm, closed in steadily from the northeast. Breakers pounded on the rocks. The dogs kept bringing him drift-wood sticks to throw into the surf.

"Not today," he told his dogs. "Not today."

He walked for almost a mile toward Cedar Tree Neck. When he rounded the point, the wind hit him full force. Sheets of low-blowing sand blasted against his trousers, which the wind flattened against his shins. Wind and spray made his eyes water. The dogs had stopped rollicking and looked over their shoulders at him. He started to turn back. Before he did, though, the dogs suddenly converged on something washed up on the beach ahead of him. They dodged as a wave broke and sent swash up around the object, then went back to it. The object was too flexible to be driftwood. He thought at first that it might be a dead shark or a seal.

As he approached, the dogs backed off and began to howl. And then he realized what the sea had washed up.

Chapter 10

Victoria walked the quarter mile from her house to the police station, which had been a one-room school in her mother's time. The overcast had thickened and the wind had backed around to the northeast. The large rosebush in front of the police station, a tree really, was full of red berries, rose hips, actually, and was noisy with birds gorging themselves before heading south. Fallen leaves skittered along the road as she walked. She carried the lilac-wood stick Elizabeth had carved for her, not because she needed it, she told herself, but because the stick was a gift from Elizabeth.

Casey looked up from the telephone as Victoria entered, out of breath and rosy from her hike. Casey put her hand over the mouthpiece. "You should have called. I'd have picked you up."

Victoria indicated the phone in Casey's hand. "The line was busy." Breathing heavily, she sat in the wooden chair in front of the chief's desk and unbuttoned her blue coat.

Casey spoke into the phone. "Thanks for checking. Sorry to bother you," and hung up with a sigh. "None of the Milwaukee Nortons has any connection with the Vineyard. None of them knows of a cousin named Mary Jane Smith, and none of them heard of any suicide in the family over the past twenty years."

"Did you contact the Island Nortons? Not Ben and Junior's branch, but the Middletown branch?"

"Same thing. No suicide, no Mary Jane Smith. They referred me to the Nortons who'd moved to San Francisco. I called them. No suicides in the family. They were outraged that someone had desecrated the family plot, and outraged that the cemetery commissioners hadn't notified them." Casey stood up, fastened her heavy belt around her waist, and slipped into her jacket. "You ready to go to the funeral home? Denny's already there with his pickup."

When they arrived, Denny, Toby, and Toby's helper Nick were loading the empty coffin onto the back of Denny's red truck.

"Where's the new guy?" Casey asked Toby.

Toby stopped to wipe his forehead. "Red. He'll be in later. Still recovering from the flu."

"Do you need another hand?"

"We can manage. The box is light." Toby put his handkerchief back in his pocket. "Red picked a hell of a time to get sick, what with this coffin nonsense."

"Just slide it on," Denny said. "Won't hurt my truck. Certainly won't hurt the coffin."

"Can't put the tailgate up," Nick said.

"Won't matter," Denny replied. "It's not as if we're worried about scratching the mahogany."

Nick examined the part of the coffin that extended over the back of the truck. "You want me to tie a rope around that panel? It's loose. Screws rusted through."

"Nah," said Denny. "Not worth the effort."

Nick shrugged and got into Denny's truck.

Casey started up the Bronco. "I'll follow."

Denny saluted her with a cupped hand, and he and Nick took off. They turned onto the Edgartown-Vineyard Haven Road and passed the high school, crowded with Island vehicles, all sporting purple and white banners, balloons, and ribbons.

Instead of turning left at the blinker, Denny went straight.

143

Victoria glanced at Casey. "Why is he going this way?"

Casey lifted her eyebrows. "Who knows?"

Denny turned onto the dirt track that wound behind the strawberry farm and the commercial vineyard.

"I can't imagine where he thinks he's going," Casey said. "Unless he knows a shortcut around the dump fire."

"This heads right *to* the fire."

"The blaze flared up again this morning. The main road is full of equipment. Denny probably wants to see what's going on."

"Maybe so," said Victoria, settling her coat under her. "This is worse than the back road to the dump." Her voice jounced as they went over rocks and roots and holes.

Ahead of them, the coffin bounced and slid on the bed of the truck, with metallic clanks and the scritch of sand sandwiched between metal and metal. The coffin had been an economy model, and the effect of its ten-year interment showed. The box shimmied and skittered in the back of the truck.

"Stupid to come this way," Casey muttered.

"I suppose it doesn't matter what happens to the coffin now." Victoria pointed to the back, which was resting on the tailgate. "That section is working itself loose."

"Nick was saying those screws were rusted." Just as Casey finished speaking, Denny's truck jounced over a large hole. The back panel of the coffin wrenched loose, and hung by one screw, swinging back and forth. Casey honked her horn, but Denny held up a hand and continued to drive.

Casey let up on the accelerator. "I'd better drop back in case that falls off."

At the next rough spot, the coffin bounced and slid and shimmied, and the back panel dropped onto the road.

"Shit," said Casey, jamming on the brakes.

"Lucky you weren't immediately behind him."

Casey got out of the Bronco and picked up the piece of coffin. The panel was about three feet wide, two feet high, and about five inches deep. What once had been the inside of the box was lined with mildewed sateen glued onto the thin metal, which was riveted together to make the coffin seem more substantial than it actually was. A rusty sheet metal screw fell onto the ground, and Casey picked it up. She carried the panel to the Bronco, opened the back door, and slid the piece in.

By the time they got going again, Denny's truck was out of sight. "You'd think he'd have noticed," Casey muttered.

They continued down the road, past the fields of hummocky dried brown strawberry plants. Victoria smiled as she thought of picking berries for the church's annual strawberry festival, of the sweet red stain on her fingers and the voices of children calling to one another.

The heavy clouds that had been gathering all morning were lowering. A few raindrops splashed on the windshield.

Beyond the strawberry fields they passed the greenhouse that produced summer-tasting tomatoes in the winter. Tomatoes belonged to August, not November, Victoria thought.

The radio crackled. Casey adjusted the squelch and lifted the transmitter.

"Chief, you're needed at Howland Atherton's place, immediately," Junior reported.

"What's the trouble?"

"I think you'd better see for yourself."

"Do you have him on the land line?" said Casey.

"Affirmative."

"Tell him I'm on my way." She turned on her flashing lights. "Hang on, Victoria."

Rain was blowing horizontally by the time Dahlia rounded the last bend in the dirt road leading to Howland's and her house. She was about to park her rental car in front when Howland strode around from the side, dressed in his yellow oilskins.

He gestured to the garage some distance away. "Leave the car over there, Dahlia."

"Why so far from the house?"

"The police are on their way."

"Would you mind parking it, darling? I don't want to get wet." She slid out from behind the wheel and before she ducked into the shelter of the front doorway asked, "What's the trouble?"

Howland got into her car and shoved the seat back as far as it would go.

"A body washed up on the beach."

The rugged clay cliffs between Howland's beach and the rocky point where the body had washed up were slick from rain and spray, and were laced with hairy poison ivy vines. The closest access to any road was across Howland's property. The state police, who'd responded to his call, had no

147

choice but to walk along the mile of beach and carry the body back to his house the same way. Toby had been notified, and he and his assistant, Red, were on their way with the Rose Haven hearse.

When the state police cruiser arrived, Howland and the troopers headed toward the beach. Before they were out of sight, Casey parked behind the cruiser.

By now, rain had turned to sleet, which spattered on the windshield. Casey shrugged into her yellow slicker and pulled the hood over her hair.

"Better wait here, Victoria. It's going to be a long, cold, wet, windy walk. I doubt if there's anything we can do except bring the body back."

Victoria held up a paperback book. "I've got my crossword puzzles. When Toby gets here, I'll tell him where you've gone."

After Casey left, Victoria worked on her puzzle, but within a few minutes, she was thoroughly chilled and was sorry she hadn't brought along an extra sweater. She found one of Casey's windbreakers on the backseat, and pulled it over her legs. Wind worked its way through the closed windows and into Victoria's muscles and joints and bones. She finally decided to wait in Howland's house, which was probably unlocked. She wished she'd thought of that sooner.

Shivering with cold, she put Casey's windbreaker in the backseat again and turned to see Dahlia hustling toward her, holding a newspaper over her head.

"Victoria, I'm so sorry! I didn't realize you were out here. You must be frozen. Come in and I'll make us a pot of tea. We can see the police from the dining room windows when they return," she added.

Victoria dabbed at her dripping nose. "A cup of tea would be wonderful." When she opened the Bronco's door, the wind slammed it against the hinges. Victoria held the door frame tightly to keep from getting blown over herself.

Dahlia offered Victoria her arm, and Victoria took it.

"I haven't even spent one night here," Dahlia said, "and already I wish I'd stayed at your house. I never realized how desolate this place is off-season. It's a mausoleum."

"November can be bleak."

"I have December, January, February, and March to look forward to. I'm not sure I can stand the wind, the way it howls and moans."

Once inside, Victoria sat at the newly

149

polished dining room table where she could view Vineyard Sound spread out far below her. Sleet and snow slashed at the windows. On the sound, steep breaking waves stretched as far as she could see, tops torn off and flung backward by the wind.

Victoria had to speak up to make herself heard over the steady roar. "I'm glad I'm not down there."

"I don't like to look out the window. The scene is quite awful." Dahlia set a tray with a silver teapot, two cups and saucers, and a plate of shortbread on the table, and sat across from Victoria.

"Howland keeps his things in the oddest places," she said. "I've been reorganizing his kitchen to make it more convenient."

Victoria frowned. "Hadn't you better ask him first?"

"You know the way men are," Dahlia said. "I doubt if he will even notice. I like to have my things in order."

Victoria curved her stiff hands around the hot teacup and closed her eyes in the steam. "How's Bacchus?" she asked. "I don't hear him."

"I covered his cage. The house is so drafty, I'm afraid he'll catch cold. The storm has upset him." Dahlia got up again from the table. "I'm going to get my coat. Would you like a sweater, Victoria?"

"No thank you. This is toasty compared to the police car."

Dahlia returned, buttoning her coat. "I suppose the body must be a fisherman. Washed overboard. Or perhaps his boat capsized." She shuddered and tugged her hat down over her ears. "What a dreadful life."

"This would not be a good day to be out there," Victoria agreed. The tea was comforting, and the teacup had warmed her hands. "How did you acquire Bacchus?"

"A friend gave him to me when I was posted in Colombia. I was there for three years. A beautiful country. Nice and warm." Dahlia laughed.

"I know very little about Colombia. Drugs and coffee, that's about it." Victoria set her empty cup down, and Dahlia refilled it.

"Drugs, coffee, oil, emeralds, and tourism. There's a great deal of wealth in Colombia." Dahlia wrapped her hands around her own teacup. "During the time I was posted there, I was invited to stay at some gorgeous estates and got to know the owners quite well."

A gust rattled the windows. The house

was pleasantly warm, but Dahlia huddled in her coat and put her hands in her pockets.

Victoria watched her with concern. "I understand that feeling cold is a side effect of chemotherapy."

"Sometimes I think the side effects of the cure are worse than the disease." Dahlia patted her hat. "I expected to lose my hair, and I knew I might feel nauseated. But the cold! At the same time my fingers and toes tingle and feel hot."

"Wouldn't you be better off in Washington?"

"I wanted to be treated here at the Vineyard hospital. The Vineyard was my childhood summer home." Dahlia glanced down at her hands. "I've never insisted on my rights to this house before now. It's my home every bit as much as Howland's."

Victoria nodded. "The new drug you're taking, Taxol, sounds promising."

"It's terribly expensive."

"So I understand."

"Originally, Taxol was made from the bark of the Pacific yew. But each tree yielded only twenty pounds of bark and it took sixty pounds to make enough Taxol to treat one person."

Victoria stood and went to the window, wiped off moisture with her napkin, and peered down. The beach was empty.

"I'm probably talking too much," Dahlia said.

"No, no," Victoria replied. "We can't do anything until they show up, and I'm not sure what we can do even then." She returned to her seat. "I suppose thousands of people need the drug. There'd be no Pacific yews left in short order."

"Exactly," Dahlia went on. "Recently, a chemistry professor at Florida State University discovered a way to synthesize a similar drug from the needles of the English yew."

"That's the yew we have here on the Vineyard."

Taxus baccata." Dahlia shuddered. "I'm sick of that wind."

The Elizabeth Islands had disappeared in flying spray and sleet. Rain lashed against the windows.

After a moment Dahlia continued. "It's a shame my cancer didn't wait ten years. The price will undoubtedly come down. I've thought of brewing tea myself from the bark or needles or berries of that enormous yew tree in the cemetery."

"That's not a good idea. Not a good idea

153

at all." Victoria shook her head. "Yew is terribly poisonous."

The next time Victoria went to the window, she could make out, but just barely, the group rounding the point with the stretcher. She watched them move cautiously up the icy slope in front of the house, and when they reached the front door, she opened it, Dahlia behind her.

The body on the stretcher was lying facedown, dark clothing plastered with sand and wrack. His shoes were missing, and his feet were a ghastly blue.

"Is it a fisherman?" Victoria asked Howland, who was at the front of the stretcher. "Where are his shoes?"

"Shoes fill with water and drop off." Howland shook his head. "Not likely that he's a fisherman. He's wearing a suit and tie and lightweight windbreaker."

The bearers set the stretcher down, and everyone went inside to wait for the hearse with Toby and his assistant.

Howland checked his watch. "Doc Jeffers should be here any minute. Toby ought to have gotten here by now."

"Toby probably got lost on your road," Dahlia said.

"Have you any idea how long the body's been in the water?" Victoria asked.

"At least a couple of days. Doc Jeffers will know."

"Suit and tie," Victoria murmured. "I wonder if he fell overboard from the ferry. Did they ever locate that missing hearse driver?"

Dahlia coughed.

Just then, a huge motorcycle roared down the long driveway. The driver was wearing a helmet with tiny flashing blue lights above the clear eyepiece. White wings protruded from either side. He had on a short black cloak, black gloves, and black leather boots festooned with shiny steel chains. He unfastened a black leather satchel from the carrier. When he turned, his cloak swirled around him. Victoria could see a caduceus embroidered on the back, two silver serpents twined around a silver and blue staff.

"Good heavens!" said Dahlia.

Howland turned to her with a smile. "Meet our Doc Jeffers."

At Town Hall, Lucretia put down the phone. "That was Meyer," she said, her cheeks pink.

Denny looked up from the form he was filling out. "Congratulations."

Rain beat on the windows. Outside, bare trees swayed in the wind.

"When did he get in?" Ephraim asked.

Lucretia smoothed her ponytail. "He'll be here on the four o'clock boat."

Ephraim looked at the wall clock. "Ten of. You'd better leave now."

"He said he'd catch a ride to my house."

Denny snorted.

Lucretia snapped at him. "What was that for, Denny?"

"Who, me?" Denny pointed at his chest.

Mrs. Danvers looked up from her computer screen. "Invite him over. We'd all like to meet him."

"He's a figment of Noodles's imagination," said Denny. "Her way to deal with Atherton's rejection."

Mrs. Danvers turned to face him. "That wasn't necessary."

Denny snorted again. "I suppose he's going to the game with you tomorrow?"

"I don't know. Probably not."

"You decided to go to the game after all?" Ephraim asked.

Lucretia nodded. "I hope it's not canceled because of the storm."

Denny said, "He can stay home with the kid, smoke dope."

Lucretia stood, knocking over her chair. Her face was bright red. "I demand an apology."

"Hah!" said Denny.

Ephraim swiveled in his seat to face Denny. "Won't hurt to apologize."

Denny stood up and put on his yellow slicker. "I'm going out for coffee. Can I get anyone else a cup?"

"Black for me," said Mrs. Danvers. "Watch it when you go out the door, will you."

When Victoria saw Dahlia's rental car splashing through the ruts in her driveway that evening, she turned the thermostat up.

"Are you all right?" Victoria asked when she saw Dahlia's face. "You can hang your raincoat over the kitchen door."

"Howland made a terrible scene when he saw how I'd reorganized the kitchen." Dahlia stepped down into the cookroom and plopped into a chair.

Victoria sat across from her.

"He was quite beside himself. He slammed doors, dumped out the contents of drawers, and used some language I didn't think I'd ever hear from him."

Victoria said nothing.

"There was no way I could work in that kitchen the way he kept it."

"I'm sure finding the body upset him."

"We're all upset. More than you can imagine. Bacchus, of course, started calling out. He's sensitive and Howland doesn't seem to understand. Then Howland's dogs started barking. That house is pandemonium."

"Where's Howland now?"

"He took the dogs for a walk on the beach. The dogs have been acting up ever since they found the body." Dahlia stood up, turned around in a tight circle, and sat down again.

"Can I get you a glass of sherry? Or something stronger?"

"I'm not supposed to drink, but thank you. May I have a cup of tea instead?"

By the time she'd finished her second cup of tea and had eaten several gingersnaps, Dahlia had calmed down. They talked a bit about the weather and finding the body and then Victoria asked her about her Foreign Service assignments. "You must be close to retirement."

"I was to have one more posting. To Paris. But the assignment has been postponed temporarily. In the meantime, I've put my things in storage until I can move up here. Amazing how many possessions one can accumulate over a lifetime."

Victoria laughed. "Imagine what it's like

living in this house with seven generations of pack rats before me."

Dahlia smiled. "I don't know what to do about Howland. He's impossible."

Victoria said nothing.

"I hope you don't mind my calling on you and venting," Dahlia said.

"Of course not. I understand how you must feel."

"Thanks for tea, Victoria. I'm sure I'll be back."

"You're always welcome, Dahlia."

Chapter 11

Lucretia left Town Hall early to be home when Meyer arrived. Her house was one of several two-bedroom Capes strung out along Amos Coffin Road, an unpaved dirt track that angled off Old County Road.

Her front door opened directly into her living room, which served as Lucretia's dining room as well. She and Sonny ate their meals, when he was home, at a small round table in a bay window. The window overlooked a patch of worn grass and a sea of shoulder-high scrub oaks that stretched eastward to the airport.

At eight o'clock, long after Lucretia had come home from Town Hall, Meyer showed up.

When she heard his knock, Lucretia rushed to the door, arms open. Meyer embraced her, then held her away from him.

"Good to see you, babe." Meyer was tall, lean, and hard. His face was the color of oiled teak. His hair was a streaky sun-bleached blond, and his eyes were pale blue.

Lucretia pouted slightly. "I thought you'd caught the four o'clock boat."

"I did. I had something to tend to."

Lucretia had set two glasses, a bottle of Scotch, and a bowl of ice, now floating in a pool of melted water, on the coffee table in front of the couch.

They sat and she snuggled against him. "I've missed you. All sorts of stuff is going on, and I've had no one to talk to."

Meyer undid the elastic of Lucretia's ponytail, lifted her hair, and nuzzled the back of her neck. "I'm here now. You can tell me." He smelled of fresh air, sunshine, and salt water.

She sat up suddenly. "You must be starved. I've got two steaks. Baked potatoes, if you can wait."

"You haven't eaten yet?" Meyer asked

"I waited for you."

He laughed. "How long will the potatoes take, an hour?"

Lucretia smiled. "Maybe longer, if I turn the oven down."

An hour later, while Lucretia was broiling their steaks, she told Meyer about finding the coffin under Simon Norton's stone, and about the sandbags in the coffin. "Apparently Howland Atherton is a drug enforcement officer. Our police chief knew he was, and yet she never told me."

Meyer smiled.

"*Mr.* Atherton told us not to mention the sandbags to anybody." Lucretia looked up. "But you're not just anybody."

Meyer patted her shoulder. "I should hope not." He looked at her with his far-seeing eyes. "What are they going to do with the sandbags and the coffin? I don't suppose they can recycle a used coffin?"

She laughed. "Denny locked the coffin in the shed behind Town Hall. Casey — the police chief?"

He nodded.

"Casey wants the mystery of the Norton girl cleared up before they dispose of the coffin."

"That makes sense," said Meyer. "Those steaks smell great."

"Rare, right?"

"Right."

Lucretia had set the table with a white linen cloth, tall candles in polished brass candlesticks, and a spray of orchids she'd bought at the flower display at Cronig's. Silver and china and crystal sparkled in the candlelight, and were mirrored in the night-dark windows. Brahms played softly in the background.

Meyer looked around at the framed prints of Island scenes, at the comfortable armchairs and braided rug, at the pictures propped up on the bookcase of Sonny in his football uniform. A clutter of teenage boy stuff was piled off to one side — a football jersey, sports magazines, earphones for a Walkman.

The storm had kept up all afternoon and was continuing into the evening. Sleet rattled against the windows. Meyer pulled out a chair for Lucretia, and sat down at the table. "It's peaceful here on the Island. Not like Seattle. I don't know how recently you've been there, but the traffic is lousy." He unfolded his napkin and reached for the salt shaker.

Lucretia passed the hot rolls. "How was the fishing?"

"King crab. The catch was so-so." He gestured with his hand, palm down. "I'll never get rich working as deckhand on someone else's boat."

Lucretia sighed. "Ephraim was saying just this morning, you ought to try for a berth on one of the Island boats."

He shook his head. "The fishing is even worse on the East Coast." He held up a chunk of almost raw steak on his fork. "Perfectly cooked."

163

Lucretia smiled. "I hope you'll look into getting a job here. You could work for the Steamship Authority. They always need deckhands."

Meyer gazed into her face, his eyes going from her eyes to her nose to her lips. "Let's talk about something else."

Lucretia felt the exquisite quivering his eye contact always aroused in her and looked down quickly.

"Where's Sonny?" Meyer asked.

"I loaned him my car and gave him enough money to treat his buddies to pizza." She straightened her napkin in her lap. "I don't know if I told you about Sonny getting kicked off the football team?"

Meyer nodded. "That's a shame. Right before the big game."

"He's taking it hard. Sonny and four others were involved. They've decided they don't want to go to Nantucket tomorrow."

"I don't blame them." Meyer broke off a piece of his roll and mopped his plate. "You're going, aren't you, babe?"

"If they don't cancel the boat because of the storm. As a town official, I almost have to go." She gazed at him over her glass. "Is there any chance you can come? Everybody's going."

"I'd rather spend a quiet day. Do some man-to-man thing with Sonny. Bonding, you know."

"You *are* a dear." Lucretia got up from the table and put her arms around his neck. "Thank you. Sonny would love that. He needs a role model."

Meyer folded his napkin, leaned back, and looked up at her. "I'm hardly a role model."

"You didn't know Sonny's father. My ex."

Meyer cleared his throat. "I think Sonny and I can find some stuff to do tomorrow to keep him occupied."

Lucretia bent down and kissed his forehead. Her hair fell in a cascade over his, blond mixing with blond.

"I'll talk to him when he comes in tonight," Meyer said, brushing her hair out of his face.

"It's Mort, all right," Red told Dahlia. "Beat up by rocks and surf, but no doubt about it." Dahlia and Red were the only customers at the ArtCliff Diner the next morning.

During the night the wind had died, and the sleet turned into a steady rain that was predicted to continue for at least another day.

Dottie hustled over. "You folks aren't going to the game?"

"Afraid not," said Red.

"Me neither." Dottie sighed. "We drew lots to see who'd work today, and I lost."

"Tough luck," said Red.

Nodding, she took their order and left.

Dahlia played absently with her fork. "When you realized the body was Mort, did you mention his name to anyone?"

Red shook his head. "They'll identify him soon enough. Toby drove the body to Falmouth late yesterday afternoon."

"I understand they canceled a couple of boats yesterday."

Red nodded. "Too windy. Toby wanted to go to the game today. He was afraid he'd be stuck on the mainland overnight, but they ran the last two ferries."

Dottie returned with a pot of coffee and Red was silent while she filled their mugs.

"I don't know what the hell is going on," he said after Dottie left. "Where could Tremont be? You don't suppose he had anything to do with the funny business that's going on, do you?"

"Never," said Dahlia. "Not Tremont. I've worked with him for years. He's completely reliable. Incorruptible."

Red laughed. "With what's at stake? Everybody has a price."

Dottie returned with orange juice, pancakes for Red, a toasted English muffin for Dahlia, and filled their coffee cups again. She jerked her head toward the steady rain pounding the parking area in front of the diner. "I wouldn't like to be playing in that mess. I wouldn't want to do the laundry when they come home." She laughed and went back to the kitchen.

Red poured syrup over his pancakes. "Things change, Dahlia. You and me, Tremont and Mort, Herb. Look at you. We moved the schedule up because of your," he cleared his throat, "illness."

"Cancer," said Dahlia. "You can say the 'C' word to me."

"Sorry." Red looked down at his plate. "I figured that Mort and Tremont split off from the group, were going on their own. Looks as though I was wrong about that."

"I hope you don't seriously suspect Tremont of having anything to do with Mort's death. That seems to have been an unfortunate accident."

"Accident, Dahlia? Hardly." Red set his fork on his plate. "Here's my latest scenario. Tremont wants Mort out of the way. That leaves four of us. So who's next? Dahlia and Red, that's who. That leaves two, Herb and Tremont."

"No," said Dahlia. "I won't believe that of Tremont. All five of us went through too much together."

"A bond?" Red sneered. "Doesn't take much to dissolve bonds. And we're dealing with a lot of much." He chewed, holding his fork in his left hand, his knife in his right. "By the way, have you heard from Emery yet?"

"No, but we don't need him right now."

"I don't trust that guy. Never did. I was never sure what he did for the Agency."

"Contract work," said Dahlia. "They call on him when they need highly sensitive work done."

"A contract killer, maybe?" Red said. "I wouldn't be surprised. How come you picked him?"

Dahlia laughed. "You had some dealings with him, too, didn't you?"

"Not directly. I ran into him in Afghanistan when I was posted there. We had a few drinks together. Quiet guy. And you? Where did you first meet him?"

"I can't really recall. It seems as though I've always known who he was. Washington, I guess. I saw him when I was in Vienna, then again in Colombia."

168

"I guess you know what you're doing. We've trusted you with one hell of a lot so far." Red shook his head. "I think you're right. We don't want him involved until we're ready for him, and we're not. In the meantime, we've got to find Tremont."

Dahlia picked up the second half of her English muffin, and spread it with marmalade. "You're paranoid, Red. Tremont would never, never undercut us. Never."

"Well, hardly ever," Red said, and laughed again. "Why am I quoting Gilbert and Sullivan?"

Their table looked out onto Beach Road and the harbor beyond. A car pulled into the gas station across the road and an attendant wearing a black slicker came out.

Red watched. "They wouldn't be able to get service that quickly in summer. Nice this time of year."

Dahlia shivered and pulled her coat around her.

Red took another bite. "What about Herb? Have you heard anything from him?"

Dahlia shook her head. "I don't expect to. He's been in Brazil for a little over a month now. Collecting orchids."

"That's what he wants us to think."

Dahlia set the uneaten part of her muffin on her plate.

"What *is* the matter with you, Red? You were suspicious of me when you called me in Washington. Then you were sure Mort and Tremont were in cahoots. Now with Mort dead, you suspect Tremont alone. And now you think Herb is scheming against us."

"The matter with me is that something damned funny is going on, and I don't like it. The coffin goes missing. Old Simon Norton's gravestone moves mysteriously. They find a coffin, not old Simon's, but ours, under his stone. The hearse arrives on the boat without the driver. Tremont disappears. Now we've got Mort's body. Fell off the ferry? Accidentally?" He shook his head. "Herb's so-called trip to Brazil is a pretty convenient way to stay out of touch, I'd say."

Dahlia threw her napkin down on the table. "Stop it, Red. Stop it!"

"I have reason for being paranoid, Dahlia. You do too."

Meyer dropped Lucretia off at the Steamship Authority dock. The rain had let up briefly. The air itself seemed to be purple and white. Banners, sweaters, balloons,

170

pennants, ribbons, even purple and white cars. Kids had daubed purple and white paint on their faces. A dozen heads of hair were dyed purple.

"Where are your colors?" Meyer asked.

Lucretia pulled a purple and white stocking cap out of her pocket, and opened her raincoat to show a long purple and white scarf.

Meyer laughed. "Stay dry! I'll listen to the game on WMVY." He turned to look at the traffic piling up behind him. "Gotta go, babe, see you when you get back."

Lucretia leaned over and kissed him. "Thanks for looking out for Sonny."

A girl with dripping hair thrust a cardboard sign in front of Meyer. HARPOON THE WHALERS!

Meyer waved and moved on.

When Meyer pulled up in front of Lucretia's house, Sonny slouched over to the driver's side and leaned in. He was wearing a Vineyarders sweatshirt with its arms cut off, and smelled of beer and stale sweat.

"We borrowed the pickup, but we've only got it for two hours," Sonny said.

"That should be plenty of time. Who owns the truck?"

Sonny spat to one side and shoved his

hands into his jeans pockets. "One of the guys on the team."

"Were your buddies able to come?"

"Two of them, Rusty and Peek. Me. That's all."

"That's enough. You guys are pretty tough." Meyer reached out of the car window and punched Sonny's upper arm. Sonny tensed both arms and his muscles bulged. Meyer grinned. "All right!" He started up the car again. "You know where they stored it, don't you?"

"Sure, man. The shed behind, like, Town Hall."

"And you found your mother's keys?"

Sonny held up a ring of keys and shook it. "She even labeled them."

"She's pretty well organized, your mom."

Sonny muttered, "That's about all she's got going for her."

Meyer scowled at him. "We're doing this as a favor to her, you understand. They want to get rid of the coffin to make room for the mower."

Sonny lifted his sweatshirt and hiked up his beltless jeans. "Whatever."

"Can I trust you guys to get the coffin into the pickup, take it to my storage place at the airport, and return the pickup?" He looked at Sonny with his unsettling eyes.

"Don't leave a mess, understand?"

"Yeah," said Sonny.

"I'll be at the storage unit. When you get there, I'll give you the money. Agreed?"

"Yeah," said Sonny.

"Better get under cover. It's starting to rain again."

Meyer had left some basic tools in the small storage unit he'd rented at the Airport Business Park — an electric saw, a drill, hammer and chisel, screwdrivers, tin snips — and had installed a hundred-watt bulb instead of the forty watt that was included in his rent.

Three quarters of an hour after he unlocked the unit, Sonny and his buddies splashed up in a pickup truck emblazoned with orange and red flames, its body perched on gigantic tires, its muffler tuned to the loudest possible frequency. Sonny and another kid flipped back a blue plastic tarp that had covered the dirty coffin, and the three ex-football-team members lifted the coffin out of the back of the truck.

"Where you want it?"

Meyer held the door open. "There, on the sawhorses."

Rain pelted on the metal roof of the shed. The three kids set the coffin down and waited. Meyer walked around, examining it. "What happened here?" he said, pointing to the missing section.

Sonny shrugged. "That's how we found it."

"You sure?" Meyer straightened up. "You didn't leave that end panel in the shed, did you?"

"No, man. We, like, checked the place out, left it nice and clean like you said."

"Where the hell is that piece?" Meyer said, almost to himself.

The kids looked at each other uneasily.

"You, like, said for us to take the coffin out of there. You're paying us, right?"

"Right," said Meyer, reaching for his wallet. "You don't need to say anything to your mother about this."

"You already told us that."

One of Sonny's buddies said, "We're, like, clams, man."

Sonny held out his hand, and Meyer slapped money into it.

"If you find out what happened to that missing piece, it's worth an extra bill."

"You collect coffins or something?" the other kid said.

"Something like that."

The three dodged through the rain, their collars up over their heads, got back into the truck, and roared off.

After the noise had died away, Meyer studied the coffin for several minutes. He opened up the hinged lid, which was held on with sheet metal screws. He stepped back when the mildewy smell hit him, then set to work, tearing out the decaying sateen lining, stained brown where water had seeped into the coffin. Worms and beetles fell onto the floor and scurried or humped into the dark corners of the shop. The creatures had chewed and digested the cheap cloth and had left their casts in folds of the rotten material. The lining had been glued onto the metal of the coffin, the smallest amount of glue and fabric possible. Meyer felt the fabric carefully before he tore it into thin strips and dumped the strips into a large plastic trash container.

The coffin itself was made of double sheets of thin waffle-patterned metal riveted together around the edges, with about five inches of air space to make the coffin look substantial.

Meyer was able to rip the metal side panels off without using tools. He slit the panels open, one by one, and shook whatever was inside onto the floor. The stuff that fell out consisted of curls of shiny metal, gobs of black dust, pieces of steel wool, a greasy rag, rivets, screws, two beer bottle caps, and a corrugated cardboard liner.

Meyer systematically cut the thin metal into strips, first with the electric saw, then, because the saw was noisy, with the tin snips. He felt each dust gob, tore the cardboard liner into postage-stamp-size pieces, and deposited his work into the trash container. When the container was full, he put on his slicker and lugged the trash to a Dumpster fifty feet from his storage unit, returned, and continued his dissection.

His face was expressionless while he worked. He neither smiled nor frowned. He worked silently without whistling, muttering, or cursing.

Morning passed into afternoon, and he worked until only dust and lint and metal scraps were left, and he swept those into a dustpan and deposited them in the Dumpster.

He checked his watch, locked the door of his storage unit, and drove through the steady rain to Vineyard Haven to meet the boat that was bringing Lucretia and a large percentage of Islanders back from Nantucket. He hadn't bothered to listen to the game, but it didn't matter. He could hear the boat's whistle, not the usual coming-into-port whistle, but a series of blasts that left no doubt about who'd won. As the boat approached the dock, he could hear hoarse cheers and noisemakers and rattles and whistles and firecrackers.

The Island's six fire companies met the ferry, even the exhausted crews that had been battling the West Tisbury dump fire. So did the Island's six police departments. After all, the Vineyarders had beaten Nantucket.

Meyer saw the West Tisbury Bronco with the police chief and her ancient side-kick. Red, white, and blue lights strobed across the scene, reflecting off the rain, and cutting through the dusk. Sirens and bells vied with the noise arriving on the boat.

Once the boat docked, purple and white high school kids poured off carrying mud-covered team players on their shoulders.

Meyer waited in Lucretia's car, parked near the bank building, some distance from the West Tisbury police vehicle.

Lucretia appeared, rosy-cheeked, her raincoat soaked through, her ponytail askew. "Meyer, darling, you should have come with us to Nantucket! What a game!" Her voice was a hoarse whisper. "It was a rout! Forty-nine to six!"

"Let's get you home," said Meyer. "Unless, of course, you'd like to go to the celebration at the high school?"

"We celebrated for two hours on the boat. I'm beat." She leaned back in her seat. "Let's get takeout for supper."

"I've already ordered. Chinese from the Golden Dragon."

She sat up straight. "How's Sonny? He wanted so badly to be part of a big win. Poor kid."

"He went off with his buddies," Meyer answered.

"I think the coach overreacted." Lucretia slumped back into her seat. "They were only smoking a joint."

Meyer said nothing.

"I'm exhausted. A hot shower, supper, and . . ."

"Early bed?" Meyer finished.

Chapter 12

From the parking lot outside the gym, the noise was awesome. Inside, the noise was deafening. Gory Blues, the rock band, had turned its amplifiers to full volume, and the music echoed off the high ceiling and bounced off the walls. The gym was crowded with celebrating teenagers and a scattering of adults, shouting, dancing, tossing purple and white streamers, inflating balloons, and letting them go to sail overhead with a rude sound that was swallowed up by the general din.

Sonny sidled into the gym and looked around. Someone pounded him on the back, shouted something he couldn't hear, and moved on. He was pushed and shoved by muddy and wet, purple and white high school kids. Someone poured a can of Coke over his head. The Coke ran down his forehead, and he swiped his hand across his face to keep the stuff out of his eyes. The gym smelled like wet dogs, stale sweat, and cheap perfume.

He searched for Denise, moving around

the floor in a rough circle with the amorphous mass of kids. She was here somewhere, but where?

Suddenly, like a flight of birds or a school of fish, the mob formed into a single line and started moving in one direction. Without consciously doing anything, Sonny was absorbed into the snake dance. He looked behind him and saw a long chain of kids, most of whom he recognized. A girl from his homeroom pushed in front of him, grabbed his hands and placed them around her waist, and the line whirled around the gym, faster and faster until Sonny felt dizzy and drunk.

Where was Denise?

Someone threw confetti. The paper dots stuck to Sonny's Coke-wet hair and face. The music made his chest throb, his head pound.

Finally, as the line curved in on itself, he saw her. He took one hand off the girl's waist and waved frantically.

"Denise!" he shouted. "Denise!"

She looked at him at first blankly, then smiled, and the line whipped past her.

The girl in front of him called back, "Hold on, Sonny!"

And then, as suddenly as the line had formed, it broke up into a mob again.

There was a brief lull, and then Sonny saw her, standing with a group of three other girls. He pushed his way through the sweaty crowd.

"Denise!"

She looked around and smiled. She'd combed out her braids, and her dark hair, held away from her face with a purple headband, hung below her shoulders.

"I gotta talk to you. Outside." He jerked his head toward the nearest exit, and didn't wait for her response. He shouldered his way through the crowd to the door, leaned his hip against the panic bar, and waited for her to catch up. Outside, the lack of noise was a relief. He still heard the celebration, but behind the closed door the noise had sorted itself out into music and singing and laughter. The rain had let up, and puddles in the parking lot reflected the lights from the school.

Denise was close behind him. "You should've come to Nantucket, Sonny. The coach was looking for you."

Sonny hiked up his pants and spat to one side. "I had stuff to do." He strolled down the row of parked vehicles in the lot.

Denise faced him. "Like, what kind of stuff?"

"My mother's boyfriend needed me to move something."

She reached up and plucked a dot of confetti off Sonny's lower lip. "Move what?"

Sonny shrugged. "He told me not to say anything."

"I can keep a secret." Denise leaned against the fender of a pickup truck.

"I guess." Sonny set his foot on the truck's front bumper.

"So?"

Sonny leaned forward. "You know that coffin everybody's talking about?"

"What about it?"

"The boyfriend wanted me to, you know, move it to the airport. To a storage unit."

"Jee-sus, Sonny. Is that what you dragged me out here to, like, tell me?"

"*You* asked *me*." Sonny glared at her. "That wasn't what I was going to say."

Denise moved away from the truck, lifted her hair with one hand, and started toward the gym. "I'm going back inside."

"Wait," Sonny said. "I was going to ask you to the show."

"Tonight?" Denise looked down at her mud-spattered jeans. "No way. I got to get something to eat. I'm starved."

"We can go to the late show. Get a hamburger at the Standby."

Denise eyed him suspiciously. "You treating? Since when?"

Sonny reached into his back pocket, pulled out a Gore-Tex wallet, and showed her a sheaf of bills.

Denise frowned. "From the boyfriend? He must have, like, wanted that coffin pretty bad."

Sonny put his wallet back in his pocket. "He said my mom wanted it out of the shed. To make room for the mower."

"So he paid you that kind of money just for moving some old coffin, and then, like, tells you to keep your mouth shut? What's going on, Sonny?"

"You want to take in a show with me or not? I can always ask Vicki."

Denise made a face. "Vicki. Sometimes I wonder about your taste in women." She kicked at a stone that landed in a puddle with a splash. "You can't go like that." She indicated his filthy T-shirt and jeans.

"I'll grab a shower."

"You got your mom's car?"

Sonny nodded.

"Well, take me home, then, so I can change."

The morning after the game, Casey and Victoria were on their way to the dump to check the fire, which the Island fire departments now had more or less under control.

"What do you know about West Virginia, Victoria?"

"It's wild and wonderful," Victoria replied, "and it's got country roads and coal mines. Why?"

"The hearse coming from Milwaukee to pick up the coffin?"

Victoria nodded.

"The hearse has Wisconsin plates, but it's registered in Petersburg, West Virginia."

"Oh?" Victoria cranked down her window and looked at her reflection in the side mirror.

"Vehicles have identification numbers, that's how they tracked down the registration."

Casey drove across the narrow bridge over Mill Brook and turned right in front of the big split oak. Victoria heard something slide on the metal floor in the back of the Bronco.

Casey glanced in the rearview mirror. "I've got to get rid of that piece of junk."

"Were the Wisconsin plates stolen?" Victoria asked.

"That's what's curious. The plates are from a Dodge van owned by a Mortimer Chaffer who lives in Milwaukee."

184

"Have you been able to reach him?"

Casey shook her head. "I called several times, but got his answering machine."

Victoria thought for a moment. "Who owns the hearse?"

"It belongs to a Herb Plante, who runs a greenhouse in Petersburg."

"What does he have to say about all this?" Victoria asked.

"He's apparently out of the country. I talked to the Petersburg police chief, who knows Mr. Plante. The chief says Plante is a retired government official who grows orchids and other flowers for sale."

"Odd that he should own a hearse," Victoria mused.

"Maybe for funeral flowers?" Casey slowed for the turn onto the dump road.

"You don't use a hearse for flowers," Victoria replied.

"Well, maybe he rents the vehicle to churches or funeral homes. Who knows." Casey stopped near the still smoking stump pile, which had been bulldozed almost level with the ground.

A weary-looking fire chief greeted them.

Casey leaned her elbow on the window frame. "Did you get any rest, Anthony? When you're not putting out fires, I see you greeting returning football heroes."

Anthony took his cap off and scratched the back of his head. "I got a few hours here and there. I can probably call it a day, now. The fire should burn itself out in a week or so. The embers are in a pit that goes down five, six feet."

"Did you ever find out what made the fire blaze up the way it did?" Victoria asked.

"Someone doused the pile with kerosene or fuel oil. Probably whoever left the body. I suppose he figured we wouldn't bother fighting the fire, and the body would burn beyond recognition." Anthony settled his cap back on his thick hair.

"Let me know if you need any help from us," Casey said.

"Thanks, Chief."

"No, Anthony. Thank *you*."

When they turned back onto the main road, the metal piece shifted again. Casey grunted. "I'm taking that to Town Hall now so they can put it with the rest of the coffin."

They recrossed Mill Brook, passed the arboretum, and Casey slowed for Deadman's Curve, the sharp turn next to the cemetery. Victoria sat up straight so she could see around Casey. Someone had pruned the big yew that overhung the

Norton plot. She could see pale reddish circles of fresh-cut wood on the massive trunk. Branches lay in a heap on the ground.

Victoria settled back in her seat. They passed the art gallery and the old parsonage.

"I suppose they'll take the yew cuttings to the dump," Victoria said. "To burn?"

Casey laughed. "I guess they need some place to dump tree limbs. Aren't yews a symbol of death?"

"Of immortality," Victoria corrected. "That's why they're planted in cemeteries."

At Brandy Brow, Casey continued up the hill past Alley's store and the white-steepled Congregational church. She pulled into the small parking lot in front of Town Hall. "I'll be right back, Victoria, as soon as I find out what they want me to do with this coffin piece."

Victoria took her crossword puzzle book out of her cloth bag and had begun a new puzzle when Casey returned, holding up a key attached by a wire to a long block of wood. "Mrs. Danvers says to put the panel in the shed. I'll be right back. You might as well work on your puzzle."

Casey fit the key into the padlock and pulled the door open. She stared into the dim shed, then returned to the Bronco, shaking her head and muttering something.

"What's the trouble?" Victoria asked.

"The coffin's not there. Denny must have put it somewhere else. I'm taking the key back to Mrs. D."

But when Casey returned, she looked baffled.

"Mrs. D. says Denny definitely put the coffin in the shed. It was there on Saturday, the day before yesterday. I'm going to check the shed again, see if there are any traces of something having been there."

Victoria slid out of the passenger seat and joined Casey.

"Denny probably put the coffin in his own shed and forgot," Casey said. "What's with that guy, anyway?"

Victoria smiled. "He's just like his grandfather."

The shed had the usual cans of motor oil, old bottles, rakes, grass clippers, stacks of newspapers, and frayed ropes. There were also marks that looked as though the coffin might have made and some blurred muddy footprints.

"I'll call Denny from Mrs. Danvers's phone and find out if he moved the coffin, and if so, where he put it. You might just as well get back in the Bronco, Victoria."

When she returned after calling Denny, Casey was shaking her head. "Denny said he put the coffin in the shed. Definitely. When he found the end piece missing, he retraced his route from the funeral home. I told him we saw the piece fall off when we were following him, and we picked it up."

"What did he say to that?"

"That I might as well keep the panel in the Bronco until the rest of the coffin turns up." Casey got back into the Bronco, started it up, and backed out. "I don't want that thing scraping up the back of my vehicle, and I certainly don't have room in the police station."

"There's room in my woodshed," Victoria said.

"I don't suppose you can lock the woodshed, can you?"

"Of course not."

"The woodshed is the ell off the cookroom?"

Victoria nodded.

"Okay," said Casey. "I suppose it doesn't matter whether the shed is locked or not."

Victoria smiled. "You're more of an Islander every day."

Mrs. Danvers looked up from her computer screen as Lucretia came into Town

189

Hall. "The coffin's missing again."

"What do you mean?" Lucretia's voice was even hoarser than last evening.

"Casey found the coffin missing this morning."

"What are you talking about?" Lucretia sat in the chair next to Denny's desk and turned to face Mrs. Danvers.

"When Denny was bringing the coffin here from the funeral parlor, a piece fell off on the road," Mrs. Danvers explained patiently. She crossed her arms over her narrow chest. "Casey picked the piece up and has been carrying it around in the police car all weekend. About an hour ago she brought the section here to reunite it with the rest of the coffin." Mrs. Danvers shrugged.

Lucretia cleared her throat. "But the coffin's missing?"

"That's what I said."

At that point, Denny shuffled into Town Hall. "Great game," he said cheerily. "Pretty good coverage on WMVY."

Mrs. Danvers looked up at him. "Have you talked to Casey?"

"I sure as hell did. What's going on?"

Lucretia stood up. "That's what I want to know, too. Where did you put the coffin now, Denny?"

"Oh for God's sake," said Denny. "Get off my case, will you, Noodles! I left it in the shed." He shuffled over to his desk and sat down.

Lucretia's voice was barely audible. "Sounds like the refrain 'two plots over from Old Simon' to me."

"If the coffin's not in the shed now, somebody must have moved it out." Denny opened a desk drawer and retrieved a pencil.

"There are only four sets of keys," Mrs. Danvers said to Denny. "Yours, Ephraim's, mine, and Lucretia's."

Lucretia turned away from Denny. "Why would anyone want that filthy thing, anyway?"

"Same reason somebody moved Old Simon's stone," Denny said. "They thought there was something in that coffin."

"Bags of sand," Lucretia said.

Denny looked over the top of his glasses at her. "They probably didn't know that."

"Did you get a 'small gratuity' again for your shenanigans, Denny? Another five thousand dollars?"

Denny thumped his desktop with the palm of his hand. "I sure as hell didn't," he said, then added, "I wish." He shifted some papers in front of him, and without looking up said, "By the way, how's the boyfriend? He like that sexy voice of yours?"

"None of your business," Lucretia snapped. "You seem to be the key to this 'who's got the coffin' game, Denny. I suppose you arranged for all the permits needed to dig up the cemetery?"

"*I* certainly didn't," said Mrs. Danvers.

"The Norton family is talking lawsuits," Lucretia went on.

Denny riffled through his papers. "That's their problem."

"What is Chief O'Neill doing with that broken-off piece?" Mrs. Danvers asked.

"She told me," Denny said, with exaggerated patience, "that she's keeping it until we find the rest of the coffin."

Lucretia leaned back in her chair. "Where, in the police Bronco?"

"That's where she said. In the Bronco."

"Here's the chief now," said Mrs. Danvers.

Casey opened the door and checked the new glass. "Safety glass?"

"Meets code," replied Mrs. Danvers.

Casey handed her a manila folder, and said to Lucretia and Denny, "The feds analyzed the sand. Howland Atherton . . ."

"I don't want to hear another word

about Atherton," Lucretia interrupted. "Don't you get too cozy with him."

"He's not *my* type," Casey said.

Lucretia flushed. "You don't need to be flip."

"Sorry," said Casey.

"What about the sand?" Denny asked.

Casey laid a paper on his desk. "Quartz sand, angular, almost pure quartz. The soils scientist narrowed the source down to some place in West Virginia."

"*West Virginia?*" Lucretia said. "Why West Virginia? How can they tell?"

"The report said it's consistent with a type of sand they use in West Virginia for glass making."

"And the hearse came from West Virginia," Lucretia rasped.

"Right," said Casey.

Lucretia continued. "The coffin, according to *Mr.* Rhodes, was buried ten years ago. Is that right, Denny?"

"Yup," said Denny.

Lucretia said, "Presumably with the West Virginia sand in it then?"

"Unless someone dug up the coffin and altered the contents sometime during that ten years," Denny said.

"And you don't happen to know anything about that, do you, Denny?"

Casey headed toward the door. "I gotta go. Victoria's waiting for me out there." She indicated the new glass in the door. "Looks nice," and shut the door gently behind her.

Lucretia cleared her throat. "Is there something special about that sand, Denny? A West Virginia hearse arrives to pick up a coffin with West Virginia sand inside? And the hearse driver is missing? You have a lot of explaining to do, Denny."

"Not me," said Denny. "You know as much as I do."

Victoria's rutted drive circled a clump of lilac bushes and the trunk and roots of a large tree that had been blown over in a storm. Casey parked the Bronco off to one side under a maple, and unlocked the back while Victoria was getting out.

From the main road, Victoria's house looked like a conventional old farmhouse, gray-shingled, with five windows on the second floor, four on the first floor, and, in the middle, the elegant front door that was seldom used. Two brick chimneys stood above the roof, one on either side of a space in the center where there used to be, in Victoria's childhood, the "lookout," a platform her sea-captain grandfather re-

194

fused to call a "widow's walk." Her grand-father had kept buckets of sand up there to put out fires, in case sparks from the chimney should land on the cedar shingles.

From the back, Victoria's house was far from conventional. It rambled on and on, one addition after another. The kitchen wing led to the cookroom, which led into the woodshed, where her grandfather had kept firewood and coal. Victoria's husband Jonathan had added a workshop and ga-rage to the woodshed.

Casey looked up at the crazy cascade of roofs, as she always did when she came to Victoria's. "I'm glad I don't have to keep this place up."

She carried the coffin panel to the wood-shed, expecting to find a dark dusty storage space. Instead, when Victoria opened the door, Casey saw that the room had been turned into a sort of solarium. Morning sunlight poured through the wall of south-facing windows. Green plants filled the room, which smelled of rosemary, lavender, and scented geraniums.

McCavity, who'd been dozing on a daybed pushed against the wall, awoke, yawned, stretched, jumped off the bed and darted past them out the back door.

"Where do you want me to put this, Victoria? It seems a shame to clutter this room up."

"We used to store coal here. I don't think a piece of coffin is any worse," Victoria said. "Set it against the wall behind the woodstove. It'll be out of sight, and out of the way. When I light the stove the panel will make a good heat shield."

When Lucretia returned home that afternoon, she found Meyer watching television, his shoes off, his feet up on the couch.

He muted the sound. "Hey, babe. How's the voice?"

Lucretia tossed her coat on a chair, and stalked over to the television and flipped it off.

"What's the matter, babe?"

"Everything's the matter." She told him how the coffin had disappeared from the shed.

"That's strange," Meyer murmured. "While you were gone, babe, I fixed the dripping faucet in the upstairs bath."

"Thanks. The back fell off the coffin when Denny moved it from the funeral home. That man can't do anything right."

"Really?" said Meyer.

"Casey is making a big fuss. She picked

the piece up from the road and has been carrying it around in the Bronco."

Meyer glanced at her. "She's got a piece of that coffin in the Bronco?"

"She doesn't want to dispose of it until the rest of the coffin is found." Lucretia paced to the end of the living room and back.

"I rehung that picture next to the fireplace," Meyer said.

Lucretia nodded, her hands on her hips.

"I pasted up that strip of loose wallpaper in Sonny's room. And I plastered over that mouse hole under the kitchen sink."

Lucretia smiled slightly.

"I made lasagne for supper."

Lucretia moved his feet aside and sat on the end of the couch. "I'm sorry, Meyer. I'm being a pill. Thank you."

"I fixed Martinis and put them in the freezer. That will cure your voice."

Lucretia nodded.

He stood up quickly and went into the kitchen. Lucretia heard him open the freezer, heard the clink of glasses, and then he returned with two frosty drinks on a tray.

"I don't know how I managed without you." Lucretia lifted her glass to him. "Don't leave me again, Meyer. You make living worthwhile."

"I can't make a living without leaving you," Meyer said. "When you win the Massachusetts Lottery, babe, I'll think about staying." He put his arm around her.

The stars were brilliant when Casey left her house to confront Junior. She looked up and saw Orion and the Big Dipper, the Pleides and the North Star. Victoria had pointed the constellations out to her. In Brockton, Casey had never noticed the stars. Here on the Island, they were as bright and clear on the horizon as they were overhead. When she looked up, she felt dizzy. She could practically feel the world wheeling around the universe with the constellations.

She parked in the oyster-shell parking space, went up the steps, and faced Junior, her hands on her hips.

"Did you take something out of the back of the Bronco this afternoon, Junior? When it was parked at my house?"

Junior looked up from his paperwork. "Certainly not, Chief. What's up?"

"I found the back unlocked."

Junior laughed.

Casey sat with a plop in her chair and flicked on her desk light. "I believe in locking up stuff, and I'll never change. You

Islanders are crazy, the way you leave everything wide open." She gestured around the small room. "We still don't have a key to this place. The *police station*, of all places."

Junior looked more like a fifteen-year-old than a thirty-five-year-old. His hair was as short as Bert's Barbershop was willing to cut it. His eyes turned down and his mouth turned up, almost meeting when he smiled. "As Victoria says, the police station is a public building," he said. "The public has a right to walk in."

"Lord!" Casey opened her desk drawer and slammed it shut again. "Someone broke into the Bronco."

"Maybe you left the door unlocked. Maybe you're getting acclimated?"

"Oh no," said Casey. "I locked all the doors, all right. Furthermore, I had a tarp and a coil of rope in there, and they've been moved."

"Oh?" said Junior.

"Somebody folded the tarp carefully, but not the way I fold it. And the rope was off to one side."

"Anything missing?" said Junior.

Casey shook her head.

"Then there's nothing to worry about. If you didn't lock up stuff in the first place, you wouldn't need to worry about people breaking in." Junior straightened his already lined-up pencils. His face was serious. "By the way, we got a call from Falmouth. The doc identified the body from the dump fire."

"A local man?"

"Nobody I ever heard of. A Tremont Ashecroft."

"Dental records?" Casey asked.

"They didn't need them. He had his wallet on him. Retired State Department guy. Lived outside Washington, D.C."

"How did he die?"

"The doc thought Ashecroft might have been hit on the head with something like a tire iron. He's making tests as we speak."

"Have the state police notified his family?"

Junior stood, hitched up his trousers, and looked out the window at the ghostly swans sailing on the dark pond, riffling the reflections of the stars. "He had no family. Wife died several years ago, no kids."

The next morning was so clear, Red and Dahlia, who were sitting at their usual table by the window in the ArtCliff Diner, could see the thin line of the mainland in the distance. A ferry rounded the jetty and slowed as it entered the harbor. They heard the whistle.

"I told you so, Dahlia." Red pounded the table, rattling their coffee cups. "They identified the body at the dump. Tremont. Tremont's dead. Mort and Tremont. We're down to three of us. You know who's next, don't you? Do you believe me now?"

Dahlia put her elbows on the table and cupped her chin in her hands. Her cap was low on her brow.

"Do you have any suggestions?" she asked.

"That we get out of here while we can. Forget the whole deal." Red swirled the coffee in his heavy mug.

"I've got to have the money, Red." Dahlia pushed her hat up on her forehead. "I've *got* to have the money," she repeated.

Dottie, the waitress, bustled over to their table. "More coffee, folks?"

Red slid his mug across the table. "Thanks."

"Can I get you anything else? Sure you don't want breakfast?" Dottie tugged her pencil out of her hair and held her pad ready.

"No, thank you," Dahlia said.

"Fresh blueberry pie? You liked that the other day."

201

"No, thank you," Dahlia said.

Dottie shrugged, put her pencil back in her hair, and left.

"I don't know about you, Dahlia, but I'm jumping ship."

"Ten million dollars," Dahlia murmured.

Red laughed. "You ever hear the Jack Benny routine where the robber says, 'Your money or your life,' and Benny pauses? That's you."

Dahlia didn't smile.

Red stirred sugar into his coffee. "We apparently haven't been careful enough. Herb is still unaccounted for."

"There's also you and me," Dahlia said. "I don't suspect you of murdering anyone."

"What about that cemetery commissioner, Rhodes?"

Dahlia shook her head. "Denny Rhodes thought a girl who'd committed suicide was in that coffin. He couldn't have known."

The door opened and three burly men sauntered over to the round table in the corner. "Morning, Dottie!"

"The usual?" Dottie called out, already filling heavy white mugs at the coffee urn.

Red looked down into his own mug, which he was holding in both hands.

"Rhodes may not be as dense as we imagined. How much did you tell Emery Borders?" He spoke quietly.

"As little as I could. Not much."

"How much, exactly, Dahlia?"

"I said I'd come into possession of some uncut gemstones, and asked if he had contacts who could cut them for me. He said he did. Of course."

"Of course. And?"

"And I said I would give him a percentage of the value of the cut stones, if he could sell them, too."

"And?"

Dahlia shrugged. "He agreed. Said for me to get in touch with him when I was ready."

"Did he know how much money was involved?"

"I probably dropped the ten-million-dollar figure."

Red pushed his chair back and stood up, facing the window. "My God, Dahlia. Borders could be killing us off. Or Herb and Borders together."

A slender, almost cadaverous, man joined the three at the corner table, and someone shouted, "Hey, Beanie! How's things?" Someone laughed.

Dahlia moved her mug in circles on a

wet spot on the table. "There's another problem you may not have heard about, Red."

"Can't be any worse. Go ahead."

"The coffin is missing again."

"Jee-sus Christ! You're kidding!" Red sat down again, and leaned toward her. "I'm getting out of here, Dahlia. First boat tomorrow. If you know what's good for you, you will too."

"I've got to find the coffin," Dahlia said. "I've got to."

"Be my guest," said Red. "The ten million is all yours. I'm outta here."

Chapter 13

The morning was clear, brisk, and sunny, so Victoria walked to the police station. When she got there, Casey was on the phone. Victoria waited by the window that overlooked the mill pond, watching the swans bob their heads into the water in search of food. Most of the foliage on the shrubbery surrounding the pond was gone now, the last leaves beaten off by the nor'easter. A few splashes of dark red showed where sheltered forsythia sprays had kept their leaves.

Casey finished her call and hung up. "Falmouth has identified the body that washed up near Howland's beach."

Victoria turned away from the window and settled into the armchair in front of the chief's desk. "Who was it?"

Casey leaned forward. "Mortimer Chaffer."

"Chaffer? The man who owned the Wisconsin license plates on the hearse?"

Casey put her arms on her desk. "His wallet was in his back pocket, car keys in his side pocket, and a waterlogged envelope in his inside jacket pocket."

Victoria unbuttoned her coat and frowned. "With his wallet and keys still in his pockets, perhaps he did fall overboard by accident." She thought for a moment, and Casey waited. "I'm surprised an envelope survived several days of soaking."

"It had five thousand dollars in it. Cash."

Victoria raised her eyebrows. "That seems like a lot of money to be carrying around loose."

Casey nodded.

"Where's the hearse now?" Victoria asked.

"The state police towed it to Tiasquam Repairs."

"Why not to the Rose Haven Funeral Home? Weren't they supposed to coordinate the removal of the coffin?"

Casey grunted. "That was before all these unanswered questions. Like, why were sandbags in the coffin instead of a corpse? And where is the coffin? And how did the hearse driver just happen to fall overboard?"

"I suppose no one saw him fall because of the fog," Victoria said.

"Boat railings are high, designed so people can't fall overboard by accident." Casey folded her arms on her desk. "The medical examiner in Falmouth determined that Chaffer had drowned. But she also said he had a bruise on his neck, right below his left ear. Chaffer got the bruise before he died, the ME told me."

Victoria rested her hands on the arms of the chair. "Perhaps he hit his head on something and lost his balance?"

"More like someone knew where to hit him and then chucked him over the rail."

"Not robbery," Victoria mused. "We don't get much robbery on the Island."

"We get enough." Casey scowled. "But no, not robbery. He had five thousand dollars in an envelope in his pocket, and several hundred dollars in his wallet."

Victoria slipped her arms out of her coat and laid it over the back of her chair. "I wonder how difficult it is to hoist someone over the rail?" She thought for a moment. "I suppose it's a matter of balance. Stun your victim with something heavy when he's leaning against the rail, then lift his feet up, and slide him over. I could probably do that."

"I'm sure you could," said Casey.

After lunch, Casey dropped Victoria back at her house, and shortly after, Dahlia called. "I've got to talk with you, Victoria.

Will you be home this afternoon?"

"Come for tea," Victoria said. "How about a game of Scrabble?"

"I don't know if I can concentrate enough to play," Dahlia replied. "But a friend sent me some Brazilian tea. I'll bring it with me."

When Dahlia showed up around four, she was obviously distressed about something.

"Come in," said Victoria. "I've lit the fire in the parlor and set up the card table for Scrabble, in case you change your mind."

Dahlia smiled. "Thank you." She gave Victoria a metal canister. "This is the yerba maté my friend sent."

Victoria examined the canister. "I don't know what yerba maté is, exactly."

"It's a tea made from the leaves of a South American evergreen."

Victoria set the canister next to the stove and put the kettle on to boil. "Put your coat in your old room, Dahlia. Unless you'd rather keep it on."

Dahlia sat in the chair next to the kitchen table. "Maybe later."

Victoria removed the top of the canister. Inside was a package labeled *Yerba Maté, La Olimarena*. She opened the package and peered inside. "This came from your friend in Brazil?"

"Yes, the same man who gave me Bacchus." Dahlia reached into her large purse. "Let me show you what else he sent." She unwrapped tissue paper from a decorated drinking gourd embellished with a silver rim. She held up a slender metal pipe with a flattened sieve at the bottom. "This is a *bombilla,* a drinking straw."

Victoria took the gourd in her hand. "How beautiful, with all those intricate carvings. Is this typical of drinking gourds?"

"Yes. The maté gourds are all different, and all interesting. One brews maté in the gourd like conventional tea. Then it's drunk through the *bombilla.*"

"Like a tea strainer," said Victoria.

"Exactly. We used to drink maté every afternoon when I was in South America."

"It looks as though your friend intended this just for you, with the one gourd and one straw," Victoria said. "I shouldn't be sharing your tea."

"It's my pleasure," Dahlia said. "My friend sent a brand I'm not familiar with. I'm sure it won't be sacrilegious to brew the maté in a china teapot and drink it out of cups."

Victoria sniffed the contents. "Did this come from Brazil?"

"The package was in our mailbox."

"Do you know if it was actually mailed from Brazil?" Victoria persisted.

"The outside had Brazilian stamps. The cancellation was blurred, so I couldn't tell the date or place it was mailed from. Why, is something wrong?"

"I don't know." Victoria shook some of the tea into her hand. "You say yerba maté is made from an evergreen tree?"

"From the dried leaves of a type of holly."

"Broad leaves?"

"Victoria, I don't know." Dahlia's voice was petulant. "I'm not a plant person the way you are. I guess so. Holly trees have broad leaves. Why?"

"Look here, Dahlia." Victoria showed her the tea in the palm of her hand. "Evergreen needles, not dried broad leaves. Does this look like the maté you're accustomed to?"

Dahlia looked at the tea in Victoria's hand. "No, but I've not had this brand before. What are you implying?"

"Do you still have the wrappings?" Victoria asked.

"I threw them out. I'm sure they're still in the trash."

"Is it possible that someone put the package in your mailbox, rather than its being delivered by Dave?"

"Dave?"

"Dave in the post office," Victoria said.

Dahlia gathered her coat around herself.

"I'll call him," Victoria said, getting to her feet. "He'll remember delivering a package with foreign stamps." She went into the cookroom and dialed. Within a few minutes, she returned. "We'd better not drink your tea. Dave hasn't delivered a parcel of any kind to Howland's and your mailbox for the past three or four weeks."

Victoria tucked the package labeled "Yerba Maté" back into the canister. "I'll ask Casey to have the tea analyzed."

The kettle whistled. Victoria rinsed out the blue china teapot and spooned tea leaves from her own cupboard. "I hope you'll settle for Earl Grey this afternoon."

Dahlia sat back in the chair. "I can ask Howland to have the maté analyzed. He has contacts at the federal lab."

Victoria lifted down a tray and set the teapot and cups and saucers on it. "I'd prefer to ask Casey."

Dahlia carried the tray into the parlor.

The low sun illuminated the painting of Victoria's great-grandfather's ship that

211

hung above the old drop-leaf desk. The firelight seemed pallid in the mellow sunlight.

Dahlia seated herself on the couch under the portrait of the half-drowned woman and Victoria sat in her wing chair.

They sipped in silence. The fire crackled. The sun settled behind the lilac bushes to the west of the house. Victoria turned on the lamp next to her chair.

Finally, Dahlia spoke. "This isn't easy for me, Victoria. You're the only person I can possibly confide in."

Victoria waited.

Dahlia sat forward, her skirt looping to the floor, her hands clasped. "You knew I was in the Foreign Service," she started. "Stationed in Colombia for several years."

Victoria watched Dahlia through half-closed eyes.

"I met some extremely wealthy people and through them — I won't go into details — I acquired a few uncut emeralds."

Victoria raised her eyebrows.

"I was the typical beginning gem collector. I got the bug, and started buying stones from various sources, some legitimate, some not quite."

Victoria poured more tea. "How did you get them into the United States?"

"That's where my problem lies. I sent home a few at a time in the diplomatic pouch, either to myself or to a friend." Dahlia sat back on the sofa and crossed her arms over her chest. "This is difficult for me to talk about, Victoria."

"You needn't go on." Victoria rested her gnarled hands on the arms of her chair.

"Yes, I do. I've got to let someone know the story." Dahlia picked up her cup and saucer, and Victoria heard them rattle as Dahlia's hands shook. "Over the years I amassed a large quantity of stones."

Victoria turned her head to look at the fire. "Where did you keep them?"

"That's what I'm coming to," Dahlia said, setting her cup and saucer back on the table. She blotted her lips with a napkin, and was quiet for a long time.

Victoria finally asked, "Didn't you want to sell them?"

Dahlia shook her head. "I didn't realize what sort of trouble I had made for myself. I hadn't declared them when they entered the U.S. I was concerned about calling attention to myself because of that. And because of the way I acquired them."

Victoria tried to keep her face expressionless, but Dahlia must have seen something.

"I don't mean I stole them, Victoria. I didn't. Except for gifts, I paid for every stone. But sometimes I bought from people who had no right to sell to me."

"I see."

The room was getting quite warm, and Dahlia unbuttoned her coat. "The word got around the department's underground that I was collecting raw gemstones, and I learned about a few other people who were doing the same thing. Emeralds, rubies, and sapphires. Diamonds."

"Diamonds? I thought the diamond market was tightly controlled."

"In South Africa, yes. But a fellow Foreign Service officer stationed in Afghanistan learned about an untapped diamond source there. An Afghani group planned to develop a mine with U.S. aid. They hadn't begun when he was there, and then of course . . ." She waved her hand.

"Was the Afghan government involved?"

Dahlia dabbed at her eyes with her napkin. "The government was more concerned about flooding the market. The volcanic pipe in which the diamonds occur in Afghanistan is very, very rich. The stones are found in a sort of blue-black mud. If diamonds ever become common, their value will drop."

214

Victoria levered herself out of her chair. "I think we need some cookies to go with our tea."

When she returned, Dahlia was flattening her napkin in her lap. Victoria set a plate of gingersnaps on the coffee table, and Dahlia took one.

"How did your associate acquire the diamonds?" Victoria asked.

"He bought most of them from people who found pretty glass-like rocks in streambeds downstream from the ancient volcano. The people from whom he bought the stones had no idea what they were selling. Even if the sellers had known they were dealing with diamonds, they would not have wanted the Afghan government to know about the transactions." Dahlia bit into her cookie.

"And the sapphires and rubies — where did they come from?"

"The rubies came from colleagues posted to Burma, the sapphires from Sri Lanka."

"And these were all uncut stones?"

"All of them."

"How did you get together? Who was in charge?" Victoria asked. "The stones must have been worth quite a lot of money."

"Among us, about ten million dollars' worth."

"Good heavens!" Victoria said.

"I contacted the others. There were five of us altogether. I suggested that, since we all had the same problem of realizing any money from the sale of the stones, that we should form a close group, band together."

Victoria was thinking about the small diamond in the engagement ring that Jonathan had given her. The diamond had cost more than a month's salary.

Dahlia went on. "You understand, the stones were worthless to us because we couldn't dispose of them without getting into serious trouble."

"I think I understand," Victoria said. "So at your suggestion the five of you met."

"About ten years ago. We discussed our dilemma. Getting the stones cut was a major issue."

"I don't suppose you could sell them to museums or mineralogy groups?"

Dahlia shook her head and pushed her hat back. "We'd have had to explain how we obtained them and how we got them into the country. That would have jeopardized our careers." Dahlia shook her head again. "We thought of everything. Finally I suggested that we hide the stones in a safe place until we retired."

Victoria started to get up to put another log on the fire, but Dahlia rose first. "Here, Victoria. Let me do that."

Once Dahlia was seated again, Victoria asked, "Weren't you concerned that one of the group might betray the others? Ten million dollars is a powerful incentive."

"We talked frankly about precisely that, and agreed we had to stick together, we simply had to. It was our only hope."

Victoria was beginning to see where this was leading. "And the safe hiding place?"

"The coffin in the West Tisbury cemetery."

"I suppose that's about as safe a place as you can find," Victoria said. "And you decided on the West Tisbury cemetery because of your family ties?"

"Yes."

"I'm afraid I know who at least one of the group was," Victoria said. "The hearse driver, Mortimer Chaffer."

"Mort and I were two. A third member was Tremont Ashecroft."

"I thought Mr. Ashecroft might have some connection with you, Dahlia. I found a toucan-shaped pin near where his body lay."

Dahlia turned back the lapel of her coat. Victoria saw a pin identical to the one she'd found. "All five of us had toucan pins."

Victoria took a deep breath. "I see why you're concerned. Two of the five of you are dead."

"A fourth is Red Crossley, who got a job in the Rose Haven funeral parlor a few weeks ago so he could monitor the transfer of the coffin."

"And the fifth?"

"Herbert Plante, who lives . . ."

"In Petersburg, West Virginia," Victoria finished. "And runs a greenhouse. Owns the hearse that had Wisconsin license plates that belonged to Mr. Chaffer's Dodge van, and is collecting orchids in Brazil right now." Victoria looked up. "And I suppose he's the one who sent you the yerba maté?"

"His name was on the package," said Dahlia.

"And he gave you Bacchus."

Dahlia nodded.

"Well," said Victoria. "I don't know what to say."

"After I was diagnosed with cancer, my physician told me she planned to treat me with Taxol, a promising new drug. When she explained the costs involved, I called the others in the group. My insurance doesn't cover the treatments. I was desperate."

"And that triggered the call to the cemetery commissioners to unearth the coffin?"

"Several years ahead of time. We contacted Herb to make sure he agreed with the plans, which he did. Herb said he was leaving for Brazil, so Mort went down to Petersburg to pick up the hearse."

"That's been a puzzle to me," said Victoria. "Why does a greenhouse operator want a hearse?"

"We bought the vehicle jointly ten years ago," said Dahlia.

"I see. To bring the coffin to the Vineyard."

"We bought it secondhand and expected to use it when we moved the coffin again." Dahlia helped herself to another gingersnap and settled back on the sofa. "Herb rented the hearse to local churches for funerals, and that seemed to tie in nicely with the greenhouse. He kept the hearse rental money, which paid for maintenance."

The sun set and the last glow faded from the sky. The fire had built up a bed of fluorescent coals, and the room was so warm, Victoria took off her sweater.

"How did you plan on selling the gemstones now? It seems to me you're faced with the same problem of explaining how you acquired them."

Dahlia straightened her hat. "In my job, I meet all sorts of people," she said. "I got in touch with a jack-of-all-trades who does contract work of a sensitive nature for the government. He agreed to have the stones cut in Amsterdam and sold, on the condition that he would have a percentage of the money."

"And the other four agreed?"

Dahlia smiled ruefully. "Reluctantly. I had to convince them."

"Do you trust him?"

"Yes and no. None of us was comfortable with him, but he had the credentials we needed."

"This is a lot to absorb." Victoria sat quietly for a few moments. "I'm not sure what you want of me."

"To be totally frank, Victoria, I'm frightened." Dahlia dabbed at her eyes again with her napkin. "The coffin is missing, you know. I have to share my problem with someone. Red and I met this morning over coffee, and he's leaving the Island tomorrow. He's willing to abandon his share of the gemstones."

"I can see why."

"He believes that Emery, the sixth person . . ."

"Your fence," said Victoria.

Dahlia smiled at that. "Yes. Our fence. Red believes that he and I are scheduled to be the next victims, and that Emery and Herb are killing us off, one by one." Dahlia blotted her eyes. "I must say, Red has me concerned, too."

"Where is Emery at this moment?" Victoria asked.

"I don't know. I've put through several calls to him, and get only his answering machine. Red and I agreed that we don't need to involve Emery until we have the stones in hand. We don't want to involve Emery, in fact."

"Yet you say he knows about the gems?"

"Only in a general way. We haven't really told him our plans." Dahlia paused. "I didn't mention this to the others, but it was Emery's idea to conceal the stones in a cemetery."

Victoria pursed her lips at that.

"I never told him that I followed his advice," Dahlia said.

"You don't doubt that Mr. Plante is in Brazil?"

"I didn't until this morning, talking to Red. He's shaken me badly. When I got the

221

yerba maté and the gourd, there was no question in my mind that it came from Herb in Brazil. One doesn't commonly see maté gourds in this country."

"I've never seen them before now," Victoria agreed.

McCavity stalked into the parlor from some hiding place, and sat in front of the fire, cleaning himself, one leg high in the air.

Dahlia watched him for a few moments before she spoke again. "I have a favor to ask of you, Victoria."

"Of course."

"I am very uncomfortable at Howland's. His house is cold and drafty, he's hostile, neither he nor his dogs like Bacchus, and, I don't know. I'm uneasy with him, frankly."

Victoria noticed that Dahlia called the house "his."

"You'd like to stay with me again," Victoria said.

"I hate to put you to the trouble, but I don't know where else to turn."

"I understand. Of course you and Bacchus may stay here, as long as you wish." Victoria added, with a smile, "You needn't pay me until your ship comes in."

"Is tonight too soon?"

"I think that's a good idea," Victoria said.

★ ★ ★

When Elizabeth came home, Victoria explained to her that Dahlia would be moving back with them.

Elizabeth glowered at her grandmother. "How could you!" She paced. "That bird!" She opened the kitchen door to let McCavity in, and when the cat rubbed against her leg she said, "Scat!" McCavity looked up at her with his yellow eyes and when Elizabeth sat down, he sat by her feet.

"We'll roast to death!" Elizabeth fixed drinks for Victoria and herself. "We'll be her servants again. Cleaning up after her bird's bath."

Dahlia and Bacchus moved in after supper, and Dahlia went quietly to her room. Bacchus made a soft chortling noise.

When the phone rang, Elizabeth and Victoria were playing Scrabble. Elizabeth answered and brought the cordless phone into the living room.

"It's Casey for you, Gram." She handed the phone to Victoria.

"I hope I didn't disturb you," Casey said.

"Heavens, no. I'm twenty points ahead of Elizabeth at the moment, and I'm waiting for her to move."

"I just got a call from Ira, who's now caretaking the Rose Haven funeral parlor. He says there's a problem there. He didn't say what."

"I'll be at the door when you get here," Victoria said, and rang off.

Elizabeth looked up from the Scrabble board with a grin. "Maybe I'll be ready with my word by the time you get back." She looked down. "I'll take care of our guests while you're gone."

Victoria put on the heavy Canadian sweater her granddaughter-in-law Fiona's parents had given her, and Elizabeth helped her into her blue quilted coat. By the time Victoria had settled her baseball cap on her head and checked its angle, the Bronco was turning into the drive. Flashing blue lights flickered across the shingled sides of the house and reflected in the small windowpanes.

The night was raw, and Victoria, in her bulky sweater and coat, felt stuffed. Casey turned on the heater, which blasted out cold air.

"I wonder what the trouble is," said Victoria.

Casey turned up the heat control. "Sorry. I had it on air conditioning."

"I meant at the funeral home."

"Ira sounded upset. Said he wanted me to see what he'd found before he called anyone else."

They passed the high school on the right. Deflated purple and white balloons drifted around the lighted sign out front, which read, HARPOON THE WHALERS! and underneath in large numbers, 49 to 6 and under that in gigantic capital letters, WE DID IT!!!!!

They turned into the funeral parlor parking lot. Ira's pickup was next to the loading platform. Casey pulled in beside him, and she and Victoria climbed up the steps and into the chilly room where they'd opened the coffin three days before.

Ira met them, a grim expression on his face.

"Something to do with the coffin?" Casey asked.

"I wish." Ira grimaced. "Better come with me. You want to wait in the parlor where it's warm, Mrs. Trumbull?"

"I'm with Chief O'Neill," Victoria said, adjusting her cap.

"I better explain first how I check this place," Ira said. "Toby gave me the keys, and I go into every room, including the refrigerator."

"Refrigerator?" Victoria asked.

"Actually, a big walk-in cooler, where he keeps bodies."

"Oh." Victoria pulled her coat around her.

"Someone had turned the temperature way down. Below freezing."

"Yeah?" said Casey.

"When I opened it, there was a body inside."

"A body that wasn't scheduled to be in there?" Casey asked.

"You got it," said Ira.

Chapter 14

The refrigerator was set into the wall opposite the door that led to the public viewing room. The temperature controls on the wall next to the heavy stainless steel door had been turned down to the lowest setting, well below freezing.

Ira tugged on the handle and the heavy door opened slowly. A cloud of frigid air billowed into the room. Victoria wrapped her arms around herself. When the icy mist cleared she could see the inside of the cooler, stainless steel, about six feet wide, eight feet deep, and six feet high. Rime frosted its walls. The freezer was empty except for a stocky figure curled up rigidly close to the door. His knuckles were skinned. His fingers had bled pinkly into the white frosting. His powdery blue face contrasted weirdly with his bright hair.

Casey stepped back from the cold air that poured out of the refrigerator.

"Red," said Ira. He slammed the door shut with a heavy thud. "Like that when I found him."

Victoria leaned against the metal table in the center of the room. The overhead light shone on her blue cap. "There's no hope of reviving him?"

Ira shook his head. "The doc has to give the final word, but I'd say Red's well beyond saving."

"How did it happen?" Victoria asked.

"He didn't lock himself in by accident, that's for sure." Ira pointed to a plastic trash container next to the table. On the floor beside it was a stainless steel handle. "Somebody took the inside handle off and tossed it over there."

"You didn't touch anything, did you?" Casey asked.

Ira shook his head. "Not after I found him, I didn't."

"Lord," said Casey. "I've got to call the state police." She tugged her cell phone out of its case on her belt. "They'll be here in ten minutes," she said after she hung up.

Victoria headed toward the door to the loading platform and paused, her gloved hand on the doorknob.

"What is it, Victoria?" Casey asked.

"I need to talk to you."

"Outside?"

Victoria nodded.

Ira took a folding chair out of the closet.

228

"I'll wait." He folded his arms over his chest and crossed his legs.

Outside, yellow lights illuminated the loading platform. Beyond, black night closed in, crisp with glittering stars. Victoria shaded her eyes against the dazzle of light. Above her Orion, the hunter, strode across the sky.

Casey's face was in shadow. "What's the matter, Victoria?"

Victoria's words came out in misty puffs. "Red Crossley was a friend of Dahlia's." She leaned against the frosty iron railing that ran along the side of the loading dock.

Casey stood with her feet apart, hands in her jacket pockets. "Yeah?"

"The hearse driver was her friend, too."

"Oh, yeah?"

"So was the body at the dump. The man with the toucan pin."

"When did you learn this, Victoria?"

"This afternoon. Dahlia and I had tea. She's frightened."

"I should think so." Casey paced the dock and back, her shadow growing and shrinking as she moved under the lights.

"That's not all," Victoria said. "Someone left a parcel addressed to Dahlia in Howland's mailbox. The wrappings had Brazilian stamps with a blurry cancellation. The package inside was labeled 'Yerba Maté,' which is a kind of tea."

Casey paced. "I know what yerba maté is."

"I invited Dahlia over for tea this afternoon, and she brought the maté to share with me. Said she used to drink it every afternoon in Colombia. When I looked at the tea, something seemed wrong."

Casey stopped pacing. "Is the maté still at your place?"

"Yes. I suppose Howland could have it analyzed, but I'm not quite sure what's going on between him and Dahlia."

"What was wrong with the tea?"

"According to Dahlia, yerba maté is made from a kind of holly, a broad-leaved evergreen. The tea she brought over had evergreen needles in it."

"Let's go," said Casey. "Get into the Bronco, Victoria. I'll tell Ira we'll be back in a half hour."

Casey returned. "Junior can take the yerba maté off-Island to the lab first thing tomorrow and wait for the results." She headed out of the parking lot and stopped before turning onto the main road.

"There's something else," Victoria said. "Dahlia told me in confidence, but you need to know about it."

Blue lights flashed in the distance. "I need to talk to the state guys before you tell me whatever you have to say."

The state vehicle slowed, turned in, and stopped next to the Bronco.

Casey rolled down her window and told the driver, "Ira found a body in the funeral parlor's cooler."

The state trooper leaned his elbow on the door frame. "What's Ira doing here?"

"He's caretaker." Casey started up again. "I'll be back shortly. I have to get something from Mrs. Trumbull's."

"Doc Jeffers is right behind us," the driver said. "How long will you be?"

"A half hour," Casey replied.

"Right."

The state vehicle moved up the drive and Casey headed toward Victoria's. As they turned onto the main road Victoria saw a second set of small flashing blue lights and the single headlight of a large motorcycle.

"Doc Jeffers?" she asked Casey, who nodded.

Casey flashed her headlights at the motorcycle, turned on her own set of blue lights, and hit the accelerator.

"Dahlia's not likely to brew herself a cup of that tea, is she?" Casey asked.

231

"I told her I didn't like the looks of the maté, and put it in the closet under the stairs."

"Three guys killed, all off-Islanders, all friends of Dahlia's. Now Dahlia gets sent some suspicious tea. You were going to tell me something. What, Victoria?"

"I can only tell you part of it," Victoria said.

Casey swerved around a slow-moving car and turned left at the blinker. They passed the tall dead pines of the state forest. Silvery trunks reflected their headlights. Light glinted off the eyes of a small creature by the side of the road.

"A skunk," said Victoria, bracing her hand on the dashboard. "Slow down."

Casey jammed on the brake, and the skunk waddled across the road in front of them followed by four baby skunks.

As they continued toward West Tisbury, the few cars they overtook pulled to the side of the road to let them pass. Victoria told Casey all she could of Dahlia's story.

"The five colleagues left something valuable in the coffin," she said, without explaining more.

"We've got to locate that damned coffin," said Casey. "You've still got that piece that fell off, don't you?"

Victoria nodded. "Behind the wood stove. The panel looks like a heat shield that's always been there."

Casey turned off the flashing lights when they reached Victoria's driveway. "We have more important things to worry about at the moment than the missing coffin. Namely, the maté."

Elizabeth was sitting in the rocking chair, reading, when Victoria and Casey entered the parlor. The fire had burned down to a low bed of glowing coals, and Elizabeth had moved the Scrabble table to one side. When she looked up from her book her smile faded. "Bad news?"

Casey nodded.

Victoria stood next to her wing chair. "Is Dahlia asleep?"

"I guess so. She hasn't come out of her room since she came home. Why?"

Casey shut the parlor door. "Mr. Crossley, the Rose Haven assistant, is dead."

"He was a friend of Dahlia's," said Victoria.

Casey explained what Ira had found in the cooler.

"The hearse driver and the body on the stump pile were also friends of Dahlia's," Victoria added.

Elizabeth stood up, dropping her book

on the floor. "Shall I wake her up?"

"No," said Victoria. "She needs all the rest she can get. Tomorrow's going to be a rough day for her."

Elizabeth bent over and picked up her book. "You both look as if you could use a drink."

"Not me," said Casey. "Give me the maté, Victoria, and I'm outta here."

Victoria went into the kitchen, opened the door to the closet under the back stairs, and handed Casey the canister.

"Let me have a plastic bag to put the canister in, Victoria. I doubt if there are any prints on it except Dahlia's and yours, but we'd better have it checked."

After Casey left, Victoria returned to the parlor and sat in her wing chair with a sigh. "I could use a glass of brandy now, Elizabeth. A generous helping."

Elizabeth brought in the apricot brandy, set the bottle on the coffee table, and built up the fire again. Victoria sipped her drink and felt some warmth returning.

Dahlia was up early the next morning. She came into the kitchen, where Victoria was opening a can of cat food. "That was the best night's sleep I've had for days." She smiled and adjusted her cap.

Victoria debated whether or not to tell her about Red Crossley's death, and decided not to, at least not yet. She filled the coffeemaker and set out the toaster. "What are your plans for today?"

Dahlia pursed her lips. "I have to go to the hospital for my Taxol treatment."

"How long will that take?"

"Most of the afternoon," Dahlia said. "It's not as unpleasant as I expected. I can read or doze. I often feel nauseated afterward, but that passes."

"Do you need someone to take you there?" Victoria seated herself at the cookroom table where she could see the church steeple in the distance.

"No, thank you. I can drive."

Victoria waited until they'd finished breakfast and were drinking the last of the coffee before she brought up the death of Red. "After you came in last night, Casey and I were called out on an emergency."

"You do lead an interesting life," Dahlia murmured.

Victoria gazed into her yellow mug. "The call was from Ira, the caretaker at the Rose Haven Funeral Home."

"Oh?" said Dahlia. "Have they located the missing coffin?"

Victoria shook her head. "Ira found a

body in the refrigerator. A body that wasn't supposed to be there."

Dahlia looked up. "Red?"

Victoria nodded.

Dahlia stood abruptly. "When I talked to him yesterday Red was frightened. He was going to leave the Island this morning." She sat again and put her elbows on the table.

"I'm so sorry," Victoria murmured.

Dahlia's cap had fallen over her brow. The cheerful colors that had seemed like a light way to deal with her missing hair now seemed grotesque.

"Three of the five of us. Dead."

"Tell me again, who is the fifth person?"

"Herb. Herb Plante."

"Are you convinced he's still in Brazil?"

Dahlia put her head in her hands. "I was sure he was, but now I don't know. I don't know what to think about anything."

"What does Herb Plante look like?" Victoria asked.

"He's in his late fifties, medium height. Thinning gray hair that he wears quite short. He's a physical fitness buff. Heavyset, but not fat." Dahlia toyed with her empty coffee mug.

"Would you like me to make more coffee?" Victoria asked.

"I've had plenty, thanks." Dahlia adjusted her cap. "Herb is a sweet, generous person. It's like him to send me maté for old times' sake."

"Casey is having the maté analyzed today," Victoria said.

"I've known Herb for years. I would trust him with my life."

"Someone is killing you off," Victoria said.

"Red told me he didn't care about the gems any longer. He wanted to leave the Island." Dahlia stood and absently straightened her long skirt. "At this point I'd abandon the gems too. But I don't even know where they are."

"Did you tell Howland about the stones?"

Dahlia shook her head. "He and I don't talk much to each other. There's no way he could know. Howland can't be the killer, Victoria."

"Someone put that yerba maté in the mailbox."

"I'm sure it wasn't Howland."

"What about the man who was going to sell the stones? Emery? Did he know you were coming to the Island?"

"I left a message on his answering machine that I would be on the Vineyard and gave him Howland's number. I didn't tell him why I was here."

"He undoubtedly guessed," Victoria said. "Could he be on the Island now?"

"He's the sort of person who could be anywhere." Dahlia walked back and forth in the small room, her skirt swaying. "I don't know what to do."

"I'll ask Casey to have someone escort you to the hospital. You'd better not be alone, Dahlia."

Meyer put down the copy of the *Island Enquirer* he was reading and got to his feet when Lucretia came in carrying two bags of groceries.

"Let me help you. Are there more groceries in the car?"

"Thanks. Two more bags. It's amazing how much food a teenager can eat."

"Which reminds me," Meyer said, taking his wallet out of his back pocket, extracting a hundred-dollar bill, and putting it on Lucretia's desk. "I want to pay my fair share."

"You're doing more than your share by fixing everything in the house that needs fixing. But thanks. I can use it."

"Did they ever locate that missing piece of the coffin?"

Lucretia looked puzzled. "I thought I told you. Casey said it was in the back of the police car."

"Yeah, of course, right," Meyer said. "I'll bring in the groceries." He paused at the door. "Speaking of Casey, who's the old lady who rides around with her all the time?"

Lucretia was shelving groceries, and said over her shoulder, "That's Victoria Trumbull. Casey's deputy."

"She's pretty old to be a police deputy, isn't she?"

"Ninety-two. Casey appointed Victoria her deputy after realizing how much Victoria knows about life in this town."

"Sounds as though West Tisbury is a good place to settle if you want to live a long time." Meyer laughed. He returned with the two last bags of groceries. "By the way, I need to do some errands of my own this afternoon. I'll be gone a couple of hours."

"Do you want the car?" Lucretia asked.

"I can walk. Or hitch a ride."

Lucretia laughed. "You and Victoria Trumbull."

Victoria was eating her lunch and reading a book when she heard a knock on the door. She wiped her mouth. "Come in!"

Her visitor was a tall, broad-shouldered man with sun-streaked blond hair and clear blue eyes.

"Excuse me for not getting up," Victoria said, indicating McCavity, who was ensconced in her lap, paws dangling over her knees. "You can see I can't move."

"I don't want to interrupt your lunch," said Meyer. "I've been wanting to meet the famous Victoria Trumbull, and since I was passing by your house, I thought this might be a good time."

"Won't you sit down?"

"Thanks," said Meyer. "I hope this isn't inconvenient. I can't stay long."

"I don't believe I know your name," said Victoria.

"Sorry — I'm Meyer King."

Victoria held out her knobby hand. "How do you do."

Meyer shook her hand gently. "I've heard a lot about you."

"You must be Lucretia's fisherman friend. I suppose she mentioned me?"

Meyer shifted in his chair. "Only good words."

"Of course," said Victoria with a smile. "Would you like a cup of tea? You'll have to fix it yourself, but the water is still hot."

"Thank you." Meyer stepped up into the kitchen.

"The cups are in the cabinet over the sink," Victoria said. "The tea is over the stove."

"Found them. May I get you a cup?"

"No, thank you," Victoria said, then changed her mind suddenly. "Yes, please, after all. Constant Comment."

Meyer returned with two mugs and sat again.

Victoria looked at him over the steaming brew. "I enjoy trying different teas," she said. "Not only the conventional types, but the herbal teas."

"I do too," said Meyer. "Tea seems more comforting than coffee."

"Do you have a favorite type?" Victoria asked.

"Plain old Red Rose brand. Salada. Or Tetley. Nothing fancy," said Meyer.

"A friend gave me some tea to try the other day."

"What kind?"

"A type they drink in South America."

"Really?" said Meyer. "I've spent time in Brazil. What was it, yerba maté?"

Victoria held her mug close to her face and peered through the steam. "That was what my friend said it was. Yerba maté."

"They drink a lot of maté in South America. The caffeine content is about the same as coffee. It's usually drunk out of a decorated gourd."

"I've never seen maté before," Victoria said.

"You can probably buy it in specialty shops, or maybe health food stores. I imagine you can get it over the Internet." He sipped his own tea. "Did you enjoy it?"

"I haven't tried it yet," Victoria said.

"It's brewed like regular loose tea." Meyer lifted his mug in salute to her. "I like this. Constant Comment. By the way, I enjoy your poetry. It reminds me of Robert Frost."

Victoria patted her hair. "Thank you. Do you read much poetry?"

"I have a few favorites that I like. You and Frost are among them."

Victoria smiled. "How long do you plan to stay on the Vineyard?" she asked.

Meyer looked past her out the window, across the field, toward town and the church steeple. "I'm not sure, Mrs. Trumbull. I have some things I have to attend to, then I'll probably go out on the boats again."

"Did I understand you fish out of Seattle?" Victoria asked.

"I fish wherever I can," Meyer replied.

"The Vineyard fishing fleet isn't as active as it used to be," Victoria said. "We had quite a few swordfishing boats at one time. It would be nice for you and Lucretia if you could find a job on one of the remaining boats."

"I'm too much of a wanderer," Meyer said. "I'm not ready to settle down."

"This is a good place to settle if you ever do decide," Victoria said.

"Isn't it pretty quiet around here in the off-season?"

Victoria smiled. "The off-season is when things happen. You heard about the missing coffin, didn't you?"

"Everyone's heard about it. I've never seen anything so efficient as the grapevine on this Island. Have they located the coffin yet? I heard a piece broke off and that's missing, too."

Victoria smiled again.

"Wasn't Chief O'Neill carrying that piece in the Bronco?"

"Where did you hear that?" Victoria asked.

Meyer grinned. "The grapevine."

"Does the grapevine know where the coffin is now?"

"Haven't heard yet, either the coffin or

the part that's missing. But I'll keep listening." He stood. "I don't want to overstay my welcome. But I did want to meet you. Don't get up," he said as Victoria started to push McCavity off her lap. "Would you like me to clear your dishes for you?"

"Thank you," said Victoria. "Are you a Scrabble player?"

"Absolutely," said Meyer. "Invite me over for a game some time. See if my mind can compete with yours."

"You'll have to beat two of us. I have a guest who's as avid a player as I am. Dahlia Atherton."

Meyer choked on something. "Excuse me," he said. "Swallowed something the wrong way." His eyes watered, and he blotted them with his handkerchief.

"Put your arms up over your head." Victoria demonstrated. "That sometimes helps. Straightens your esophagus."

Meyer coughed again. "Where is your guest now?"

"She's out for the afternoon," said Victoria.

Junior had gone off-Island on the first boat that morning with the canister of yerba maté. Casey had driven Dahlia to the

244

hospital in the Bronco after breakfast and promised to pick her up after she finished her treatment.

After Meyer left, Victoria hiked the quarter mile to the police station. On her way, a car stopped and the driver offered Victoria a ride. She shook her head and waved her thanks. When she reached the station house, Casey was working on her computer.

"What's up, Victoria?"

"I had a visitor after lunch. Meyer King."

"Lucretia's boyfriend?"

"Yes. He knows all about yerba maté, has spent time in Brazil, and was interested in the missing piece of the coffin. He knew you'd had it in the Bronco. He doesn't plan to stay around the Island once he's finished some mysterious business he referred to." Victoria sat down in her usual chair and unbuttoned her coat.

Casey leaned away from her computer.

Victoria fanned herself with her open coat. "Where did Meyer come from, anyway? Do you know anything about him?"

Casey shook her head. "I've had no reason to even wonder about him."

"The other night I was playing Scrabble with Elizabeth. You know how you line up seven letters and try to make a word?"

The phone rang, and Casey answered. "Let me call you back." She hung up. "Go on, Victoria."

"I had drawn Es and Rs and an M. Then I drew a Y. Do you realize the name 'Meyer' is an anagram for the name 'Emery'?"

"What?" Casey sat up straight.

"I suppose it could be a coincidence."

"You know how I feel about coincidences, Victoria." Casey tapped her fingers on her desktop. "Emery is one of Dahlia's partners, right?"

"Not exactly. Emery is their fence. Dahlia's been trying to reach him and hasn't been able to."

"Not what you'd call bright to use such an obvious alias."

Victoria's lips tightened, forming radiating lines of wrinkles. "I don't believe it's so obvious."

Casey smiled. "Have you said anything to Dahlia about this?"

Victoria shook her head. "There's more. When Meyer came to call, I told him I had a guest named Dahlia. He choked on something. He wanted to know where she was. I didn't tell him, of course, and then he left."

Casey leaned back in her chair and looked at her watch. "I'm supposed to pick up Dahlia at the hospital around four-thirty. Junior hoped to catch the three o'clock boat. If he did, he'll be here any minute."

When Junior arrived a few minutes later carrying the maté canister, Casey was on the phone. He set the bag on her desk without saying a word. His blue baseball cap shaded his eyes. His mouth was a thin, straight line.

Victoria was sitting at Junior's desk assembling reports. She pushed the stapler aside.

Casey hung up the phone. "Well?"

"It's yerba maté, all right, but mixed with *Taxus baccata*. English yew."

Victoria started to get up.

"Don't get up for me, Victoria. The lab says a cup of tea brewed from this would kill anyone who drank it, probably within a couple of minutes." He gave Casey an envelope. "Here's the report. The poison is taxine, an alkaloid."

"Wouldn't the taste give it away?" Victoria asked.

"Not necessarily. The taste of the maté is strong enough to mask the yew, the lab said, but even the yew by itself may not be unpleasant tasting. Something like pine needles. Probably bitter."

Casey opened the envelope and studied the report. "Who the devil sent the maté to Dahlia?"

"The package had Brazilian stamps with a blurred cancellation," said Victoria.

"Roughly thirteen percent of the Vineyard's year-round population is Brazilian," Junior said. "No problem finding Brazilian stamps. Doesn't matter whether they're canceled or not." He stood at the window with his hands clasped behind his back. "I understand Dahlia's moved back in with you, Victoria."

"Temporarily." Victoria straightened the reports in front of her and lined up the stapler with the blotter, the way Junior usually kept it.

"We're going to have to watch Dahlia," Casey said. "Looks as though she's next on the hit list."

"She or Herb Plante," said Victoria.

"I suppose whoever killed the hearse driver planned to drive the vehicle off the boat," Junior said.

"And remembered the keys as the body went over the side," Victoria added.

Chapter 15

Casey drove Victoria home before she went to the hospital to pick up Dahlia. "I'll wait in the parking lot until Dahlia comes out, get caught up on paperwork. Where's Elizabeth?"

"She should be home in a couple of hours." Victoria looked at her watch. "By seven."

"You'll be here when I bring Dahlia back, won't you?"

Victoria nodded. "I have to write my column."

Before Victoria set out her typewriter, she decided to make soup to have ready when Elizabeth came home. She put a marrow bone in the kettle with barley, onions, and water, and was scraping carrots when she heard a knock on the kitchen door.

"Come in!" She dropped the carrot she was holding into the sink and wiped her hands on a kitchen towel.

The man who opened the door was no one Victoria knew. He was wearing an overcoat over a suit coat, white shirt, and patterned tie. He removed a shapeless tweed hat exposing pink scalp thinly covered by short gray bristles.

"May I help you?"

"I hope I have the right place." The man was shorter than Victoria. He peered at her through thick gold-rimmed glasses. "You're Mrs. Trumbull, I assume?"

Victoria nodded and waited.

He shut the door behind him, folded his soft hat, and took off the dark leather gloves he'd been wearing. "I'm visiting the Island for a few days on business. Do I understand you occasionally rent rooms?"

Victoria laid her towel on the side of the sink and leaned back against the counter. "How did you hear about that?"

The man unbuttoned his coat. "I'm a fan of yours, Mrs. Trumbull. I have several of your poetry books and I read your column in the *Island Enquirer*."

Victoria looked down at her knobby hands and smiled.

"I got the impression from your column that you accept paying guests occasionally. I had hoped to stay here while I'm on the Island." He lifted the flap of his overcoat pocket and tucked his hat and gloves inside.

"I sometimes rent my downstairs room," Victoria said, "but it's not available right now."

At that moment, Bacchus started to bark.

The man's face brightened. "You have a dog."

Victoria moved away from the sink. "It's a bird."

Bacchus stopped barking and Victoria heard him slash his beak against the bars of his cage. Then he started barking again, over and over and over.

"Your bird?" the man asked.

"It's not mine." Victoria spoke above the clamor of the toucan. "I have a cat."

"You mean the cat has you," he said, and Victoria smiled at that. "Cats certainly make less noise than tropical birds."

"Won't you sit?" Victoria indicated the captain's chair.

"Thank you, but I can't stay," he said.

Victoria pulled out a chair at the kitchen table for herself. "How long do you plan to be on the Island?"

"That depends on how soon I can transact my business."

"What sort of business are you in?"

"Import-export," he explained. "Oriental art objects."

Victoria nodded. "Many old Vineyard

homes have everyday furniture mixed with oriental objects the whalers brought home."

"Interesting," he said. He opened his overcoat and put his hands in the pockets of his trousers. Victoria caught a glimpse of a bird-shaped lapel pin on his suit jacket. She looked down at her hands, which were clasped together on the table edge.

"My sea-captain grandfather brought home all sorts of things from his trips to the Pacific."

He shifted slightly and leaned against the door frame. "Do you still have those things?"

"Yes, indeed. Around 1845, my grandfather brought home two potted plants from China. 'Trees of Heaven' he called them." Victoria looked up at the man and smiled. "Ailanthus trees."

The man laughed. "The tree that grew in Brooklyn. They're nuisances now."

"One of the two trees was blown down during the 1938 hurricane, but the other is at the entrance to my driveway."

"I saw it as I came in. It must be close to four feet in diameter."

"Are you sure you won't sit down?" Victoria asked.

"I really can't stay," he replied. "Did

252

your grandfather bring home other objects? Some of those are quite valuable now."

"They're priceless to me," Victoria said. "I would never think of parting with them."

"I'm sorry." The man tilted his head, and the kitchen light reflected off his glasses, hiding his eyes. "I didn't mean to imply that I was interested in purchasing them. But I *am* interested in seeing anything of that sort you might care to show me." When Victoria hesitated, he said, "This is a bad time for you, I see. I must go. If I were to come back with copies of your poetry books, would you autograph them for me?"

Victoria unclasped her hands and smoothed her hair. "I'd be glad to."

After he left, Victoria realized the man hadn't told her his name. But she was sure she knew who he was.

After closing the door behind him, the man put on his hat, pulled on his dark leather gloves, and slipped into the seat of the rental car he'd parked under the maple tree. Black wind clouds were moving in rapidly, and had already covered the new moon, a pale sliver in the darkening sky to the west. He turned on the dome light, adjusted his glasses, and studied first a map of the Island, then a handwritten letter, which he refolded and put back in its envelope. He turned off the light, started the car, backed out of his parking spot, and drove slowly away from Victoria's, looking both ways before turning toward Edgartown.

He obeyed the speed limit until he passed the Youth Hostel, where the speed limit changed to forty-five miles an hour, then he sped up to ten miles over the limit, holding both gloved hands high on the wheel and leaning forward, staring straight ahead. His lips were pressed together so tightly the skin around his mouth was a bluish-gray. He was so intent, he didn't see the deer that bounded across the road behind him. He followed the straight road as it dipped into the frost bottoms that had been formed by glacial meltwater, then up the other side to flat land again. On the outskirts of Edgartown he passed Morning Glory Farm and Sweetened Water Pond, and finally slowed as he reached the school. He turned right onto Main Street in front of the white clapboard jail, then before Main Street plunged down to the harbor he turned left again onto North

Water Street, which he followed until the road turned past the Harbor View. He drove into the hotel's parking lot, locked his car, and strode into the lobby.

The concierge greeted him. "Good evening, sir."

He nodded and continued past her, up the carpeted stairs to the second floor, and to a room halfway down the hall. He drew out his card key and unlocked the door, shutting and locking it behind him. He zipped open his suitcase, tugged a sports coat and two pairs of slacks off hangers in the closet, scooped up his shaving kit from the bathroom, his pajamas from the back of the door, opened drawers, looked in the wastepaper basket, shut his suitcase, and returned his key to the desk.

"Checking out, Mr. Plante?"

"Afraid so," he said.

"Was everything all right, sir?"

"Fine." He signed the papers the desk clerk set in front of him, and when she continued to look concerned, he said, "A family emergency," and looked up at her with a small smile.

"I'm so sorry, sir. If we can help in any way . . ."

"Thank you," he said, walking quickly out of the lobby, into the parking lot. He got back in his rental car and drove through Edgartown into Oak Bluffs, where he parked briefly by the harbor, bought a copy of the *Island Enquirer* from a newspaper dispenser, found an ad for a room at a bed-and-breakfast a couple of blocks from the center of Vineyard Haven and the ferry, and continued on into Vineyard Haven.

He found the place, parked under a large oak tree in front, and studied the house for several minutes before he got out of his car. The building, an old one, was set back from the street and had three rattan rocking chairs on a large front porch. A concrete walkway, buckled by tree roots, led up to the front steps. Before he went up to the house, he walked to the end of the block, then turned and walked the other way, studying the houses across the street and on both sides of the bed-and-breakfast. Only one car came down the street while he reconnoitered.

Finally, he went up the wooden stairs to the porch. He noticed a bowl of water to the left of the door, and just then a dog started barking, the deep-throated bark of a very large dog.

A woman's voice said, "Hush, Sammy. Quiet." Then, "Sorry about that," and she appeared at the door holding the collar of a gigantic dog that seemed to be mostly black Lab with a smattering of Great Dane and St. Bernard. The woman, who had shoulder-length light brown hair and brown, soulful eyes, looked as though she weighed less than the dog. "Sorry," she said again. "He's not a mean dog." She nudged the dog with her foot. "Sit, Sammy." The dog sat for a few seconds, then rose again, tail wagging. "Sammy!" she scolded. Then, "Can I help you?"

The man explained that he wanted a room for possibly as long as a week, and she led him up a narrow staircase to the second floor, down a short hallway, and into a clean room with rose-printed wallpaper, frilly curtains, a double bed, an easy chair, and a bureau.

She turned on the light next to the chair. "This is a pretty good reading lamp. The bathroom's down the hall." She turned the light off again. "I'm Edna Vincent."

"How do you do," the man said. "My name is Bob Jones."

"Are you from the Boston area?" Edna asked.

He nodded. "Cambridge."

"You're my only guest. This time of year things are pretty quiet."

The man who now called himself Bob Jones drew out his wallet and paid her in cash. "Lovely home," he said. "Do I need a key?"

She shook her head. "I only lock up at night. If you come in after midnight, ring. Sammy will wake me."

Jones ruffled the fur on Sammy's flank. "He seems to be a good guard dog."

Edna nodded. "Nobody can sneak up on this house."

Mr. Jones took his suitcase up to the room, unpacked what needed to be hung up, turned on the reading light next to the easy chair, shut the door behind him, and went down the stairs. Sammy stood at the bottom, tail wagging. The dog dropped a stuffed toy at the man's feet.

"Hey, boy." Mr. Jones tossed the toy animal into the air, and the great dog caught it with a snap of large bright teeth.

"Sammy!" said Edna, coming into the hall. "Mr. Jones doesn't want to play."

"I won't be late." Mr. Jones looked at his watch. "Probably back by ten or so."

"Have a good evening," said Edna. "I'll leave the porch light on."

Victoria continued her soup-making after her visitor left. She added cut-up

258

carrots and celery leaves and a can of tomatoes and lowered the heat under the kettle. She tossed in dried herbs from her summer garden, sage, thyme, and lavender.

By the time Casey returned with Dahlia, the kitchen was fragrant with the smell of soup and Victoria had written several items for her column. Darkness had settled, and the wind was beginning to rise. Victoria pushed her typewriter aside as she heard Dahlia trudge slowly up the steps. Casey followed.

"Something smells great," Casey said.

"I've got plenty of soup. Can you stay for supper?"

"No thanks, Victoria. I wish I could. I'll take a cup of tea now, though."

Dahlia paused inside the doorway and leaned against the frame. "I think I'll lie down, Victoria." She straightened her cap. "Thank you for the limousine service, Chief."

"No problem," said Casey.

Victoria got up stiffly. "Can I get you some tea, Dahlia?"

Dahlia shook her head, walked to her room, and shut the door behind her. Bacchus chuckled softly.

Victoria brewed tea for Casey and herself, and Casey carried the teapot and mugs into the cookroom.

"Dahlia looks terrible," Casey said after she had added her usual heaping spoonfuls of sugar to her tea.

"Is that a normal reaction to the Taxol treatment?"

"Apparently so. People react differently. Taxol kills specific types of cancer cells. I guess the wrong dose can kill the patient."

"I'm beginning to feel as though everything around me is deadly," Victoria said. "Dahlia came close to drinking that yew tea. If she had, would an autopsy show that English yew killed her rather than Taxol?"

Casey shrugged. "I have no idea. Whoever sent the tea probably knew about her treatments."

"She certainly makes no secret of her illness. I suppose a medical examiner could differentiate between something a victim drank and something injected into her bloodstream?"

"I guess so," Casey said. "The doctor would have to suspect deliberate poisoning before running tests to determine which specific poison was involved."

Victoria was quiet for several moments. "Three people dead and an attempt on Dahlia's life. The killer must be someone the five people knew and trusted." She peered absently into her mug. "Who made that attempt on Dahlia's life, and why?"

"Ten million dollars is strong motivation," said Casey.

"But Dahlia's group had good reason to stick together. Now three of the five are dead, and the gemstones are missing."

"Divide ten million by five, and it's two million each. Divide it by one and it's ten million. You can do a lot with ten million dollars. If we eliminate Dahlia as a suspect, that leaves this mysterious Herb Plante."

Victoria set her mug down with a thump.

"What's the matter, Victoria?"

"I had a caller about an hour ago. He didn't give me his name, but I noticed he was wearing a toucan-shaped lapel pin like Dahlia's and the one I found near the stump fire. He knew I rent rooms occasionally, although I haven't told many people. He said he saw it in my column, but I don't think that's true." Victoria traced the pattern of the checked tablecloth with her thumbnail. "Bacchus started barking when the man came in, and when I said it was a bird, not a dog, he knew Bacchus was a tropical bird."

"You're thinking your visitor might be Herb Plante?"

"I'm sure he was. He told me he was in the import-export business, which means he's probably well traveled."

"As in Foreign Service?"

Victoria nodded. "Herb Plante now knows that Dahlia is staying here."

"He heard Bacchus. Of course."

"Mr. Plante gave Bacchus to Dahlia. Bacchus undoubtedly recognized his voice."

"He was the one who sent Dahlia the yerba maté."

Victoria nodded. "Supposedly sent from Brazil, where Herb Plante claimed he was hunting orchids. Dahlia didn't suspect a thing. It was a fluke that she brought the tea here to share with me."

"Suppose you hadn't been suspicious of the tea." Casey stood. "We've got to find Herb Plante. Did you see what kind of car he was driving?"

Victoria shook her head. "He said he'd be back to have me sign my books. He was looking for a place to stay, so perhaps you can check hotels."

"He probably was looking for Dahlia, not a place to stay." Casey paced the small room. "You know how many hotels there are on the Vineyard? Hotels and bed-and-breakfasts and people who rent rooms occasionally, like you?"

"Then we've got to guard her."

"Forget the 'we' stuff, Victoria."

"Either we guard Dahlia," Victoria continued, "or we send her back to Howland's, where Herb Plante can't find her."

"The maté was left in Howland's mailbox, remember?"

"Well, Dahlia's in no condition to be moved, anyway. Can one of your police officers stay at my house tonight?"

"I'll call Junior."

"Will you change your mind about staying for supper?"

"Thanks. I guess I will."

Chapter 16

Dahlia was still in her room when Elizabeth left for work the next morning. Junior had parked the police cruiser under the maple at the end of the drive, and was sitting in the driver's seat, door open. Wind had sprung up during the night and was scattering leaves across the driveway.

"What's *he* doing here?" Elizabeth asked her grandmother.

"It's too complicated to explain right now. On your way out ask him in for coffee, if you will please, Elizabeth."

"But . . ."

Victoria cocked her head. "I hear the phone. Have a good day," and she went into the cookroom to answer. Elizabeth shrugged and headed toward the police cruiser.

After Junior had drunk his coffee, socialized a bit, and left for the police station, Victoria cleared up the breakfast dishes. She was thinking about Herb Plante when she saw someone at the door, and was not prepared for Denise, the teenage girl who stood there holding a glass jar. The girl's long hair was windblown, and she combed her fingers through it.

"Hi, Mrs. Trumbull."

"Come in, Denise. What do you have there?" Victoria indicated the jar. A square of flowered cloth covered the top and was secured with a blue ribbon.

Denise shut the door carefully against the wind. "My mom's been making jelly and told me to bring you some."

"Thank you." Victoria held the jar up to the light. "What a pretty color."

"Vineyard purple. From our own grapes." Denise grinned. "My mom freezes the juice in October and makes jelly around now."

"Have you time for a cup of tea?" Victoria asked. "Herbal tea with lemon and honey."

"I'd love some. Thanks." Denise unzipped her down jacket. "It's gotten cold again." She sat in the captain's chair and watched Victoria set the jar on one of the glass shelves in the window over the sink where the morning light would shine through the jelly. When the tea was ready Victoria led the way into the cookroom. Wind rattled the window frame and bent the tops of the cedars in the west pasture.

"How's the grave digging business going?" Victoria asked.

Denise shrugged. "It's okay."

"What made you decide to become a grave digger?"

"My dad made me."

"Really!" Victoria looked up from her yellow mug in surprise. "Why?"

Denise stirred honey into her tea. "Like, community service?"

"Oh?" Victoria waited.

"He's cemetery superintendent, you know?"

"Yes, I know."

"Me and Sonny?" Denise looked up.

"Yes, Lucretia's boy."

"Well, last Halloween we got to messing around in the cemetery?"

"I see," said Victoria. "Tipping over gravestones, I suppose?"

Denise flushed and looked down again. "Yeah."

"Digging graves seems like an appropriate punishment. I've seen you at the cemetery. But not Sonny."

"I got caught. He didn't."

"That doesn't seem fair," Victoria said.

Denise shrugged. "My dad told me to set the stone back up and plant stuff around it. Sonny moved the stone, so I didn't have to."

"Those stones are heavy."

"I could of moved it. I'm pretty strong. But I guess Sonny felt guilty or something."

"How much time are you supposed to put in digging graves?"

"Forty hours. Actually, I like the work. It's not so bad."

Victoria nodded. "How many stones did you tip over?"

"Just one."

"And you got caught?"

"We didn't exactly get caught. We thought it would be, like, fun, you know? But after we tipped over the gravestone, it didn't seem like so much fun after all. So I told my dad."

"You were right to do that. I take it you didn't tell on Sonny, though."

Denise shook her head.

Victoria studied the girl. She was pretty with her long dark hair and high cheekbones. Denise was gazing down into her tea, bright blue eyes partly hidden by long lashes.

"Was the gravestone you tipped over near where you were digging the other day?" Victoria asked finally.

"I don't really remember. Halloween night was really, really dark, you know? We were on that side of the cemetery, though, near the big pine tree."

"Yew tree," Victoria corrected. "I see."

Branches of the maple whipped back and forth, and there was an occasional snap of a branch breaking.

"My dad told me where to get sod, you know? Grass to put around the stone so it looked like nothing happened?"

Victoria nodded. "Sonny must be quite strong to have moved the gravestone."

"He's on the football team," Denise said. "He can pick up the front end of a car."

"Heavens!" said Victoria. "I'm glad he was playing on our side Sunday."

Denise's face sobered. "The coach wouldn't let him play in the big game. Sonny was smoking a joint in the boys' lockers, and the coach caught him."

"That's too bad," Victoria said. "Did he go to Nantucket to support the team?"

Denise shook her head. "His mom's boyfriend asked him to do a job for him."

"Lucretia's boyfriend?" Victoria's interest picked up. "Meyer?"

Denise nodded. "He gave Sonny a lot of money. Sonny took me to dinner and a show after I got back from the game."

"That was nice. What sort of job did he pay Sonny to do?"

"Sonny told me not to say anything, but I guess I can tell you. The boyfriend had him, like, move that old coffin out of the shed behind Town Hall, you know?"

Victoria held her breath, then let it out slowly. "Really? Where did he take the coffin?"

"To the storage place at the airport."

"Oh?"

"Meyer told Sonny that his mom wanted to, like, make room in the shed for the mower." Denise rolled her lovely blue eyes. "Now she's acting as if she doesn't know anything about the coffin."

"More tea?" said Victoria.

Denise looked at her watch. "No thanks, Mrs. Trumbull. I gotta go. My mom wants me to stop at the senior center." She carried her cup and Victoria's into the kitchen and put them in the sink. "Thanks, Mrs. Trumbull. Bye." A gust of wind blew papers off the table as she opened the door to leave.

Victoria picked up the papers, put them back on the table, and weighted them down with a stone. As soon as she saw Denise pull out of the driveway in her father's car, Victoria reached for the phone.

Casey arrived a few minutes later. "There aren't that many storage units at the airport, Victoria. I don't think it will be difficult to locate the one he rented, even if he used another name."

Victoria set her blue cap on her head and held it in place against the wind as she seated herself in the Bronco.

"I knew there was something about that man," Victoria said as they sped toward the airport. "Showing up when he did, just as people are being killed right and left, cozying up to Lucretia, and having the effrontery to use an anagram of Emery for an assumed name."

"We don't know he's the same person, Victoria."

Victoria didn't reply.

Casey turned onto the road that led to the business park at the airport. She parked in the shelter of the office building and they went inside.

"Can I help you?" The manager stood up from a battered fake leather recliner where he'd been watching soaps on TV, and touched his baseball cap in acknowledgment. His trousers hung well below his belly, and he hiked them up.

Casey introduced herself and Victoria.

"Pleased to meet you, Mrs. Trumbull. I read your column every week."

Victoria studied the name embroidered

on his shirt. "You must be Carl."

"Yes, ma'am. Carl Fisher. The manager here."

When Casey described Meyer, Fisher said, "Sure. Mr. King rented the storage unit for three months, the minimum. Meyer King. Said he might need it a month or two longer. Nice gent."

"Can we look inside his unit?" Casey asked.

The man lifted his cap and scratched his head. "We got a privacy clause, Chief. You'd need a warrant, I'm afraid. Sorry about that."

"You're quite right," said Casey. "Which unit is it? I'll just look around."

He pulled on a windbreaker that had been hanging on a nail next to the door and led them to a low cement block building with a shingled front. "Mr. King asked for an end unit because he wanted more light, he said. The end units have windows high up. Can't stop you from peeking in, can I?"

Casey brought out the milk crate she kept in the back of the Bronco and stood on it. She shaded her eyes and examined the interior of the unit.

Victoria held her hand against her face to protect her eyes from blowing dust.

271

"Can you see anything?"

"Doesn't look like anything's in here." Casey sounded puzzled. "You're sure this is King's?" she asked the manager.

"Yes, ma'am."

"Is someone on duty here most of the time?"

"Only during working hours, nine to five, Monday through Friday." Fisher straightened his cap. "We're not dealing with what you'd call a high crime area."

Victoria snorted.

Casey asked, "Was anyone here on Sunday?"

"No, ma'am. Most of the Island was over to Nantucket. At the game."

Victoria left Casey and Mr. Fisher and studied the ground. She stopped at the nearby Dumpster, stood on tiptoe, and looked inside.

"How often do you empty this?" she asked Mr. Fisher.

"We take it to the dump on Mondays," the manager replied.

"Do you transport the rubbish yourself?"

"No, ma'am. We have a contract with IRC."

"IRC?" Victoria repeated.

"Island Rubbish Corporation. They've got garbage trucks with arms like pinchers

272

that lift up the Dumpster, turn it upside down, and dump the contents into the back of the truck."

Victoria pointed to something shiny in the bottom of the Dumpster. "Can you tell me what that is?"

"Looks like a piece of metal," he said.

"Is there some way you can get it for me?"

He looked at her strangely. "Sure, Mrs. Trumbull. I can probably reach it with a broom. What do you want that junk for?"

Victoria leaned on the lilac-wood stick she was carrying. "I'm curious, that's all." She waited.

He looked at her again, shrugged, went to his office, and returned with the broom.

Casey watched as Mr. Fisher retrieved a flat piece of thin metal with jagged edges, roughly four by six inches. He handed the metal to Victoria, who turned it over, examining it.

Casey moved closer and brushed her hair away from her face. "What have you found, Victoria?"

Victoria glanced at Mr. Fisher and back at Casey before she replied. "I don't know. What do you think?" She handed the metal to Casey.

"You can keep that if you want," Mr. Fisher said. "No reason not to. You need any help, let me know. Got to get back to my soaps." He grinned and lifted his cap.

Casey flexed the piece of metal she was holding, bending it back and forth.

After Mr. Fisher was out of earshot Casey said, "I know exactly what you're thinking, Victoria."

Victoria nodded. "The piece that fell off the coffin is made of the same kind of metal, isn't it? A sort of waffle pattern."

"Sure looks like it." Casey handed the piece of metal back to her.

"Lucretia's gentleman friend Meyer knew something was hidden in the coffin."

"Changes everything, doesn't it?" Casey shifted her heavy belt to a more comfortable position. "Sonny brings the coffin here, Meyer cuts it into small pieces so he can search thoroughly, and discards the pieces in the Dumpster."

"I wonder if he found the gemstones?" Victoria mused.

"When did he call on you, Victoria, after the game?"

Victoria stared at Casey.

"Lord, Victoria. We have to find a better place to store that end panel of the coffin than behind your wood stove."

274

Chapter 17

"Ten million bucks." Back in her office, Casey paced the narrow space behind her desk. "We're not storing that piece of junk in the police station." She gestured around the small room. "We're not storing it in the shed behind Town Hall, definitely not in the back of the Bronco, and absolutely not behind your wood stove." Casey struck the side of her head with the palm of her hand. "You've got me saying 'we' now."

Victoria watched from her usual chair by Casey's desk.

"I know you don't trust Howland, Victoria, although I think you're wrong. But I don't trust Dahlia."

"She's hardly the killer," Victoria responded. "She seems to be the next one on the killer's list. Furthermore, she's too weak physically."

Casey stopped pacing. "I don't suspect her of killing anyone. I just don't think you should tell her anything about the coffin, that we think it's been destroyed, and that we are pretty sure we know where that ten million bucks is." Casey started to pace again. "Ten million is awfully tempting, especially when you've got medical bills like hers must be."

"What about my cellar?"

"What cellar?"

"The bulkhead doors under the dining room windows open into my cellar."

"That's too obvious."

Victoria shook her head. "Maybe not."

Later that afternoon, Meyer borrowed Sonny's bicycle and rode partway down New Lane, the western boundary of Victoria's property. He left the bike under the overhanging branches of a large spruce tree and squatted where he could see Victoria's door from the semidarkness of the spruce cave. Two cars were parked under the maple at the end of Victoria's driveway. One was the police cruiser, the other was a blue Toyota he didn't recognize. He sat down, pulled his leather jacket tightly around himself, leaned his back against the tree trunk, and waited.

He had waited a half hour when he saw Dahlia come out of the house. She was buttoning her coat and adjusting her knit cap. He heard her speak to someone in the house, Victoria, he assumed, but he was too far away to understand what she said.

Then Victoria came to the door, her sweater thrown over her shoulders. She called out, "On your way back from the movie, would you pick up a package of dried Navy beans, please? And a jar of molasses."

Dahlia waved a hand in acknowledgment, climbed behind the wheel of the Toyota, and left. The cruiser followed, and Meyer could see that Junior, the police sergeant, was driving. He waited a few minutes more, then pedaled against the wind to the end of the lane, turned onto the Edgartown Road, turned again into Victoria's driveway, and rode up to her house. He hadn't worn gloves, and his hands were blue with cold.

Victoria answered his knock. "It's Meyer, isn't it?" She smiled broadly, wrinkles spreading across her face. "Are you here for our Scrabble game?"

"I've brought my copies of your books and hope you'll sign them for me," he said.

"I'd be delighted. Anyone who compares my work to Robert Frost's . . ." Victoria shut the door behind him, and he stepped up into the warm kitchen. "How about a cup of tea? I may still have some of that yerba maté we talked about."

"That would be great. I love that stuff," said Meyer. "But any kind of tea would be fine, as long as it's hot. I biked over. That north wind is brutal."

"We're going to have more weather," Victoria said. "Another snowstorm, I should guess. Now, where did I put that maté?" She glanced at him.

"It does feel like snow," Meyer said.

Victoria fussed about in the closet under the back stairs. "No, I guess the maté is used up." She turned again. "I had several women over for a tea party."

Meyer nodded. "I bet you served them maté. Did they like it? Not everyone does."

Victoria said, "I didn't hear any complaints."

"When you're not used to it, maté tastes pretty good with milk and sugar."

Victoria plugged in the teakettle. "Why don't you sit in the cookroom, and I'll join you as soon as the water's hot."

Meyer leaned against the kitchen counter. "Want some help?" He watched as Victoria looked him up and down, from his blond hair to his bright eyes to the leather jacket that stretched across his broad chest. She checked his slim hips, his pressed jeans, his clean running shoes. He grinned, big, white, crooked teeth in his tanned face.

"Well, yes," she said finally. "You can help. I'll sign your books while you make tea. There's the tray."

"Sounds like a deal," said Meyer.

Victoria seated herself at the cookroom table with her pen. "The teapot is next to the stove. The tea is in the cupboard."

"Found it," he said.

Victoria tested her pen on a piece of scrap paper and opened one of the books to the title page. "How would you like me to sign?" She turned in her seat to face him. " 'To Meyer'? Or 'To Emery'?"

Meyer dropped a spoon on the kitchen floor, coughed, picked the spoon up, and laughed. "We've got to have that Scrabble game, Mrs. Trumbull."

Victoria set down her pen. "We've got to talk."

"Right you are." Meyer poured the now boiling water into the teapot and took the tray into the cookroom.

"I know all about the uncut gems," Victoria said, once he'd seated himself across from her. "I know you know Dahlia Atherton, and I know you know she is staying with me. I also know that Dahlia has been trying unsuccessfully to reach

Emery, who is supposed to have contacts in Amsterdam, where he is supposed to have the stones cut." She paused.

"Go on," said Meyer.

"I know Meyer appeared about three months before Dahlia arrived on the Island, and is now Lucretia's mysterious suitor." She studied him. He was studying her just as intently. "That's a good way to gather inside information, by the way. Courting a village official."

Meyer leaned back in his chair, tipping it.

"Don't do that," said Victoria, and Meyer set the chair back on all four legs.

"To begin with, nobody could find that coffin because your helper, Lucretia's boy Sonny, had tipped over an old gravestone as a Halloween prank last month, then moved it to a different place as a further prank."

Meyer raised his eyebrows.

"I know you cut up the coffin, evidently looking for the gemstones, and didn't find them."

Meyer started to lean back in his chair, thought better of it, and put both elbows on the table. He gazed at Victoria with a faint smile.

"Shall I go on?" said Victoria.

"Please."

"I know you've been trying to locate that missing part of the coffin. The stones probably are hidden there. You traced the coffin part to the police Bronco, and now you've lost track of it. That's why you've come to me. Am I right so far?"

Meyer leaned forward on his folded arms. "You tell me."

"Yes, I'm right." Victoria considered him. "In the meantime, three people have been killed and there's been an attempt on a fourth. You seem to be a logical suspect. You've certainly got motive and opportunity."

Meyer sat back in his chair and sighed. "I don't suppose you'll believe me if I say I had nothing to do with the killings."

"I'm keeping an open mind," said Victoria.

"If you think I'm the killer, drinking tea with me face to face is not exactly a wise move on your part."

"I'm not worried," said Victoria.

"I didn't kill them."

"I know something about your background. I suspect you wouldn't hesitate to kill someone if you needed to."

Meyer looked away.

"In this case, I think you're simply an opportunist, a petty crook hoping the principals will kill one another so you can take off with the jewels."

Meyer made a wry face and looked up at the whitewashed rafters. "Not exactly flattering. 'Petty crook'?"

"I intend to find that killer." Victoria slapped the table with the palm of her hand. "I care about Dahlia, and Dahlia may be the next victim." She looked up. "The jewels are only money."

Meyer laughed.

Victoria continued. "I assume you came here to find the coffin part. Well, I can't tell you."

" 'Can't,' Mrs. Trumbull? Or 'won't'?"

"Does it matter?"

"Good grief! Ten million dollars?"

"The money doesn't belong to you."

"A share of the money does. I'm essentially a sixth partner. The original five needed me to sell the stones. They were right. I don't know of any other person with my contacts." He watched her closely. "Where's the rest of the coffin hidden, Mrs. Trumbull?"

"What makes you think I know where it is?"

"Come, now, Mrs. Trumbull. You've been candid so far, and so have I. Where is it hidden?"

"How do you plan to get me to divulge the information, assuming I have it?"

Meyer laughed again, started to tip his chair back, then stopped. "I suppose I can get the information out of you by using blackmail, torture, threats, or seduction. I'm not sure any of those will work on you."

Victoria smiled. "What's wrong with seduction?"

Meyer sighed. "What if we make a bargain?"

"What sort of bargain?"

"I'll help you find the killer. You help me find the stones. I'll take only my share."

"What's your share?"

"Originally, one-sixth. Now it's increased to one-third. That's three and a third million. You help me, and I'll cut you in. How about one-fourth to each of us, you, me, Dahlia, and Herb Plante?"

Victoria fished an envelope out of the wastepaper basket. The envelope read, in glittering holographic letters, *"Victoria Trumbull has just won $5 million!!!"*

Meyer grinned.

Victoria looked up at him and scowled. She turned the envelope over and scribbled something on the back. "Two million five hundred thousand," she murmured.

Meyer nodded.

"I have to think about it," said Victoria.

Meyer drummed his long fingers on the table. Somewhere in the house a board creaked. McCavity strode in, looked around, went to his bowl of cat chow, and crunched noisily.

Meyer waited. "I'll catch the killer, and I'll make sure you get the credit."

Victoria smoothed her corduroy trousers over her knees.

He went on. "I'm more qualified as a manhunter than you are, Mrs. Trumbull — meaning no disrespect to you." He looked out of the window at the weather-beaten shingles on the south side. "Maybe you'd prefer to wait a bit."

Victoria said nothing.

"Who knows," Meyer continued. "In a few days or a week your cut may rise from one-quarter to one-third. Three-point-three million." He drummed his fingers. "That's a lot of shingles for this old house."

Victoria turned the envelope over and drew circles around the dollar sign in front of "5 million." Finally she said, "Suppose someone tells you where the stones are, and suppose you aren't able to catch the killer?"

"I'll catch him first. Once I've done that,

you can tell me where the stones are."

"What makes you think you can trust me?"

"I can trust you, all right. We'll shake on it. A gentlemen's agreement."

"I need to think about it," said Victoria. Meyer stood up. "This matter is still in the negotiating stage. We're not discussing it with anyone else, right?"

"You mean like the chief of police?" She smiled. "I'll think about that, too."

Meyer got back on the bicycle, pedaled out of Victoria's driveway, and turned left onto New Lane. He stowed the bike under the spruce tree, and sat down again with his back to the trunk, his hands in the pockets of his jacket.

His wait was longer this time. His breath steamed around his face. He could see Victoria go from the cookroom to the kitchen, turning on lights as the evening came on. It was almost dark when Elizabeth's ancient convertible finally clanked into the drive. Meyer sat up so he could see better.

Elizabeth went into the house, and Meyer waited. Occasionally Elizabeth and her grandmother passed in front of the windows. He saw a light go on in an upstairs window, then go out again. Victoria walked past the kitchen window again and he could see she was carrying what looked like an old blanket. The two disappeared from his sight briefly. He stood up. Within three or four minutes, they returned and passed in front of the window again. Elizabeth was carrying a large flat object wrapped in the blanket. The object was about the size and shape of a good-size oil painting. Meyer laughed to himself and moved closer, from the cover of the spruce to the cover of the lilac bushes in the driveway, where he could see better.

Victoria held the kitchen door open and Elizabeth sidestepped into the narrow entryway with the bulky object, then down the stone steps into the darkening evening. Meyer could see her clearly. He heard Elizabeth ask, "Can you see okay?" and Victoria's firm response, "I'll go first with the light."

Meyer froze. If they flashed the light around, they would be able to see him and his steaming breath through the bare lilac branches. But they moved steadily toward the sloping bulkhead doors below the dining room window. Victoria propped one of the doors open with a stick. Meyer saw the flashlight beam waver as Victoria went down the steps. Elizabeth followed, carrying the blanket-wrapped object. He heard something creak, probably a door at the foot of the steps.

Meyer waited. A few flakes of snow landed on his jacket.

Ten minutes later, the same door creaked, then slammed shut, and he heard the metallic scratch of a latch slid into place. Victoria emerged from the cellar with the blanket, folded now. She held the flashlight while Elizabeth shut the bulkhead door, and both of them went back into the kitchen. The snow was falling heavily now.

Meyer grinned.

He waited a few minutes more, then slipped back to the spruce tree, retrieved Sonny's bicycle, and pedaled toward Lucretia's.

The snow fell steadily. Meyer rode cautiously on the slick surface. Few cars passed him. Suppertime, he guessed. There was a game on tonight that would keep people indoors, but he didn't follow football and didn't much care who was playing.

A dark Ford in the left lane dimmed its headlights, slowed to pass him, then moved on. Meyer raised a hand in thanks. The driver probably hadn't seen his gesture.

The snow spiraled in the wake of the car before the wind blew it across the road in long gauzy streamers. He brushed snow out of his eyes, put his head down, and pedaled.

Lucretia's house was only a couple of miles from Victoria's, but tonight the ride seemed longer. Another car came toward him, its headlights long lances of dancing snow, and passed him. The road in front of him was illuminated briefly as a car came up from behind him. He hadn't ridden a bike since he was a kid, and he felt a stab of fear. Would the driver see him? Did that damned Sonny have reflectors on his bike? He steered onto the grass shoulder. The snow had begun to stick and the bike skidded. The car slowed. He felt a surge of relief. The driver must have seen him. Another approaching car passed, and the car behind him waited before pulling around him into the left lane. Meyer was thinking he would never again underestimate the hazards of bike riding when he noticed that the car was the same dark Ford that had passed him going the other way.

He ticked off in his mind the reasons for the dark Ford passing him twice in just a few minutes. The driver had forgotten something. He'd passed his turnoff. Or maybe the driver was a she. She'd taken her kid's playmate home, and was on her way back to her own place.

Or was someone playing games? Did anyone besides Mrs. Trumbull know who the man called Meyer and Emery was and what he was doing on the Island?

The snow was coming down harder, blowing horizontally across his field of vision, stinging his face. He had less than a half mile to go before he reached Lucretia's road. He pedaled as hard as he dared on the slippery surface.

He was almost there. The white gate that marked Lucretia's road was only a hundred feet ahead of him.

He could see the headlights of an approaching car. Would he reach her turnoff before the car got to him? He played the sort of game he played as a kid. Which of us will get to the road first? The car came toward him, slowed, and before it sped up and vanished behind him, he could see it was the same dark Ford.

Chapter 18

Herb Plante continued to the end of Old County Road and turned right onto the Edgartown Road.

The man he'd passed on the bicycle was Emery. Herb had no doubt about that. He'd seen Emery a half dozen times during his postings abroad. The biker wasn't wearing a helmet, and there was no mistaking that streaky blond hair and long, bony face.

Herb turned his windshield wipers on high, but the snow was coming down thickly and the wipers barely cleared a patch before snow blotted his view again. He could hardly make out the road. He turned on the high beams, but the beams reflected off a dense wall of white. Just as well, he told himself. No one will venture out in this weather.

What was Emery doing here? In West Tisbury? As far as Herb knew, no one had told Emery where the stones were hidden. Certainly no one had mentioned the hiding place in the cemetery.

Unless Dahlia had told Emery.

Herb thought about Dahlia. He'd never trusted her entirely, even when they had worked together. In fact, he checked out of his hotel and changed his name once he'd located her at Mrs. Trumbull's. Was Dahlia in league with Emery? Dahlia, after all, was the one who had recommended him to the original group of five. He, Herb Plante, had objected to the inclusion of Emery, but Dahlia had gotten her way, as usual.

The group was down to two now. Three, if you included Emery, who didn't deserve an equal share. That equal share bit was at Dahlia's insistence, and the others had gone along with her on that, too. Well, a three-way split wasn't bad. A two-way split would be better.

Did Dahlia and Emery have something going between them?

He was sure Emery had noticed the dark Ford that had passed the bike three times, but Emery couldn't possibly connect Herb Plante to the anonymous dark rental car.

He drove slowly, past the police station and the mill pond. Between gusts he could see the swans swimming in a circle of open water. Ice was forming.

He turned left at Brandy Brow, grateful

for the lack of traffic on the road. His tires spun on the icy hill, then caught, and he reached the level road by Alley's store. The store was closed. Fat pumpkins were piled on the porch next to corn shocks, where anyone could steal them. No one would, though. They'd come by tomorrow or the next day and pay for their pumpkins and their *New York Times*. Pumpkin pie for Thanksgiving.

He thought of the $10 million in stones somewhere on this Island in the missing coffin. Where could something the size of a coffin be hidden?

The hearse might contain a clue. The police had towed the vehicle to Tiasquam Repairs, finished examining it, and had notified him, the owner. Mort might have left a note of some kind in the hearse. If he had, he, Herb, would have to find and destroy the note. Herb wondered how carefully the police had searched the vehicle. Had they lifted fingerprints? That wouldn't matter. His prints would be all over the hearse, and the police would expect that. Mort's prints would be too, of course. Who else of the group had driven the hearse? He couldn't recall.

He had given one of three keys to Mort, one to Red, and had kept the third. The key could have been duplicated, of course, but for what reason? Had Red been able to transfer the stones to the concealed compartment in the hearse?

Their scheme had been a crazy one, hiding the stones in a coffin that supposedly held a suicide, buried furtively in the cemetery of a small town, to be unearthed when the five had retired. But they had decided on the scheme ten years ago when they were a lot younger. And, come to think of it, what else could have worked? He had to credit Dahlia, begrudgingly, for thinking of such an imaginative plan. The five had bought the secondhand hearse and had garaged it at his flower shop.

He could use his share of that money. Things had not been going well for him lately. With the money divided by six, if he included Emery, there'd have been only $1.6 million. Now, divided by three each share would be $3.3 million, considerably better.

There'd been no traffic on the road since Herb Plante had passed the bicyclist. He glanced in the rearview mirror to make sure the road was still clear, and turned left into the driveway that led behind Tiasquam Repairs, where the shop stored summer people's cars. He drove down the corridor between the rows of stored vehicles until he came to the hearse. He parked several rows beyond the hearse, and walked back. He tugged off one of his gloves, took the key out of his pocket, and put his glove back on.

Snow had coated the hood and windshield, and made a long low drift along the window on the driver's side. He brushed off the lock, inserted the key, and opened the door. The dome light went on. He slipped inside, shut the door, and with his penlight systematically searched the vehicle. Through the glove compartment, through recesses under the seats, in pockets behind the seats, behind the sun visors. He lifted the carpeting in back, went through compartments over the rear wheels, looked in the spare tire well. Then he moved the front seat forward and felt for the hidden compartment. It was empty. He had found a few pieces of paper, a shopping list, and a receipt that the police had missed, but no notes. Nothing that would incriminate any of them.

Unless the police already had found something.

However, as he had expected, the stones had not been transferred to the hearse.

Herb locked up the hearse and cautiously retraced his route along the still un-plowed road to his room at the bed-and-breakfast in Vineyard Haven.

Lucretia met Meyer at the door. "Darling, I've been so worried. You're soaking wet." She looked up at him. "I have drinks waiting. Why don't you take a hot shower?"

"Let me borrow your car," Meyer said. "Quick!"

"What is it? What's the matter?"

"I'll tell you when I get back. I'm in a rush." He kissed her hurriedly and held out his hand for the key. She reached into her pocketbook, her hands beginning to shake, and gave him the key. "There's trouble, isn't there?"

"Thanks," Meyer said, and went out into the storm.

He drove as rapidly as he dared. When he came to the end of Old County Road he could see tire tracks turning to the right, still visible through the new-fallen snow. He turned right, too. At Brandy Brow, the tracks turned to the left, and he followed. Before he reached Alley's, he switched off the headlights. The snow made the night bright, and he followed the tracks to Tiasquam Repairs, where they turned in.

Meyer nodded to himself.

He drove past the repair shop, made a U-turn, parked, and waited, engine running, heater on, lights off.

In about fifteen minutes, the dark Ford that had passed him on Old County Road pulled out of the driveway, stopped, then turned right toward Vineyard Haven.

Meyer followed at a distance, lights off. When the car turned left on Brandy Brow, Meyer followed. If the driver was heading to Vineyard Haven, he was taking the long way around.

Only one other car approached. Headlights flicked to let Meyer know his lights were off. When the Ford reached the outskirts of Vineyard Haven, Meyer waited for a curve that hid him from view briefly, then switched on his own lights.

The Ford turned onto Main Street, its tracks black lines on the snow-covered asphalt. Meyer dropped back until he was a couple of blocks behind. Ahead of him, he could see the Ford turn left on a side street. When Meyer reached the street, he noted the name, Daggett Avenue, and drove past. He continued to West Chop, then doubled back and turned onto Daggett Avenue. He found the dark Ford parked under an oak tree in front of an old house with a sign identifying it as a bed-and-breakfast. Meyer drove past. He heard a dog bark, saw a man's silhouette on the frosted glass of the front door, saw a light in an upstairs front window, and he retraced his route to West Tisbury.

He parked on New Lane, took a flashlight out of the glove compartment, and cut across the pasture to Victoria's. He stood under the lilac bushes again. The branches were heavy with snow. Snow continued to fall, covering his tracks. Occasionally, a gust would shake the branches, and a clump of snow would drop on him. The downstairs lights were off now, but he could see a light on in an upstairs room, Victoria's he guessed. The room was on the west side of the house; the cellar doors were on the south side where no one would see him.

He eased the cellar door open, shone his light down the steep, narrow stone steps, and lowered the door behind him. At the bottom of the steps, as he had guessed, there was a door, a homemade plywood door closed against the weather with a rusty latch. He eased the latch back, lifted the heavy door so it wouldn't scrape on the cellar floor, and pushed it gently. No sound. He left the lower door open and flashed his light around.

To his right was an old freezer, still running, but festooned with cobwebs. Did Victoria still use this thing? To his left was a stack of green-painted shutters, also festooned with cobwebs. In the thin beam of his light the cobwebs cast eerie shadows that moved as his light moved. Cobwebs hung from the low ceiling, from the hanging light he didn't switch on. Cobwebs covered rows and rows of glass jars of jams and jellies and pickles and green beans. His light picked out the purples and reds and greens of whatever was in the jars. My God! Did she use any of this stuff? It must be decades old.

The cellar smelled of mold and earth and stone and brick, not a bad smell. He shone the light on the floor, ancient brick, apparently laid in sand, because in places the flooring sagged into depressions several inches deep.

Where could she have put that coffin piece? He held the light and tilted the shutters forward so he could search behind them. He peered at the shelves — she couldn't have stashed the piece there or she'd have knocked down some of the jelly jars. He stepped carefully over piles of dishes and bricks and paint cans and jugs of water, all covered with thick white cobwebs. Wherever he moved, his head brushed into more spiderwebs that hung into his face like lace. Surely Victoria and her granddaughter must have cleared a path. He stopped and studied the cellar. A vague clearing seemed to lead to the back.

He followed and found, behind the chimney foundation, what looked like an underground seedbed contained by ten-inch-wide boards. The bed was about six feet wide and eight feet long. When he got close enough to shine his light on the seedbed, he discovered the soil was dried manure. He pondered on that for several moments before he decided he'd found a long-abandoned mushroom garden.

The surface of the mushroom bed looked as though it had been raked, and recently. He dug his hand gingerly into the dry manure, and after feeling around, found what he was looking for. The end panel of the coffin.

He removed the piece, quickly smoothed out the manure, and retraced his steps, carrying the coffin piece in both arms. He set it down on the steps while he closed and latched the lower door, then went up the stone steps until he could lift the bulkhead door. He stepped out, lowered the door gently behind him, and moved as rapidly as he could through the thickening snow back to Lucretia's car parked on the lane.

The next morning when Howland showed up at Victoria's, snow was still falling. Several inches had accumulated, and his car made deep tracks.

Victoria, who was at the sink, turned and scowled at him when he came into the kitchen. "Where have you been all this time? On business, I suppose?"

"May I have a cup of coffee, Victoria?"

"You didn't answer me."

"Where's Dahlia?"

"Asleep, I imagine. She's having a rough time." Victoria wiped her hands on a dish towel and led the way into the cookroom. "Help yourself to coffee, and pour a cup for me, while you're at it, please." She sat down stiffly. "Elizabeth made muffins, and you might bring one for each of us."

Howland carried in two mugs of coffee, two plates, two muffins, and two napkins on a tray, and sat across from Victoria.

"Well?"

"I had to go to Washington on DEA business. While I was there, I checked on the backgrounds of Tremont Ashecroft, Mort Chaffer, Red Crossley, Herb Plante, and Dahlia. They were in the Foreign Service at roughly the same time, although they served in different countries."

Victoria nodded. "I could have told you that."

"I needed to know more than that."

"I could have told you more, if you'd listened. Dahlia explained their relationship to me. They acquired their stones all over the world. Colombia, Sri Lanka, Afghanistan, Burma."

Howland sighed and rubbed his nose. "Is there anything else you could have told me?"

"Since you've been gone — who fed and walked your dogs, by the way?"

"A caretaker comes by when I'm off-Island. What about 'since I've been gone'?"

"You disappeared before we found Red's corpse, didn't you?"

"I heard about his death. How you and Casey were the first" — he paused and rubbed his nose again — "officials on the scene. Must have been gruesome."

Victoria nodded. "I wish you could be more pleasant to Dahlia. She's suffering, and you're not helping. She's sick, and those were her friends."

"Tough," said Howland. "Do you want to hear what I learned in Washington or not?"

Victoria stood, her hands flat on the table for support. "Go ahead," she said. "I'm getting the butter."

"Sorry," said Howland. "I meant to bring it in."

"I think Dahlia's up now. I hear Bacchus."

"I'm out of here," Howland said. "I'll come by later to make sure you can get out of the drive."

"Thank you," said Victoria. "Take your muffin with you."

Dahlia appeared a few minutes after Howland left. Her cap was askew and she had dark circles under her eyes. Bacchus barked monotonously behind the closed door of her room. McCavity, who'd been nuzzling his cat chow, headed for the door and waited for some house servant to let him out.

Victoria pushed the door open, but McCavity didn't move. He stood half in, half out, studying the white scene beyond the entry.

"Out!" said Victoria, nudging the cat with her foot. She shut the door firmly behind him.

Dahlia laughed. "I suppose he thinks you're inconveniencing him with all that snow."

Victoria handed a freshly poured mug of coffee to her. "How are you feeling today?"

Dahlia fluttered her hand. "So so. No worse than I expected."

"I think you're remarkably courageous."

"Do I have a choice?" Dahlia poured half-and-half into her coffee. "Do you mind if I make some raisin toast?"

"We have fresh muffins, if you'd rather."

"Much better."

When they'd settled at the cookroom table, Victoria asked Dahlia about her plans for the day.

Dahlia stared out at the snow falling steadily. "I need to talk with Denny Rhodes, the cemetery superintendent."

"Oh? I hope you don't feel you need to make arrangements for yourself, yet."

"That, too," said Dahlia. "But I have something more immediate." She broke a piece off her muffin and buttered it. "I've told you how I acquired the gemstones and where we cached them."

Victoria nodded.

"Now the coffin has disappeared." Dahlia set her piece of muffin on her plate, untouched. "Someone must know where it is."

Victoria looked away.

"I've got to locate that coffin, I must. I have to find those stones."

Victoria shifted uncomfortably in her chair.

"The only person I can think of who might be able to help me is Denny Rhodes."

Victoria coughed delicately. "Have you told him the situation? About the stones in the coffin?"

Dahlia crumbled her muffin into still smaller pieces. "The fewer people who know about the stones the better." She pushed the crumbs around her plate with her finger. "I wanted to tell you about the gems, but I don't think I told you that Denny arranged for the coffin's original burial ten years ago."

Victoria patted her lips with her napkin. "You might want to call him first to make sure he's home. Or at Town Hall."

"Good idea," said Dahlia. "I guess I'm not hungry after all. Shall I put this in the compost bucket?" She indicated her wrecked muffin.

"I'll scatter the crumbs on top of the snow for the birds," Victoria said. "Nothing is wasted in this house."

Dahlia pushed her chair back and took her plate into the kitchen.

Victoria called out to her, "You still haven't heard from Emery, have you?"

Dahlia shook her head. "He might be anywhere. I'm not worried about him. I'm sure I'll catch up with him eventually."

Victoria thought for a moment, then said, "I have some lovely lavender bath oil, Dahlia. Would you like to take a long soak before you head out into the snow?"

"Thank you, Victoria. You've been such a support to me. I only wish Howland could be" — she paused — "kinder, or more thoughtful."

While Dahlia ran her bath water, Victoria took the cordless phone into the parlor and called Casey.

"She has a right to her jewels, Casey. It's wrong to make her search for a coffin that no longer exists, when we know where the jewels are hidden."

"Do not — do you understand me, Victoria? — do not tell Dahlia anything about anything. She has to wait until this whole thing is sorted out. It's not going to kill her."

"It might."

"We're keeping an eye on her."

"Meyer came by yesterday afternoon."

"I know. We saw him on that kid's bike. I'm coming right over, Victoria. We've got to move that coffin part out of the woodshed. You can tell me then about Meyer's visit."

★ ★ ★

Denny was still eating breakfast in the kitchen with his daughter when Dahlia arrived at his house. Snowplows had cleared the main road, and Dahlia's only problem had been getting out of Victoria's long driveway.

Denise pushed her plate back without greeting Dahlia, set her elbows on the table, and glared at her father. "Mom had, like, trouble getting out of the drive this morning, you know?"

"What was I supposed to do," Denny snapped. "Shovel the drive for her? She got out okay without my help."

"The main road is nice and clear," Dahlia said. "Have either of you heard the weather report?"

"Accumulation of eight to ten inches before the storm moves on tomorrow afternoon," Denny said. "Can Denise get you some breakfast?"

Denise glared at him.

"No thank you. But I need to ask you something in private."

Denny adjusted his glasses, holding the sidepiece between thumb and forefinger. He cleared his throat.

Denise sat where she was. "You want me to leave?"

Dahlia, still standing, looked from one to the other. "I have personal business I need to discuss with your father."

"O-kay," said Denise. She pushed her chair back with a scrape and slouched out of the kitchen.

"Kids," Denny muttered.

Dahlia sat down in the chair Denise had vacated. "I'll get right down to business," she said.

"I understand you're interested in reserving a cemetery plot, but all the papers and plot maps are in Town Hall, and we're closed today."

Dahlia shook her head. "No, no. This is something different."

Denny pushed his plate away from him, tucked his napkin into a green plastic napkin ring, and folded his arms on the table.

Dahlia said abruptly, "Where is the coffin, Denny?"

He stared at her. "What are you talking about?"

"The coffin. You know what I'm talking about."

He unfolded his arms and waved his large hands. "Give me some clue."

"You don't need to play stupid with me, Denny. You dug that grave by hand your-

307

self ten years ago. You fell in. Remember?"

Denny pushed his glasses back in place. His forehead had a thin sheen of perspiration. He stroked his beard.

"We paid you five thousand dollars. Do you recall which coffin I'm talking about now?"

"It's coming back to me." Denny folded his arms on the table again. "That was a long time ago."

"Do you recall a request from the funeral home in Milwaukee, roughly a month ago, asking you to disinter that same coffin so the girl could be reburied near her family?"

"There was no girl in that coffin." Denny sat up straight. "Bags of sand. And that's all it was, bags of sand. What in hell trick are you trying to pull? I thought I was doing the family a favor, burying the girl quietly. A suicide."

"You were to get another five thousand dollars for expediting the move."

"Well I didn't, did I? I could hardly claim the money they found on that drowned hearse driver."

"So where is the coffin now?"

Denny pulled his napkin out of its plastic ring and wiped his forehead. "Who knows?"

"What do you mean, 'Who knows'?" Dahlia made a fist and pounded on the table. "There's something of great value to me, and to me alone, in that coffin. I've got to find it."

"I don't know what you expect me to do."

"Let's retrace the journey of the coffin," Dahlia said. "You finally located it, under the wrong gravestone, I understand."

Denny adjusted his glasses and stroked his beard.

"You had the coffin moved to the funeral home, where you opened it."

"Actually, Toby, the undertaker, opened the coffin."

"For God's sake!" Dahlia exclaimed. "So the coffin was opened, the police chief suspected the sandbags contained drugs and called in the DEA, and the DEA analyzed the sand, which turned out to be nothing more than sand. Then, from what I understand, you moved the coffin to the shed behind Town Hall, and the coffin disappeared."

"No one suspected that piece of crap had any value."

Dahlia's face reddened. "Ten million dollars. That's what that coffin is worth."

Denny's mouth opened, a pink gash in his black beard.

"Who had access to that shed? Who moved the coffin?"

"Anyone could have. The shed isn't exactly Fort Knox. Easy to break in."

"Was the lock broken?"

Denny thought a moment, then shook his head. "I don't believe it was."

"Who has keys to the shed?"

"All three selectmen and Mrs. Danvers."

"Where do you keep your key?"

Denny patted a ring holding about a dozen keys hitched onto his belt. "Right here. On me all the time, except when I'm asleep, and then it's on the table by my bed."

"What about the other selectmen? Let me have their phone numbers. And Mrs. Danvers's number at home."

Denny wrote out the information, handed the paper to Dahlia, and stood, dismissing her. "Wish you'd let me know the coffin had some value. You can't expect us to mind read, you know." He shook his head. "I'll do what I can to help, but I can't promise anything."

Dahlia sighed. She closed her eyes. She pushed her cap off her brow. She stood.

Denny opened the door. "You shouldn't have too much trouble backing out. Be careful on the road."

He went back inside, and Denise was sitting in the chair Dahlia had vacated.

"I suppose you had to listen, didn't you?"

"You didn't tell me not to."

Denny smoothed his hair over the top of his head. "Clear the table." He stroked his beard. "That woman gives me a pain."

Denise didn't move.

"What's the matter with you, kid?" Denny looked at his watch. "Are you waiting for lunchtime to clear the breakfast dishes?"

Denise still didn't move. She looked steadily at her father. "I, like, know where the coffin is," she said.

"What are you talking about?"

"Noodles's boyfriend . . ."

"Her name is Lucretia," Denny said. "To you she's Mrs. Woods."

"You call her Noodles."

Denny started to get up, and Denise quickly said, "O-kay. Mrs. Woods's boyfriend gave Sonny some money to move the coffin to the airport storage place."

"What!" Denny stood up. "What are you telling me?"

"Sonny borrowed his mom's key. That's how they got the coffin out of the shed."

"Christ!" said Denny. "So Noodles is up to her little tricks, is she?"

"Mrs. Woods," Denise said in a small voice.

311

Chapter 19

Sonny was shoveling his mother's driveway when Meyer accosted him. Sonny stopped, tossed the shovel aside, and kicked a chunk of ice out of the way. "So that little bitch squealed on me, did she?"

Meyer leaned against Lucretia's car, his arms folded over his leather jacket. "Seems to me you were the one who was supposed to keep your mouth shut. Had to show off, didn't you? Impress the girls."

"All I told was Denise."

"That was enough, wasn't it?" Meyer said. "I never should have trusted a kid who lets himself get kicked off the team for stupidity."

"Hey, wait," Sonny protested. "I only took a couple puffs."

"In the locker room. With the coach coming through the door." Meyer turned away from him. "What's done is done. Don't expect any jobs from now on."

"Jeesh," said Sonny. "Nervous old lady."

Meyer's eyes got a strange intensity. "What did you say?" He stepped toward

Sonny, who was several inches taller. Sonny backed away. "You want to repeat that?" Meyer reached out and grabbed the front of Sonny's sweatshirt. He twisted it into a ball and shoved it against Sonny's throat. Sonny tried to back away and couldn't.

"I didn't mean it." Sonny's voice was a croak. "Sorry, Meyer. I was just kidding. Let me go."

"You know how easy it is to kill someone?" Meyer whispered. "You know how slim the line is between life and death?"

"Sorry, Meyer. Sorry! I shouldn't of said that. I mean it. I'm sorry!"

Meyer shook his hand loose from the sweatshirt. "Get out of my sight."

Sonny scuttled away. Once he was out of Meyer's reach he shouted over his shoulder, "You didn't need to overreact like that. Jeesh!"

Meyer picked up the snow shovel Sonny had abandoned and finished clearing the driveway before he went back into the house.

Lucretia was standing at the window staring out into the backyard. Two cardinals were at the bird feeder, red against the still-falling snow. She turned when Meyer came through the front door.

"You want to explain this coffin business to me? *Is* there an explanation? What's going on, Meyer? You wanted to bond with Sonny, remember?" Lucretia's hands were in fists by her side. "You said you wanted time with my boy. A project, you said. Well?"

"I finished shoveling the driveway," Meyer said.

"Are you going to explain or not? Denny called me ten minutes ago to say you hired my son to move the coffin to a storage unit at the airport. Right?"

"Babe, there's a simple explanation."

"Surely you must know that coffin is puzzling everyone."

"Yeah, babe. I do now." Meyer hung his head sheepishly. "I thought I was being helpful, getting that piece of junk out of the shed for you and putting Sonny to work at the same time. I paid him out of my own pocket." Keeping his head down, Meyer glanced up at her with his blue eyes. "I thought I was doing the right thing, babe. I see now how wrong I was. I'm sorry."

Lucretia's fists relaxed slightly. "Where's the coffin now? Denny wants to know."

Meyer hung his head again. "It's gone,

314

babe. I cut that piece of junk into little pieces and threw the pieces in the Dumpster."

"You did *what?*"

Meyer nodded. "I figured that way you wouldn't have the trouble of disposing of it." He straightened up. "I thought I was doing the right thing."

"You cut up the coffin?"

Meyer nodded again. "I can see how much difficulty I've made for you. I thought I was helping. Getting Sonny involved like that. Taking his mind off the game." He stepped toward her, and she moved a step back.

"Why did you cut it up?"

Meyer shrugged. "You saw that coffin. It was nothing but a decayed piece of junk."

"I don't understand."

"I did the wrong thing, I can see that now. Stupid of me."

Lucretia turned back to the window. "Denny told me something else."

Meyer stared at her back. "You mean about the coffin?"

"He said someone told him the coffin had ten million dollars in it."

Meyer whistled. "No way. There was nothing in that coffin but rat shit and dead beetles."

315

Lucretia turned to him. "Tell me, Meyer. Were you looking for the money?"

"No way, babe." He crossed himself. "Believe me, if I'd thought there was money in that coffin, I'd have said something to you. I wouldn't have cut it up unless the police chief was looking on."

Lucretia sighed. "I want to believe you."

"You have to believe me when I say if I'd found ten million dollars in that coffin, nobody could have been more surprised."

"You've been such a special friend to me and Sonny. I'd hate to ever think mean thoughts about you."

He held out his hand and she took it. "Friends again?" he said.

She nodded. "I'll explain to Denny what happened. It's all so logical. I wish you'd said something to me first, though."

Meyer looked sheepish again. "I wanted to surprise you."

"You're a sweetheart. Thank you. I'm sorry I snapped at you," and Lucretia threw her arms around Meyer's neck.

Dahlia was able to get out of Denny's drive easily, but when she got to Victoria's, she decided not to attempt the long driveway, and left her car parked by the

316

side of the main road. She'd have to cut across the scrapings of the plow later, but that would be only a matter of a few feet, not several hundred.

She locked the car and walked through the deep snow to the house. Once inside, she shucked off her wet clothes and snowy boots, took a hot shower, dried herself, and called Lucretia.

When Lucretia answered, Dahlia cleared her throat as a sort of formal introduction. "I'm with the State Department," she said, "and I've been asked to look into some mystery about a missing coffin."

"The State Department?" Lucretia sounded bewildered.

Dahlia cleared her throat again. "If you have time, I'd like to meet with you. I understand you may know something about the coffin."

"Yes, I do," said Lucretia. "There's no need to meet. The coffin has been disposed of."

Dahlia covered a gasp. "I beg your pardon? Disposed of?"

"A friend of mine cut up the coffin and threw out the pieces."

"Do you know where he threw them?"

"Into a Dumpster at the airport."

"Can you tell me just where?"

Lucretia paused. "I'm afraid I didn't get your name."

"My name isn't important," Dahlia said. "Do you know just where at the airport?"

"I'm sure the contents have already been shipped off-Island."

"Thank you," said Dahlia weakly, and hung up.

After lunch, Meyer borrowed Lucretia's car, topped the gas tank at the Up-Island Texaco station, and drove to Vineyard Haven. The snow had let up and the streets were clear. He went down Main Street past dozens of parking spaces, and turned onto Daggett Avenue. The dark Ford was still in front of the bed-and-breakfast. Meyer drove around the block and parked several car lengths behind the Ford.

He turned the radio on to the classical music station Lucretia liked and unfolded his copy of the *Island Enquirer*, prepared to wait all day, if necessary.

Less than an hour later a bulky man with thick glasses and a crumpled tweed hat came down the steps. Meyer heard the dog bark. The man turned, and Meyer caught a glimpse of his face.

Herb Plante, as he had suspected.

Herb had recognized him last night, riding Sonny's bicycle in the snow. Herb had checked out the hearse in the lot behind Tiasquam Repairs. Had Red had time to hide the gemstones in the hearse?

Meyer followed the Ford to the video store on State Road, and when the car turned in to Cronig's, Meyer decided not to wait. Instead of going to the flower stall at the grocery store, he doubled back to the florist shop down the hill, bought a dozen long-stemmed red roses, and delivered them to Lucretia with a note of abject apology.

After she apologized profusely to Meyer for ever doubting him, and after she arranged the roses in a tall vase and set the vase in the window where the red roses stood out against the snowy backyard, she told Meyer about the phone call.

"This woman said she was from the State Department, isn't that strange?"

"Yes, it is," said Meyer. By now they were sitting together on the couch, and he had his arm around her shoulders.

"She wouldn't give me her name."

"What did she sound like?" said Meyer.

"Sort of breathy. I told her the coffin had been destroyed, and she sounded choked up."

"I'm beginning to think I did everyone a favor by getting rid of that thing."

"I think you're right," said Lucretia.

"By the way, babe, I put a couple of sandbags in the trunk of your car. Should help give you traction in the snow."

"You think of everything, darling. Did you want the car again tonight? I have to finish up some work here at home."

Meyer tightened his arm around her. "Thanks, babe. When my ship comes in, I'll make it up to you."

"You already have," said Lucretia.

Meyer had put the coffin piece in the trunk of Lucretia's car the night before, wrapped in a blue tarp. He'd weighted the tarp down with two fifty-pound bags of sand that Lucretia was not likely to lift out.

After supper, he drove to his storage unit at the airport, parked as close as he could, unlocked the door, opened the trunk of the car, and lifted the heavy sandbags off the tarp-wrapped coffin panel. He noticed a slight smell of solvent, bicycle oil he decided. He hadn't been aware of the smell the night before, and he wondered.

He leaned the coffin piece against the wall and turned on the overhead light. He moved the sawhorses to the center of the small room under the overhead light, and set the coffin piece on top. He unfolded the tarp. The smell of oil was quite strong.

The end piece, like the rest of the cheap coffin, had been fabricated of thin waffle-patterned metal. The metal of the main coffin had been riveted along the top, bottom, and sides, leaving a hollow center. The whole was stiffened with cardboard. The piece that Meyer had laid on the saw-horses was held together with rusty bolts and nuts, not rivets. He examined the bolts. That was where the smell of oil was coming from. He smiled to himself. Mrs. Trumbull had one-upped him again.

He undid the bolts on three sides anyway. They unscrewed easily. He opened the piece as though it was a plastic doggie bag box. There were no mouse droppings or worm casts, no beetles, dead or alive. No scraps of cardboard or metal shavings. The inside was clean except for an envelope addressed to "Meyer/Emery" in Victoria Trumbull's loopy backhand writing.

Inside the envelope was a note: "Wasn't it our favorite poet who said, 'tell the stones: Men hate to die . . .'? Thank you for disposing of this. V.T."

Chapter 20

The snow stopped during the night and lay a foot deep in the driveway. Snow had piled up on the split rail fence and capped the fence posts at the back of Victoria's garden, weighed down the branches of the cedars in the west pasture, and filled the seed cups of the Queen Anne's lace.

Across her pasture, across Doane's pasture, which was on the other side of the lane, and beyond the brook, Victoria could hear the town clock ring the hour.

The sun came up in the washed sky, and the new-fallen snow turned rose, then gold, then dazzling rainbow hues. A chickadee landed on the bird feeder, snatched a seed, and fluttered to the shelter of the wisteria vine.

Victoria was watching the glorious play of colors on the snow when the police Bronco plowed its way up her driveway.

"You've made it easier for the next car," Victoria said as Casey stamped the snow off her boots. "Now I won't have to shovel."

Casey laughed. "You'd probably have conned someone into doing it for you, most likely Meyer." She rubbed her hands together. "I hope you've got coffee."

"A fresh pot," said Victoria.

Casey hung her yellow slicker over the back of a kitchen chair. "I saw smoke coming out of the stovepipe."

Victoria sat where she could continue to watch the play of colors on the snow. "I thought the temperature in the woodshed might drop," she said. "I didn't want my houseplants to freeze."

Casey started to pull out a chair, then pushed it back under the table. "We'd better move the end of the coffin away from the woodstove before we do anything else."

"I've already moved it."

"Not down the cellar?"

Victoria nodded.

"Victoria! How can you be so . . ." Casey stopped. "Well, let's retrieve it."

Victoria pulled on her black rubber gardening boots and her quilted coat. Together they trudged the short distance through the snow to the bulkhead. Casey brushed snow off the door and propped it open. Victoria led the way, carefully setting her feet sideways on the narrow steps, bracing her hands against the stone wall. She pushed against the door at the bottom of the steps. The door opened with a long-drawn-out squeal.

A broken cobweb hung from the ceiling and dangled in front of them. "Don't use your cellar much, do you?" said Casey.

Victoria stepped over and around bottles and paint cans and boxes of indescribable odds and ends, and edged around the chimney footing. Morning light shone through the high, small cellar windows, and cast wavery reflections of sunlight on snow on the cobwebby beams above.

"I put the panel in there." Victoria pointed to the six-by-eight-foot seedbed.

Casey stared at the dusty bed. "Manure? You gotta be kidding, Victoria."

"Jonathan grew mushrooms down here."

"Yeah?" Casey found a metal rod leaning against the stone wall, poked it into the dry manure, and stirred. A cloud of dust arose. Victoria sneezed.

Casey probed the length and width of the bed. "Are you sure you put that thing in here?"

Victoria leaned against the wall. "Absolutely sure."

"There's nothing here," said Casey. "Nothing."

Victoria retraced her path to the foot of the steps and turned to Casey. "I thought so," she said softly.

"What did you say?" Casey tossed the metal rod onto the brick floor with a clank. "Let's get out of this creepy place. Then tell me what's going on."

Once Casey had shut the bulkhead door, she set her hands on her hips and turned to Victoria. "What were you thinking? Did you let Meyer or Emery or whatever his name is know you'd stashed that coffin part down there?" Casey's breath came out in steaming white puffs. "I told you the cellar is too obvious. You got any more bright ideas, Victoria?" Casey's face was pink.

"It's cold out here. Let's go in and drink our coffee."

Casey didn't move. "You bury ten million bucks in manure and expect that to be a safe hideaway?"

"I suspected he'd find it," said Victoria, "but I wasn't sure." She put her hand on Casey's shoulder for support and headed toward the house.

Casey moved slowly. "How could you do that, Victoria?"

In the entry, Victoria took off her boots and with relief slipped into her shoes with the hole cut for her sore toe.

Casey plopped into a chair, and Victoria brought in coffee. "Where do you expect to go from here, Victoria?" She slapped her head. "I'm the stupid one. I never should have agreed to let you keep that thing."

Victoria started to say something, but Casey continued.

"I suppose he's long gone with those stones. We have nothing to prove they ever existed. I never saw them. Maybe there are no stones."

"But I . . ." Victoria said.

"Even if we catch him, what can I charge him with, breaking and entering? Around this place nothing ever gets locked up. Furthermore, how do we establish what he stole?"

"Wait . . ." Victoria said.

"I should have my head examined. I know you're smart, Victoria. But you are ninety-two, after all."

Victoria stood up, hands flat on the table, her hooded eyes glittering. "Will you let me talk?"

Casey stopped. "Sorry, Victoria. I didn't mean that."

"Listen to me, now. I took that panel apart before hiding it down cellar."

Casey sat back in the chair. "You what?"

"I took it apart."

"Why did we have to go through that charade, then?"

"I wasn't sure Meyer would take the bait. But he did. All he's going to find is a note from me."

"Lord!" Casey let out a deep breath and eyed the old woman. "Were there any stones in there?"

Victoria nodded.

"I suppose you've hidden them again?"

Victoria nodded again, and sat down.

"Where, Victoria? Where are the stones?"

Victoria looked down at the table. "Someplace appropriate."

"Where, Victoria?" Casey sounded exasperated.

"The woodstove."

"In the woodstove? And you lit the fire?"

"Fire won't hurt them. Anyway, heat rises, and the stones are underneath."

Casey said nothing for several moments.

"Your coffee is getting cold," Victoria said.

"So the gems actually exist?"

"Yes."

"What do they look like?"

Victoria narrowed her eyes and gazed out across the pasture at the church steeple in the distance. "They looked like ordinary stones, only angular. I probably wouldn't have picked them up if I'd found them on the beach. Most of them were small, the size of a pencil eraser. The largest ones, only a few, were about this big." She held up her knobby thumb. "Some were clear, like dirty glass, some looked black, but were actually dark red. Some were green, some different shades of blue. Some were yellow." Victoria ran her thumbnail along a line in the checked tablecloth. "I was disappointed. I expected something quite different. Pirate treasure, not ordinary-looking stones."

"We gotta get them out of there, Victoria."

"We'll have to wait until the fire dies down."

Casey sat forward. "We've got to get them to a bank vault. Or a safe-deposit box."

"I suppose I can tell Dahlia now. She owns a share of the stones, you know."

Casey shook her head. "Don't say anything to her, Victoria. Not yet. The stones need to be in police custody. At least until we know what's going on." Casey stood. "I'm going to Oak Bluffs to explain all this to the state police."

Victoria stood too. "I'll go with you. The gems are safe."

"I want you to stay here until I get back. Junior is keeping an eye on Dahlia. I'll tell him to watch you, too."

"Where is he now?"

"He cruises by here at least once an hour."

Casey had been gone less than a half hour when there was a knock on the kitchen door. Dahlia was still in her room. Victoria had been typing an item for her column. She pushed her typewriter aside, got up from her chair, and opened the door to the man who'd asked about a room two nights before, Herb Plante.

"Good morning, Mrs. Trumbull."

"Come in, Mr. Plante." Victoria looked beyond the man at the driveway. "I don't see a car."

"You know who I am, I see." He removed his hat. "I didn't want to get stuck so I parked on the road and walked in."

"Are you here with books for me to sign?"

"Not this time." His glasses steamed up in the warm kitchen and he took them off and wiped them with a linen handkerchief. "Actually, I need to talk to Dahlia Atherton."

Victoria closed the door behind him and

waited, arms folded across her chest.

Plante sighed. "I have to talk with Dahlia."

"Dahlia's not well."

"So I understand."

"She's still in her room."

"I have information I need to give her." He unbuttoned his overcoat and ran a hand over his short hair.

"Does Dahlia know you're on-Island?"

He shook his head. "I don't think so."

"You've come from Brazil?"

"I got in a couple of days ago."

Victoria noticed some movement at the entrance to her driveway. "Well, come in, Mr. Plante." The police cruiser had nosed into her driveway and stopped. Junior stepped out.

Victoria led the way into the cookroom and moved her chair where she could see the pasture and the town buildings in the distance, and where she would block Plante's view of Junior plodding up the driveway. Plante sat across from her.

Victoria shifted slightly. "You and she are the only ones left of the original five collectors, I understand."

"You know about that."

"The police do, too. They believe the three murders are connected to your gem collection."

He nodded. "That's why I need to talk to Dahlia."

Victoria heard Bacchus's first tentative barks, then she heard Dahlia's door open. She glanced out of the window to judge how long Junior would take. She put her elbows on the table, and rested her chin on her clasped hands. "It's difficult to know whom to trust."

Plante nodded, but said nothing.

"I'm sure you knew her life was threatened?"

Plante set his coffee mug down and wiped his mouth with his linen handkerchief. "I hadn't heard," he said.

Victoria waited.

"*I'm* not the one you need to worry about, Mrs. Trumbull."

At that moment, Dahlia staggered into the kitchen. She stopped abruptly when she saw Herb Plante.

"What are you doing here?" she asked.

"That's a nice friendly greeting." Plante ran his fingers through his hair and straightened his tie.

Dahlia dropped into a chair between Victoria and Plante. "I thought you were still in Brazil."

Plante looked from Dahlia to Victoria and back. "I got a message from Red."

"Red's dead," she murmured.

Plante set his elbows on the table. "So I've heard."

"Are you sure the message was from Red? How did he get in touch with you?" Dahlia was watching him intently.

"He left a message with my assistant at the flower shop."

Victoria glanced out of the window.

Dahlia sat forward. "When was this?"

Plante took his glasses off again and deliberately wiped them. "Must have been the same day he was killed."

Dahlia persisted. "What did the message say?"

"That I should get to the Island as soon as possible."

"Was that all?"

Victoria saw Junior stop to look at something in the snow. She hoped he had found something that would delay him a bit. She needed to hear the rest of the conversation. She studied Plante and then Dahlia. Was this a conversation between two possible victims? Or was it between a victim and a killer?

"Where are you staying?" Dahlia asked Plante.

"I was at the Harbor View in Edgartown, but I've moved."

"That's an expensive hotel," said Victoria.

"It wasn't the expense. I moved for another reason."

"Really? What might that be?" Victoria waited for him to reply, but Dahlia cut in.

"Where are you now?" Dahlia's cap had slipped down on her forehead, but she didn't seem to notice.

Victoria let out her breath. Junior had reached the entry just a moment too soon. He stamped his feet on the grass mat, knocked, and opened the door.

"Morning, Victoria. How's everything?"

"Fine, Junior, fine. You know Dahlia Atherton." She indicated Dahlia, then Plante. "And this is Herb Plante."

Plante stood, and he and Junior shook hands. "Nice to meet you, sir. Is that your car on the main road?"

"Did I park it illegally?"

"No, sir. But the plows will be coming through any minute, and you may have trouble getting over the berm."

"I'd better move my car then," said Plante. "Thank you." He bowed to Victoria. "I still need to talk with you, Dahlia. Perhaps later this afternoon?"

"I'll be here all day," Victoria answered for Dahlia.

Chapter 21

Victoria watched the two men follow the Bronco's tracks down the snowy drive to the main road where the police cruiser and Herb Plante's car were parked.

Dahlia cleared her throat. "Did Herb tell you where he's staying?"

"No. You came in right after he arrived." Herb and Junior were hidden now by the great trunk of the ailanthus tree, and Victoria turned back to Dahlia. "I wonder why he moved out of the Harbor View? It's a lovely old hotel, and the rates are low this time of year."

"He was quite mysterious, wasn't he?" said Dahlia. "I wonder, too, why he needed to talk with me."

"Was it Herb Plante who gave you Bacchus?"

Dahlia nodded. "As a reminder of my years in South America. We were quite close at one time. He gave all of us toucan pins."

"Do you think he sent you the yerba maté?"

Dahlia thought for a moment. "That's mysterious, too. I've always considered Herb a good friend even after we drifted apart. And yet . . ." She stopped.

"And yet he's been acting strange lately?" Victoria finished.

"I suppose you could call it that."

The phone rang and Victoria answered. "Good morning, Howland," she said.

Dahlia sighed. "Oh dear!"

"She's right here," Victoria said. "Did you want to talk to her?"

Dahlia stood. Victoria looked up and shook her head. "After lunch is fine. You won't have any trouble getting in the drive. Casey cleared a track this morning with the Bronco."

Victoria hung up, and Dahlia looked at her watch. "I believe I'll go to Vineyard Haven for lunch. I don't really want to deal with Howland."

"He's been most unsympathetic," Victoria agreed. "I'm disappointed in him. I've always considered him such a gentleman, yet he's been almost rude to you."

Dahlia smiled. "His behavior to me dates back to our childhood. Some things never change."

"It will do you good to get out. The main roads are clear," Victoria said. "Junior will be close by in case you get stuck."

After Dahlia left, Victoria started to write an item for her column about the year's early snowfalls. Then she remembered seeing an article in an old *Martha's Vineyard Magazine* about Island storms. Her item would be much livelier if she could refer to historical snowfalls. Elizabeth had taken a stack of magazines to the attic, and the one Victoria wanted was probably among them.

She made her way upstairs, holding the banister tightly, passed through the upstairs study, and paused at the window to catch her breath. She looked down on the snow-covered driveway, and the trees and bushes with their snowcaps. She opened the door at the foot of the steep attic stairs and looked up. The attic seemed high above her. She braced her hands against the wooden sides of the old narrow stairwell, which still smelled faintly of vanilla, the scent of fresh lumber even after two centuries.

Once she reached the firm footing of the attic floor, she carried a pile of magazines to the west window where she'd have plenty of light and where she'd see Howland when he drove in.

Howland had certainly been acting odd

lately. She wondered what had happened in the past to cause such ill feelings between Dahlia and him. The animosity seemed to be deeper than any conflict over ownership of their house.

Victoria found the article she'd been looking for and put the magazine aside. But she noticed other articles on other subjects, and became so engrossed, she forgot to watch for Howland's car.

Suddenly, she was aware of a sound. Her watch said it was after two o'clock. She looked out of the window and saw a new set of tire tracks. She picked up the copy of the magazine she'd come for and rose. Below her, the loose floorboard in the study squeaked, and someone started up the attic stairs.

"Hello!" she called out.

"Victoria?" Howland appeared at the top of the stairs. "You had me worried."

Victoria headed toward the stairwell. "I got involved in research."

"Do you want a hand coming down the stairs?"

"No, thank you."

"I'll carry your magazine for you."

Once they were back in the cookroom, Victoria shooed McCavity out of her chair, where he'd been curled up, and sat down.

"What was it you've been trying to tell me?"

"Where's Dahlia?"

Victoria looked up. "She's avoiding you, Howland. What's the matter between you two?"

"I won't go into that now. Where did she go?"

"Vineyard Haven, I think. What do you want to tell me? Why don't you sit down?"

McCavity had seated himself in Howland's chair, and when Howland lifted him up, the cat snarled at him. "Sorry about that, Cavvy." Howland sat down with McCavity in his lap. McCavity immediately jumped down, stalked into the kitchen, and stood by the door.

"He can wait," said Victoria, as Howland started to get up. "Now tell me."

"Something about Dahlia and her associates hasn't seemed right, so when I was in Washington, I looked up their personnel records."

"I thought that was private information."

"With three of the five murdered, I had good reason for requesting their files."

"And what did you find?" Victoria asked.

"All five have satisfactory records as civil servants, not stellar, but adequate. Then I looked up the health records of all five. All five are reasonably healthy. One had poor eyesight, corrected by glasses. Another was slightly overweight. One had elevated cholesterol levels. Four of the five are exactly what they seem to be."

"And the fifth?" Victoria asked. "What's the matter with the fifth?"

"Nothing," Howland answered. "The fifth is perfectly healthy."

"Dahlia?" Victoria asked.

Howland nodded. "There's no indication of cancer in her health records."

"Perhaps the cancer was diagnosed only recently?"

He shook his head. "Not likely. Her latest physical exam was only three months ago. She had a clean bill of health."

"But she's taking Taxol treatments at the hospital," Victoria protested. "She wouldn't be going through that if she weren't desperate. She's lost her hair. She's obviously ill. She looks terrible."

"She's faking, Victoria."

"Never," said Victoria.

Howland set his elbows on the table and clasped his hands. "I can't access her Island hospital records, at least not without going through a lot of red tape. But perhaps you can do some undercover detective work."

"What happened between you that makes you distrust her so?"

Howland sighed. "Everything," he said. "She's not what she seems. Find out for yourself, Victoria."

For the rest of the afternoon, Victoria found herself recalling what Howland had said about his cousin, and getting more and more angry with him.

When Dahlia returned before sunset, Victoria was still steaming.

"How was your meeting with Howland?" Dahlia asked.

"Aggravating," said Victoria.

"I was afraid of that."

Dahlia's face was pale. She had deep creases between her hairless eyebrows and on either side of her nose. Dark circles ringed her eyes. Victoria thought about Howland's accusation of fakery, and got angry all over again. She said softly, "How are you feeling, Dahlia?"

"I'm fine, thanks, Victoria. I expected to feel much worse. I'm tired, that's all. But then I'm not as young as I used to be." She smiled at Victoria. "When I'm around you, I feel ashamed of complaining about aging."

"When do you have to go for your next treatment?"

"Wednesday. Only once a week, thank goodness."

Victoria got up from her chair. "Let's have a cup of tea and forget about Howland."

"I believe I'll pass, Victoria. Thank you, though. I'm going to lie down."

Victoria brewed herself a cup of tea and thought again about Howland. What a cruel thing to say about his cousin, she thought. How unfair. Dahlia truly was exhausted. She certainly wasn't faking the missing hair.

She reached for the phone and called Casey at home. "Tomorrow's Sunday, I know, and it's not my usual day to read to the elderly. But . . ."

"But you'd like me to take you to the hospital, right? Okay, Victoria. I'll pick you up after church."

During the night icicles formed along the edge of the gutters. The morning had a spring-like feel to it, and Victoria could hear the constant drip of water. The ruts Casey had plowed in the snow yesterday were now sandy lines.

When Casey pulled up, Victoria was waiting.

"I don't know what this hospital trip is

all about, Victoria, but I suppose you'll tell me eventually?"

"Reading to the elderly," Victoria said primly.

"Sure," said Casey, as she pulled out of the drive. "How long do you plan to be?"

"The usual," said Victoria. "About an hour. They fall asleep if I read much longer."

The snowplows had come through during the storm, and shoved great piles of snow to the sides of the roads. The snow was melting now, leaving black scallops of wetness on the asphalt road surface.

Casey slowed as the car ahead of her turned onto a side road, then sped up again. At the end of Old County Road, they turned onto State Road, where tall pine trees shaded the road. An occasional lump of snow dropped from the trees onto the paved surface ahead of them with a splat. They drove past Main Street in Vineyard Haven, skirted the harbor, and Casey slowed at the hospital entrance.

"I have a few errands to do, Victoria. I'll meet you in front of the main entrance."

"Drop me off at the emergency entrance, if you will."

"That's miles away from the nursing home wing," Casey said.

Victoria stared straight ahead.

Casey grinned. "Okay, Deputy." She continued around the sharp curve that led to the back parking lot, and pulled up in front of the emergency entrance.

Victoria slid out of her seat with her lilac-wood walking stick and pushed through the doors into the waiting room.

Doc Jeffers was at the desk doing paperwork. He stood when she entered, lifted his motorcycle helmet off the counter, and stowed it under his chair. He was wearing a blue scrub suit. Tufts of white hair showed in the V of the shirt. "Good morning, Victoria. Is everything all right?"

"Fine," said Victoria. "I thought I'd drop by and say hello, since I was passing this way."

"Always glad to see you. Pretty quiet this morning."

"Dahlia Atherton hasn't come by, has she?"

"She usually comes on Wednesdays," Doc Jeffers said.

Victoria nodded. "Who administers the Taxol, one of the doctors or a technician?"

"Taxol?" Doc Jeffers looked blank. "What about Taxol?"

"I realize you can't discuss patients or their treatments, but I was wondering, in a

343

general way, where do you administer Taxol? And how?"

"We don't," said Doc Jeffers.

"Because of privacy?" Victoria asked.

He shook his head. "Nothing to do with confidentiality. We have no patients undergoing Taxol treatments at the hospital."

"None?" said Victoria, leaning on her stick.

"None," said Doc Jeffers firmly.

"But Dahlia is coming in on Wednesdays?"

He laughed. "She plays Scrabble with the folks in the nursing wing."

"But she's being treated for cancer?"

"I don't know anything about that," Doc Jeffers said. "I wouldn't tell you if I did know. I can confirm that Dahlia's signed up for Scrabble on Wednesday. Want to look at the volunteers' schedule? You're on for tomorrow, I believe."

Victoria sighed. "No, thank you. Do you mind if I read to the elderly today instead of tomorrow?"

"Go right ahead. The wing is a long trek from here. Want to borrow a wheelchair?"

"Of course not." Victoria turned and strode down the long hall, swinging her lilac stick.

"So what did you find out?" Casey asked, after she'd helped Victoria into the passenger seat. "Can you tell me now?"

Victoria took a deep breath and let it out slowly. "Dahlia apparently is not undergoing treatment for cancer."

"What do you mean?"

"No one is getting Taxol treatments."

"Are you serious? I've taken Dahlia to the hospital and picked her up again, myself."

"She plays Scrabble."

"Whew!" said Casey. "That gives us something to think about."

Casey drove out of the hospital's main entrance, and turned toward Vineyard Haven. The harbor was on their right. The topsail schooner *Shenandoah* rode at anchor, masts and spars silhouetted against the snow-covered town on the other side of the harbor. The ferry *Islander* rounded the jetty and Victoria heard its whistle.

"Why would she go to all the trouble of faking cancer? That doesn't make sense. Unless she is the killer."

Victoria shook her head. "She can't be the killer. Whether she's undergoing treatment or not, she's not well. Certainly not strong enough to kill three big men." Victoria wound down her window and adjusted the rearview mirror. "She wants those gemstones, that's why she pretended to need expensive treatment. She doesn't know where the stones are, and I haven't told her."

"Don't," Casey warned.

"A share of the stones is hers, legitimately. I'd probably fake an illness myself, if two million dollars was involved."

"No, you wouldn't," said Casey. "Not even if the ante was ten million. First thing tomorrow, we take the stones to the bank."

"I wish she hadn't faked her illness. She didn't need to."

"She thinks she did."

Chapter 22

Casey pulled into Victoria's driveway, splashing through meltwater rivulets. A gust of wind shook the bare branches of the maple and plopped a clump of wet snow onto the hood of Dahlia's car.

"I suppose you're going to confront her?" Casey said.

Victoria nodded.

"In that case, I'd better stick around."

"You needn't. Junior will be looking out for her."

"He's not guarding her full time, Victoria. I don't have that kind of manpower."

"This is supposed to be your day off." Victoria eased out of the Bronco. "I know how to reach you if I need you."

She waited on the steps until Casey drove off, then went inside. Dahlia was coming out of her room. Behind her, Bacchus was barking steadily.

"I'm sorry he's making such a racket, Victoria. That must be annoying to you."

"I've gotten used to him," Victoria said. "How about a cup of tea now?"

"Lovely," said Dahlia. "I'm afraid I don't have any more yerba maté to offer you." She smiled broadly at Victoria. "Do you have any Constant Comment left?"

Victoria reached into the cupboard for her collection of tea. "Earl Grey will have to do."

McCavity appeared from the dining room and rubbed against Victoria's legs. She leaned down and scratched his head, stroked the soft heart-shaped white patch under his chin.

Dahlia carried the tea tray into the cookroom. McCavity settled on Victoria's lap, his paws dangling over her knees, his eyes half-closed.

Dahlia reached over and petted the cat. "Did you have a good morning, Victoria?"

"Fine." Victoria poured tea and handed a cup to Dahlia. "After church, I went to the hospital to read to the elderly."

"Don't you usually read on Mondays?"

"Usually." Victoria sipped her tea. "I understand you've been volunteering at the nursing wing, too."

Dahlia shifted in her chair. "Yes. I've been playing Scrabble." She cleared her throat. "Age doesn't seem to affect their word skills."

"Didn't you say Wednesday is the day

you go for your Taxol treatment?"

Dahlia set her cup in its saucer. "Yes, Wednesdays."

"The same day you play Scrabble?"

Dahlia put her hands in her lap and looked down. "Have you spoken to my doctor?"

"Doctors don't discuss their cases with ordinary people," Victoria said. "But I learned that the hospital has no patients undergoing Taxol treatment."

Dahlia sighed and moved her cup and saucer away from her.

"Why did you find it necessary to lie?" Victoria asked.

"I'm sorry, Victoria. You've been good to me."

"Why?" Victoria's eyes were hooded.

Dahlia twined her fingers around each other in her lap. "I had what I thought was a good reason."

"Can you tell me?"

Dahlia nodded. "It dates back to childhood summers with Howland and our families. He was in frail health as a child, and got all the attention from both his parents and mine. You have no idea how difficult my summers were. You didn't know our family then. We were summer people."

Victoria listened, eyes half closed.

"Being seriously ill, even fatally ill, seemed like a way to even the score," Dahlia finished.

"That doesn't make any sense at all," Victoria said. "You're not staying with Howland. You're staying with me."

"Things didn't work out the way I thought they would."

Victoria lifted McCavity off her lap and set him on the floor. "You came here to disinter the uncut gemstones, not to get even with Howland."

"What can I say?" Dahlia stood up and started to pace the small room. "The stones are gone. I went to all that trouble for nothing. Years and years of collecting. Years of planning."

"The stones will show up eventually," Victoria said. "It's fortunate that you aren't ill after all, and aren't desperate for the money."

"But I *am* desperate for the money." Dahlia looked away from Victoria's fixed gaze. "Being ill seemed an acceptable reason for recovering the stones early." She stopped.

"Go on," said Victoria.

Dahlia paced, then turned and paced back. "I invested in stocks at the height of the euphoria about dot-com companies,

350

and borrowed money from a former col-
league, who turned out to be with the
Mob. They want their money. Now."

"I hope the loan was not as much as the
gems will bring you, two million dollars?"

"More. Much more. I invested in a sure
thing."

Victoria looked away from Dahlia, at the
snowy landscape, and thought about her
sweepstakes entries. "The stock market is
hardly a sure thing," she said. "What did
you use for collateral?"

Dahlia continued to pace. "Everything I
own. My house in Potomac. My summer
place in the Adirondacks. My car. My
share in a horse farm near Middleburg."

"What about Howland's house?"

"That too. Everything."

Victoria traced circles around a stain on
the tablecloth with her spoon. "It seems to
me, that explanation is more acceptable
than lying about an illness you don't have,
trivializing cancer and its treatment the
way you've done."

"What can I say?" Dahlia stopped pacing.

Victoria frowned. "Three of your associates have been murdered. Yet you seem
more concerned about the gems than their
deaths. Aren't you afraid you might be
next?"

Dahlia started pacing again. "I've got to find those stones." The cookroom was so small her pacing consisted of only three steps. "Everything went wrong," Dahlia continued. "The hearse was delayed by the snowstorm. The grave diggers couldn't locate the coffin because some boy . . ."

"Lucretia's son, Sonny."

". . . some boy moved a gravestone as a Halloween prank. When they finally found the coffin, the undertaker decided it was junk, and trashed it." Dahlia's long skirt swung about her legs. She took off her cap and tossed it onto the table. It was the first time Victoria had seen Dahlia without the hat. Dahlia's hair was growing back in short, dark bristles.

Victoria picked up the cap and smoothed it out on the table. "You shaved your head?"

"And my eyebrows." Dahlia clasped her hands behind her. Without the hat, her head looked naked and too heavy for her neck.

"The stones are safe," Victoria said.

Dahlia stopped abruptly. "What makes you think that? Lucretia Woods's boyfriend cut up the coffin and threw the pieces in a Dumpster."

"You know who Lucretia's boyfriend is, don't you?" Victoria asked.

Dahlia stood still. "Should I know?"

"He goes by the name Meyer," Victoria answered. "The name Meyer is an anagram for the name Emery."

Dahlia's face grew even paler, and she sat abruptly. "Emery!" She let out a deep breath. "How long has he been on the Island?"

"He came here for the first time about three months ago," Victoria said. "He's been off and on since then."

"Almost exactly three months ago I told Red, Mort, Tremont, and Herb that I had to have my share of the money."

"Three months," Victoria repeated. "That was when Red started working at Rose Haven, wasn't it?"

"He applied for the job so we would have one of us in place at the funeral home." Dahlia sat back and stretched her legs out under the table. "How did Emery find out?" Dahlia murmured. "Who told him?"

In mid-afternoon, at the same time Victoria and Dahlia were talking, Meyer caught up with Herb Plante at the bed-and-breakfast on Daggett Avenue. He had parked Lucretia's car halfway down the block where he could watch for anyone coming out of the house onto the porch. No cars passed. After an hour's wait, Herb Plante came to the front door. Meyer could see the dog inside, carrying a stuffed toy in his mouth and wagging his tail. Herb tousled the dog's head and closed the door behind him.

He stepped off the porch, came down the broken concrete walkway, paused, looked up and down the street, reached into his pocket, and eased around the front of the dark Ford parked under the oak tree.

Meyer silently closed the door of Lucretia's car, strolled casually down the middle of Daggett Avenue, and stopped next to the dark Ford.

Herb froze, about to put his key in the lock. "You!" His voice shook.

Meyer leaned his hand against the roof of the Ford. "Right." His pale eyes glittered.

"What do you want?"

"Three guesses," said Meyer.

"I don't have the stones."

"I know that." Meyer crossed one leg over the other and leaned on the car.

"I don't know where they are." Herb's forehead was beginning to glisten.

"I know that, too."

Herb took a linen handkerchief out of his suit coat pocket and wiped his forehead and the top of his head. "You've found them."

"Do you think I'd tell you if I had the ice?"

Herb dropped his hands by his side. "What do you want?"

Meyer grinned. "Three down. Two to go."

"You'll never find the stones by killing me."

Meyer laughed aloud. "I want you very much alive. Give me your car key." He held out his hand.

Herb didn't move. "You've got a gun?"

Meyer grinned again, baring his white teeth. "As you well know, I don't need a gun. Car key, please."

Herb handed him the key with a shaking hand, and Meyer unlocked the driver's door. "Get in," he said. "You're driving. I'll give you the key when I'm in the passenger seat."

Herb sat behind the wheel, hands in his lap. Meyer opened the passenger door, sat, slammed the door shut, and passed the key to Herb.

Meyer waved his hands like a conductor. "Start 'er up."

"Where are we going?" Herb's voice whined.

"Put the key in the ignition and turn it," Meyer said. "We're going to West Tisbury."

Dahlia snatched up her cap, stormed out of the house, got into her car, spun out of the driveway, and turned onto Old County Road. She turned again after a short distance onto Amos Coffin Road, and parked in Lucretia's driveway. She stalked up to the front door and pounded on the doorbell.

Lucretia answered immediately. "What's wrong?" She was out of breath. "You're Dahlia Atherton, aren't you? What's the matter?"

"Let me in. I've got to talk to you," Dahlia said.

Lucretia stepped aside, and Dahlia marched past her.

"What's the matter? What's going on?" Lucretia closed the door and followed Dahlia to the table by the back window. The roses Meyer had given her were bright against the remaining snowdrifts in the backyard.

Dahlia sat down and pushed her hat back on her forehead. "I've just had some terrible, terrible news."

Lucretia remained standing. "What are you talking about? What news?"

"Your friend, Meyer?"

Lucretia sat abruptly. "What about Meyer? Has anything happened to him?"

Dahlia shook her head. "His name is not Meyer."

"What on earth are you talking about?" Lucretia sat forward and clasped her hands between her jeans-clad legs.

"He's an assassin." Dahlia stared at Lucretia.

"Are you out of your mind?" Lucretia's hands tightened.

"His name is Emery. He's a contract killer for the CIA."

Lucretia pushed her chair back and stood up, bright pink splotches on her cheeks. "How dare you!" she said. "Get out of my house!"

Dahlia remained where she was. "You've got to listen to me. I was with the Foreign Service. I've known him for years."

Lucretia set her hands on her hips. "So you're the one who called me. Asking about the coffin on behalf of the Foreign Service?" She pointed to the door. "Get out of here."

Dahlia continued to sit. "You've got to listen to me. How long have you known him?"

Lucretia didn't answer.

Dahlia went on, "Three months? That was when we decided to disinter the coffin. Three months ago."

"What *are* you talking about?"

"Does your Meyer ever go out in public? Does he disappear for days with no explanation? Do you know anything about his background?"

Lucretia said nothing.

"Well, does he?"

Lucretia folded her arms across her chest. "What Meyer and I do is none of your business."

"He's a killer named Emery, I tell you. He's after those gems . . ."

"What!?" Lucretia stepped back. "You're crazy!"

"The gemstones — my gemstones — were hidden in the coffin, and he's stolen them."

Lucretia backed away still farther and started to reach for the telephone. "I'm calling the police."

"You do that. Have them arrest him for murder."

A door opened somewhere, letting out a blast of loud music. "Mom?" Heavy boots clumped down the stairs, and Sonny appeared, tucking in a sleeveless Harley-

Davidson T-shirt. "What's going on? I'm trying to study."

"Nothing." Lucretia set the phone down. "Go back to your room."

"Something *is* going on," said Dahlia. "Your mother doesn't want to know her boyfriend is a killer."

Sonny laughed. "Who, Meyer?"

"Emery," Dahlia said.

"Huh?" Sonny scratched his head.

"His real name is Emery."

"Well, he scared the shit out of me the other day, you know. Said he could, like, kill me easy, or shit like that."

"What do you mean?" Lucretia stared at her son in horror.

"I tell Denise that Meyer paid me to take the coffin to the airport. Denise, like, tells her father. Her father tells you. When Meyer finds out he goes ape-shit. Practically, you know, strangles me. Right there." He pointed to the driveway.

Dahlia turned to Lucretia. "Do you believe me now?"

Lucretia shook her head as if trying to clear it.

"Sonny?" A soft voice floated down from upstairs.

"C'mon down," said Sonny. "Denise and me been studying," he explained.

Denise came down the stairs, tightening the belt that held up her jeans and combing her fingers through her long hair.

Lucretia sat down again. "I know Meyer took the coffin to the airport."

"*I* took it to the airport," Sonny said. "He paid me, you know, to take that thing to his storage unit."

Lucretia said, "Meyer was helping the town by disposing of rubbish." She looked from Dahlia to Sonny to Denise and back to Dahlia. "That coffin was nothing but a piece of junk."

"The foot of the coffin held ten million dollars' worth of gemstones. He must have found the stones."

"There wasn't no foot to the coffin," Sonny said.

Dahlia looked at him blankly. "What do you mean?"

"Meyer got, like, mad when we delivered the coffin to the storage unit because the back was missing. We thought, you know, he wasn't going to pay up."

"What happened to that piece?" asked Dahlia.

Sonny shrugged. "Who knows?"

A pickup truck pulled into the drive behind Dahlia's car.

"Here's my father." Denise made a face.

"I gotta go. See you, Sonny."

Lucretia got up again, opened the door, and Denny limped in. She shut the door. "I need to talk to you," she said.

Denny smirked. "My little girl misbehaving again?"

Dahlia spoke up from her seat at the table. "It's about the coffin."

"I thought that was a dead issue." Denny smirked again.

"Not funny," said Lucretia.

Dahlia turned her chair so she faced Denny. "You took it from the funeral home to the shed behind Town Hall, is that right?"

Denny nodded.

"Was it intact when you got to Town Hall?" Dahlia asked.

"Nope. The back fell off on the way."

"What happened to that piece?" said Dahlia.

"At the time, I wasn't aware that it had fallen off."

"What happened to it?" Dahlia said again.

"Will you let me explain?" Denny said.

Dahlia sat back, arms folded.

"That piece was held on with rusted sheet metal screws, rusted through, you understand."

Dahlia sighed.

"Chief O'Neill, who was following me, saw the piece fall off, so she stopped and picked it up."

"Then what?" said Dahlia.

"Lady, let me talk, will you? The chief had to respond to a call about a dead body washed up on the beach, and by the time she got around to reuniting the back of the coffin with the front, the coffin had disappeared."

Dahlia sighed again. "So the piece is in the police car?"

Denny moved farther into the room, looked around, and settled on the couch. "Let me finish. The chief didn't want that piece of crap sliding around in the back of her Bronco, scratching the finish, so she put it someplace until she could figure out what was going on." As Dahlia started to interrupt, he held up his hand. "I have no idea where she put that piece of crap, and I don't much care. Does that answer your question?"

"Where is it?" said Dahlia, putting her head in her hands. "Where? Where? Where?"

The dark Ford pulled up in front of Victoria's entry. Herb Plante got out of the driver's seat and walked toward the house with his head down. Meyer followed with an odd smile that Victoria couldn't interpret.

She greeted them at the door.

Herb continued to look at the ground.

Meyer gave Victoria a bright smile. "You haven't forgotten our bargain, have you?"

"What bar . . ." Victoria started to say, but finished with, "Oh?"

She shut the door behind the two men and led the way into the cookroom. "Sherry?" she asked brightly.

"Not until our friend signs his confession."

"Confession?" Herb sounded alarmed. "What confession?"

"Write it in your own words," said Meyer. "Here's a piece of paper. Give him a pen, Mrs. Trumbull."

"Are you out of your mind?" Herb adjusted his glasses and ran his hand over his short hair. "What's going on?"

"I'm not going to influence what you write," said Meyer. "A pen, please, Mrs. Trumbull."

Victoria selected a pen from the marmalade jar next to the phone and gave it to Herb. He stared at the pen as if he'd never seen one before.

"In your own words," said Meyer. "Take your time."

Herb peered at Meyer through his thick lenses, then bent down to the paper. When he'd finished writing, he handed the paper to Meyer, who read, " 'I bought uncut rubies during my postings in Sri Lanka from people who didn't know what they were selling me. I then sent the stones back to the U.S. in the diplomatic pouch. I realize now this was probably illegal.' " Meyer laughed and tossed the paper back to Herb. "Joker," he said. "Very amusing." He drummed on the table with his fingers. "Mrs. Trumbull and I have an agreement. I agreed to hand her the killer in exchange for something she has."

"The killer? Me? You think I'm the killer? *You* trying to blame *me?*" Herb sat back. His glasses had slipped down his nose. "*Me?*" He pointed to himself. "Let's get this straight, right now. I'm getting the police chief over here, right now." He reached for the phone. "Do you mind if I use your phone, Mrs. Trumbull?"

"Wait," said Victoria.

Herb set the phone on the table. "I know who the killer is, and it's not me."

Victoria looked at Meyer. "Herb can't be the killer if he was in Brazil, as he says."

"Herb never went to Brazil. He and Mort drove the hearse from West Virginia, and on the ferry coming over, he tossed Mort overboard." He turned to Plante. "You didn't realize Mort had the keys in his pocket. That really screwed you up, didn't it, Herb?"

Herb was shaking his head violently. "My God, no. I had nothing to do with Mort's murder." He reached into his pocket. "Besides, I have my own keys."

Meyer gazed at Herb for a moment, then went on. "You and Tremont went for a drive, you killed him, took him to the dump, then doused the pile with kerosene, figuring the body would be burnt beyond recognition."

"This is outrageous!"

"You bungled both of those killings, a real amateur."

"You're wrong, all wrong!" Herb sputtered. "Mrs. Trumbull, you have to listen to me."

Victoria looked from one to the other.

Meyer went on. "The yerba maté supposedly sent from Brazil . . ."

"What yerba maté?" Herb's face was covered with perspiration.

"You were hoping we'd think you mailed it from Brazil. You bungled that, too. The maté was obviously from you. If Mrs. Trumbull hadn't noticed something wrong,

Dahlia would have been victim number four."

"I didn't send her anything. I wouldn't have known where to send it if I did," Herb protested.

"Then Red. Easy enough. He trusted you, and would have shown you that cooler, not expecting you to lock him in. Did it occur to you that with four of the original five dead, you're the obvious killer?"

"Wait one goddamned minute." Herb stood and pointed at Meyer. "You're the one." He jabbed his finger for emphasis. "I actually suspected Dahlia until I saw you on that bicycle the other night. None of us knew you were anywhere near the Island. You're the only one who needed to kill. The rest of us would get our share of the stones. One hell of a lot of money. Plenty. Not so with you. You have no compunctions about killing. You knew our plans. You got here early, as soon as you heard we were going to unearth the coffin. You cozied up to that woman official, bungled the killings on purpose so it looked like an amateur's job. No one would believe a professional like you would be so sloppy."

"I want my share of that ice," said Meyer. "But I don't waste effort, killing people when I don't need to."

"Wait!" said Victoria again. "There's something neither of you knows."

Both men stopped and turned to her. Meyer's face was set in rigid lines. Herb's face was pasty.

"Dahlia does not have cancer."

"What?" said Herb.

"What makes you think that?" asked Meyer.

"Are you sure?" said Herb.

"How do you know?" asked Meyer.

Herb sat again. "Why would she fake something like that?"

"She's desperate for money." Victoria tapped her fingers on the table.

"Where is she now?" said Meyer.

"I believe she went to Lucretia's," Victoria replied. "She was hoping Lucretia knows where to find the jewels. And she's blaming you, Meyer, for the murders."

Meyer scratched the back of his neck. "We know, don't we. Lucretia doesn't have the stones."

Victoria smiled.

Herb sat back in his chair. "I don't give a damn about the stones. They're jinxed. I don't really need the money. I hope they're gone for good. We five were naïve and stupid, and look at us now." He took a deep breath. "Opportunists, that's all we were. Opportunists."

"Wonder where I heard that before," Meyer muttered.

"So we've narrowed down the list," Herb said. "Dahlia or him," he pointed to Meyer.

Victoria had been quiet. Finally she said to Herb, "Do you still have your airplane ticket stubs?"

"You get electronic tickets these days," said Meyer. "No ticket stubs."

"A stamped passport?" Victoria asked.

"I left it at the bed-and-breakfast," Herb replied.

"Sure," said Meyer.

"That can be checked," said Victoria. "The way things stand now, Dahlia blames you, Meyer. You blame Herb. Herb first blamed Dahlia, now you."

"If I'd been killed," Herb jabbed a finger at Meyer, "everything would point to you."

Meyer shook his head. "I'm no amateur."

"Dahlia is likely to be back soon," Victoria said. "I believe I can sort things out, if she doesn't know you two are around."

Herb stood. "I'll move my car."

"I'm going with you," said Meyer. He turned and saluted Victoria. " 'Good fences make good neighbors,' " he said.

Victoria laughed. " '. . . you have done a good deal right, don't do the last thing wrong.' "

"What was that for?" said Herb.

"Frost's fan club," said Meyer.

Victoria opened the door that led into the woodshed. "You can hear anything that's said in the cookroom from here."

Dahlia returned a half hour later, her face flushed. Victoria was sorting her mail.

"Since you don't have to pretend to be undergoing chemotherapy anymore, would you care for a glass of sherry?" Victoria looked up from the sweepstakes envelope she had opened.

"Thank you, Victoria. This has been a difficult day. May I bring in a glass for you, too?"

"Please," said Victoria.

Dahlia returned with two glasses of sherry and settled into her chair with a groan.

"Did you talk to Lucretia?"

"I talked not only to Lucretia, but to Sonny, Denny, and Denise."

"Did you explain to her about Meyer and Emery?"

"She didn't want to believe me. But then Sonny told his mother that Meyer had threatened him, and she began to understand what kind of person she's been consorting with."

"Were they able to help you locate the gemstones?"

Dahlia smiled. "I think so, Victoria."

"That must be a load off your mind."

"I seem to have traced the stones back to you."

Chapter 23

"To me?" Victoria opened her eyes wide.

Dahlia took off her cap and tossed it onto the table. "It's possible you don't realize you have the stones right here."

Victoria waited, turning her untouched glass of sherry around and around.

Dahlia continued. "I learned from Denny that the police chief picked up that panel that fell off. And you were in the police vehicle at the time, weren't you?"

Victoria nodded.

"That piece contained the stones."

"Really," said Victoria.

Dahlia sat back and placed her hands on the table. "Where is that piece now, Victoria?"

"It's been destroyed," Victoria said.

"You can't be serious!" Dahlia stood, her skirt swinging around her legs. "How could that be?"

"That panel was nothing but rubbish," Victoria said.

"Where was it discarded? Who did it?"

"I believe it was Meyer — or Emery —

who found the piece in my cellar and disposed of it."

Dahlia sat again. "Oh no! No, no, no!" She put her arms on the table and rested her head. Victoria noticed a dark mole on the back of her scalp. Dahlia lifted her head again. Her eyes were red-rimmed. "What will I do now? After all the time and effort I've invested. Only to have the stones lost!"

Victoria said nothing.

Dahlia sat up. "Emery is the killer, Victoria. You realize that, don't you? When I learned the yerba maté was poisoned, I was sure Herb was responsible. But now it's clear who the killer is. You can see that, can't you? Emery. It's Emery."

"How did he kill your three colleagues?" Victoria asked in a firm voice.

Dahlia lifted her glass and sipped the sherry. "This tastes wonderful, Victoria. Just what I needed. I'm so sorry I deceived you about the Taxol treatment. But you understand, don't you?"

Victoria toyed with her glass and waited.

"I've been thinking about this for some time," Dahlia said. "Emery had the idea in the first place of burying the stones in a coffin. And he must have guessed we'd bury the coffin here in West Tisbury. You understand?"

Victoria looked up and nodded.

"As soon as he learned we were going to exhume the coffin, he came here, to the Island." Dahlia paused and drank her sherry in one long swallow.

"I'm sure you're right about that," Victoria said. "Would you like a bit more sherry?"

Dahlia rose to her feet. "I'll get it."

After Dahlia had refilled her glass, Victoria said, "And killed Mort?"

"Right. I think Emery rode the ferry to Woods Hole when he knew the hearse was due. He had a chance on the return trip, after the hearse was aboard, to lure Mort onto the upper deck. Emery could have stunned Mort by hitting him on the side of the head with something he picked up, or even with his fist. Then he could easily have lifted Mort over the rail. No one would see the body go over; it was dark and foggy that night."

"Yes, I remember," said Victoria. "Wasn't Tremont killed first?"

"Yes, he was." Dahlia finished her sherry and poured herself more. "Emery probably met Tremont at his motel and they went out to dinner together. Coming back, he could have detoured by the dump fire. The fire department wasn't at the dump all the time, you know. Not before the fire flared up again."

Victoria nodded.

"Emery must have beaten Tremont to death with a tire iron or something. Then" — Dahlia took another sip of sherry — "he'd have to have dragged the body over to the stump pile and covered it with branches. He probably splashed some kerosene around. I guess he didn't have enough to soak the body but it would have made the fire flare up."

"Did he think the fire would consume the body?"

"I imagine so."

"What about Red?" asked Victoria. "That couldn't have been easy to arrange."

"Red trusted Emery. Red was planning to leave the next morning on the early boat. So when Emery showed up, Red would have been surprised, but not suspicious."

Victoria nodded. "It must not have been easy to get Red to go inside the cooler."

"Not for Emery; he's a professional killer. He could have knocked Red out and dragged him into the cooler. All he had to do was take off the door handle — with a Swiss Army knife, even, or maybe something he found in the place there. While

Red was unconscious, I guess he'd have closed the door, turned the temperature down as far as it would go, and left him to die."

"It seems to me," said Victoria, watching Dahlia, "that the murders were terribly amateurish. Emery must be a stupid man."

"They were not amateurish at all," said Dahlia heatedly. "Not at all." She flushed. "He always planned everything carefully, months in advance. Not the work of a stupid person."

Victoria swirled her untouched sherry. "Emery destroyed the coffin panel. What about the gems?"

"I think you know where they are, Victoria." Dahlia's eyes were glazed. Her bare head seemed oddly alien. "We can work together, you and I. You're a gambler. If we can trap Emery, we can share the money."

"Trap him?" Victoria repeated.

"If he were to die, by accident, of course, that would be the end of all this." Dahlia waved a hand dismissively.

Victoria got up stiffly from her seat. "Dahlia, I'll go with you to the police station and you can turn yourself in."

"*Me?* What are you talking about, Victoria?" Dahlia pursed her lips. "I told you, it was Emery who killed them."

"You've told me in detail what only the killer would know." Victoria paused. "Details the police haven't released yet."

Dahlia stood and looked around her.

Victoria braced herself and took a deep breath. She realized her lilac-wood stick was leaning against the bookcase, just out of her reach and within Dahlia's.

Dahlia's eyes lighted up when she saw the stick. She seized it. "You're making me do this, Victoria. I didn't want to harm you." She tightened her grip on the stick. "I'm so sorry!"

"No, Dahlia, don't! Help! Somebody — help!"

"There's no one to hear you."

With a loud crash, Meyer and Herb burst through the door together, the wood around the latch splintering as they came in.

At the same moment, Victoria heard the police siren approach, wail into her driveway, and wind down to a stop. The two men seized Dahlia and twisted her arms behind her back. Victoria's stick dropped on the floor and Meyer kicked it out of the way. Casey raced up the steps, through the entry, tore open the kitchen door, and strode into the cookroom with Junior right behind her.

"Dahlia Atherton, you're under arrest," Casey said.

Victoria sank into her chair, breathless. "How did you know it was Dahlia?" she asked Casey.

Casey snapped handcuffs on the struggling woman. "I'm arresting you for threatening and intimidating Selectman Lucretia Woods."

After Casey, Junior, and Victoria had driven away with Dahlia in the police Bronco, Herb and Meyer sat down at the table.

Meyer examined the splintered door. "I suppose we'd better fix that for her."

"Right," Herb agreed. He wiped his handkerchief across his forehead. "I'm glad that's over." He dried his hands. "Sorry I suspected you, Emery." He picked up the sherry bottle and held it up to the light. "Not a drop left." He set the bottle down again.

"No harm done," said Meyer. "I owe you an apology, too. Seems like you lost out on just about everything."

"I'm alive. And I've got the hearse," said Herb. "What more can I ask?" He put his handkerchief back in his pocket, adjusted his glasses, and examined his hands. "I'd better wash up."

"Go right ahead," said Meyer. "You might want to take a shower while you're at it. After all that action, you're kind of ripe." He wrinkled his nose.

"I suppose Victoria won't mind." Herb turned before he disappeared into the bathroom. "Can I give you a ride anywhere?"

"I'd appreciate your dropping me off in Vineyard Haven."

"Be glad to. Picking up your girlfriend's car?"

Meyer smiled. "Something like that."

When Herb finally emerged, his face and hands scrubbed pink, his hair damp, Meyer was coming out of the woodshed, shrugging into his backpack.

They drove to Vineyard Haven in silence, past the Tashmoo overlook with Vineyard Sound and the mainland in the distance, past the Black Dog's railroad dining car, past the nursery, closed now for the season.

Herb turned onto Daggett Avenue and parked under the oak tree in front of the bed-and-breakfast where he was staying. The dog came to the door and barked. The two men shook hands.

Meyer walked back to Lucretia's car, got

into the driver's seat, started up the car, and drove to the ferry. He left Lucretia's car in a two-hour parking zone, went into the terminal, bought a one-way ticket, and boarded the *Islander* with several minutes to spare.

When Casey arrived at Victoria's the next morning, the expression on her face was a peculiar mixture of emotions. "Did you have to go through all those theatrics, Victoria?"

"How else could we have nabbed her?"

"Not 'we,' Victoria. The police. She'd have tripped up sooner or later."

"After she'd killed Meyer? Or Herb Plante? Or both?"

"She'd have been under custody at Noodles's insistence."

"Lucretia, not Noodles," Victoria said absently. "They'd have kept her only overnight, at most."

Casey slumped into a chair. "Ouch." She shifted her belt to one side. "What I can't figure, Victoria, is the whole yerba maté caper. Why'd she do that? Suppose you'd brewed the stuff?"

"She gambled on the fact that I know my plants." Victoria patted her white hair. "Even if I hadn't recognized the *Taxus* in

379

the canister, she'd have found an excuse not to drink the tea. She wanted us to think she was in danger, and for a while, we actually believed she was."

"Howland stopped by the police station this morning for a chat."

"Oh?"

"He told me he'd looked up the deed for his place at the courthouse. He's sole owner. Dahlia has no part of it."

"Poor Dahlia."

"Poor Howland," Casey said. "Dahlia's asked him to take care of Bacchus until she's out of stir. I think he's got the bird permanently."

Victoria started to say something, then stopped.

"What were you about to say?"

"I was going to offer to take Bacchus until I remembered McCavity's feelings."

"And Elizabeth's." Casey stood again. "We've got to get those stones to a safe-deposit box right away, Victoria. I swear, sometimes I'm convinced they don't even exist."

They went from the cookroom into the plant-filled woodshed. Sunlight poured through the south-facing windows and filtered through the leaves of Victoria's orchid plants, her geraniums, the avocado tree she'd grown from seed, the ginger plant that had never bloomed.

The fire was out in the woodstove. Victoria braced herself on the still warm cast-iron top and knelt in front of the stove. She used a potholder to open the iron door and peered in at the bed of gray ash mixed with a few unburned chunks of wood. She stirred the ashes with a stick of kindling, exposing still-glowing embers. And there, underneath the dying fire, like a giant roast potato wrapped in aluminum foil, was the metal fruitcake tin she'd hidden.

Victoria fished the tin from the bottom of the stove with the potholder and the kindling stick, and dropped it onto the cement floor with a metallic rattle.

"There it is," she said, looking up at Casey with a broad grin wreathed in wrinkles.

"This I gotta see," said Casey, moving in close to Victoria. "Ten million bucks' worth of ice. Something to tell my grandkids."

Victoria tugged off the outer aluminum foil and exposed the red and green tin with a picture of a laughing Santa Claus, his white beard and the white trim on his red coat yellowed from heat. The tin had cooled enough for Victoria to pry the lid off. Inside was a foil-wrapped packet.

"You really did it up right," Casey said with admiration. "I'd never guess you could stash anything worth that much in such a small space."

"Think of the value of a two-carat diamond and how small it is. The smallest stone in this tin is five times that size." Victoria hesitated.

"Come on, Victoria. Open up."

Victoria got carefully to her feet, holding the stove top with one hand, the tin with the foil-wrapped packet in her other hand. "Something's wrong. It seems too heavy."

She set the tin on the stove top, folded back the flaps on either side of the packet, and opened the creased centerfold.

Casey watched.

Inside were shiny rounded beach stones.

Victoria lifted the packet of stones. Underneath, on the bottom of the tin, was an envelope addressed to her in bold handwriting. She ripped off the end of the envelope and drew out the paper inside. On it was written, in the same bold handwriting:

"VT: Do you think the world will end in fire? Or in ice? Good luck with Scrabble and your next sweepstake. M/E."

"What does he mean?" Casey asked.

Victoria laughed. "It's from 'Fire and Ice,' another Robert Frost poem." She wiped her eyes with the back of her gnarled hand. "I thought I was so clever with my literary hiding place. Emery knew me too well. I wonder if we'll ever meet again?"

About the Author

Cynthia Riggs, a thirteenth-generation islander, lives on Martha's Vineyard in her family homestead, which she runs as a bed-and-breakfast catering to poets and writers. She has a degree in geology from Antioch College and an M.F.A. in creative writing from Vermont College. She also holds a U.S. Coast Guard Masters License (100-ton). This is her third published mystery.